A Paranormal Therapist's Guide to Divorce

And Falling in Love Again

Sylvia Steere

HUMAN
AUTHORED

For Miranda

Your love and encouragement inspire me every day.

Shell Shock

Standing on the pavement in front of the courthouse, Maxine pretended she wasn't having a panic attack.

This was actually happening. Throughout their year of separation, she hadn't given up hope for the phone call where he'd say something like "I'm so sorry, here's the completely reasonable and rational reason why I left, and now I'm coming back to you." But the phone call never came. His lawyers sent paperwork, her lawyer reviewed it, and it was all over but the waiting.

With a manila folder of paperwork to be signed and notarized tucked under her arm, she dabbed on the perfume she knew Jehudin liked. Maybe some of it would rub off on the paper and he'd smell it. And he'd remember how much he still wanted to be with her. No, that was insane. This was the final paperwork and the loss of hope that anything would give her back the happy ending she'd lost.

The courthouse in front of her burned her eyes, but they remained dry. She was a strong, independent woman. Strong, independent women wait to cry at home curled up on the floor of their closet; everybody knew that.

The lobby was bustling with people going about their business. She waited in line to be directed towards whatever office managed divorce paperwork. From there she would wait for her lawyer to arrive. Jehudin would arrive, they would sign the forms which told the world she was a horrible human being no one could ever love, and then they'd go their separate ways.

"Go down this hall, up the stairs on your right, and then it's the second door on your left. Give the lady your name and everyone has to arrive before being assigned an office."

Nodding, Maxine kept her eyes down as she followed the directions. Without truly experiencing the transition from lobby to waiting area, she found herself sitting in a plastic chair staring at cheap carpet.

It should have been quiet and mournful so she could brood, solemnly waiting for her last glimpse of Jehudin, but everyone else was talking as though the world wasn't currently ending. She tried to keep her head down, but every time the door opened she looked up hopefully, like a dog waiting for its owner to get home.

Thirty minutes passed.

Sixty minutes.

She kept checking her phone, texting her lawyer to ask where the hell they were. When her lawyer finally responded, it was to say they were on the phone with Jehudin's lawyers who had requested a last minute reschedule.

"Are you kidding me?" Yelling into the receiver was a necessary, if involuntary, way of making sure the lawyer knew she wasn't happy. Everyone was staring at her. They also knew she wasn't happy. Maxine made a three-quarter turn towards the wall for enhanced privacy and hissed angrily into the receiver, "He asked for this time! I've been waiting here for an hour, and he just now wants to reschedule? What, was there traffic in the fucking firmament?"

The lawyer's voice was garbled like the adults in a *Peanuts* cartoon. She couldn't make out words through the combined rage and emotional drain. She sat down, phone pressed to her ear, as she tried to make sense

of their voice. There was a long pause when they were done saying...
whatever it was. Maxine didn't know how to respond.

The lawyer's droning *"wah waaaah wah"* restarted, but her trembling
fingers pulled the phone away from her ear and ended the call. She
couldn't do it. She couldn't cope with this after everything she had
pushed through just to get herself into this room.

People probably had breakdowns in here all the time. It was fine.
Everyone else could mind their own business.

She spent at least five minutes curled into a miserable ball, holding her
breath until her autonomic system kicked in and forced her to inhale a
shuddering gasp into her lungs, expel it, then repeat the process. She was
still trying to figure out breathing when she heard two people arguing
their own way into the waiting room.

"You can't talk me out of this, Phillipe. You had your chance. You had
a million chances!"

A human woman was stiffly turning away from, presumably, Phillipe.
He was obviously a vampire, with a stereotypical ruffled blouse in a style
which had been considered gauche for years. His expression was one of
distress.

"You're not listening, Laura. This is moving too fast, please slow
down."

"Excuses, Phillipe! I've given you years of my life, and—"

Maxine tried to tune them out. They had their drama, which was
trivial compared to her drama, and they would figure it out.

"We've barely had a chance to get to know each other!" Phillipe's voice
was tremulous. Scared. "I'm trying Laura, I'm really trying!"

Maxine had tried too. She had really tried to get Jehudin to listen to
her.

"You say you're trying, but every day is the same thing. You can't talk me out of this, Phillipe. We're done."

"What do you mean? You didn't tell me you were unhappy until—"

Why hadn't she brought headphones? Maxine desperately wished she could duck her head down and blend into the wall like the other people in this waiting room.

"I've been telling you for months!" Laura's voice was shrill. Maxine could recognize physical signs of anger and exhaustion in how her hands and lips trembled. Phillipe was moving towards his almost-ex-wife with the posture of someone not aware she was a grenade without a pin.

Based on how Laura's adrenaline and fury had built up during their argument, Maxine could tell she was close to losing control. There could be more screaming, or it could get physical. It had only taken a few physical altercations between clients on the couples-couch before Maxine learned to recognize when someone was geared for violence. Another witness, a large man sitting a few plastic chairs over from Maxine, was perking up into alertness as well.

A new voice cut in. Maxine was only moderately surprised to realize it was her own.

"There's a known condition in some vampires that changes time perception." Quite a few heads turned to see what random asshole was inserting herself into an argument between strangers. Since she'd already started, she decided to continue. "Especially vampires who have been turned for more than ten decades. It becomes difficult to understand a human's sense of urgency over single-digit years."

No one else was saying anything. The silence was painful, but still better than screaming. Maxine wasn't ready to experience her own life yet, so she continued intruding into theirs.

"There are ways to coach finite time perspectives back into an immortal's daily routine. Have you seen a therapist to make sure you aren't struggling with different expectations around timelines?"

The woman's expression was blank with shock. Phillipe, looking like he'd discovered the Mona Lisa lying on the sidewalk, shifted his whole posture from one of slumped despair to straighten up and point excitedly at Maxine.

"You mean this is... this is something other people have too? It feels like I blink and suddenly she's angry at me for no reason!"

"How dare you, Phillipe! I've told you so many times—"

"There's a simple exercise you can try." If these had been her clients, she would never interrupt them like this. But she also wouldn't have let them get to this point. Right now, she could revel in the freedom of being a random asshole. "The mortal partner puts something like a bead, or a dry bean, anything small really, into a jar every day. However long you want, but it should be more than two weeks. Then hide the jar, and ask the immortal how many beans are in it."

They both blinked at her in confusion.

"If he's blending days together the way some immortals can, he might think there's just a couple beans in there. It's something you put effort into every day, but he doesn't realize how much you've put into it."

Maxine sighed, too drained to continue this small social interaction. But she pushed on. "From there I'd recommend therapy. There are mental exercises older vampires can do to understand a mortal perspective. If he's willing to commit to the work, of course."

"I will!" Phillipe held this lifeline with both hands. "I want to see things from your perspective, Laura. Please, give me a chance!"

Laura's face was brittle. She had built up the steam to initiate divorce proceedings, and her train car had been knocked off track.

But her expression and voice both softened as she looked at Phillipe and asked, "What... what sort of exercises?"

The whole waiting room seemed to relax now that the bomb was defused. Big guy a few seats over stopped paying attention.

Maxine tried to hide her own exhausted sigh as she pulled a pen out of her pocket and tore off the back half of her manila folder. She wrote out a few quick exercises and included the name of a different relationship therapist whom she recommended to clients she didn't want to work with.

"Here. Good luck with... uh... good luck." Maxine grimaced at herself while handing over the torn folder.

The two left peacefully. Maybe they'd make it, maybe not. Jehudin hadn't been willing to see a therapist no matter how much Maxine had begged him. But it looked like Phillipe would put in the work, and Laura was willing to back down and listen.

Her throat felt raw, dry and cracked from the strain of not crying. Looking around for a water fountain, this purgatory of failed marriages offered nothing but water-stains in the drywall. She swallowed around what felt like a hot coal in her throat. It was time for her to go; she had no more business being here if she couldn't even get *divorced* properly. But somehow failing at her failure felt so much worse. Maybe if she sat here longer she'd find some other, magical ending to the day. Another option might present itself, preventing her from needing to trudge home alone with her broken heart.

"Good job." The voice was directed towards her. Big guy, having leaned back and disengaged, nevertheless saluted her with a trendy gym water bottle before taking a sip. "That coulda gone bad quick."

He was big enough that he took up two seats, but he made an effort not to man-spread, which was interesting. Reading body language was second nature for Maxine, and his was overly controlled. This was a man actively trying to make himself smaller and non-threatening.

"Excuse me, could I have some?" It was a weird request, but Maxine had left her last shit somewhere outside the courthouse.

The man handed the bottle over without a word and she sucked on the silicone straw. Maybe it was poison and she could finally die.

Fuck, it WAS poison! She choked for a moment, only barely preventing a spit-take. She had expected water, so when straight gin burned down her throat her body tried to reject it. She clapped a hand over her mouth, choking and trying not to spit on the carpet while her new best friend chuckled. It was cold, but only a little watered down from ice. It was exactly what she needed to wake up.

When she got herself back under control she took a much deeper sip of gin. Quirking an eyebrow at him while she did, he shrugged and gave a pained smile. His eyes were tight and he looked stressed. Well, they *were* in the waiting room of the divorce court.

Her throat burned from equal parts breakdown and cheap gin, and her eyes still felt hot with the tears she absolutely refused to cry until she was alone. Wordlessly, she handed the bottle back. He took a sip, then handed it back to her. She must've really looked like she needed it. She did.

"I got stood up for my divorce by a celestial," she said after a moment's pause. Her voice was hoarse, and she took one last sip before handing the bottle back.

He nodded, as though this were a normal thing to say. He held a phone in his other hand, which she noticed had a flow of texts and notifications pushing each other up the screen. Without trying to read them, it was obvious most of them were profanity. He glanced at the texts that appeared then rolled away just as quickly, and took a long drink.

"My ex just trashed my place and stole my car." Although his tone was casual, like he was commenting on the weather, the tightness around his eyes only got worse and he pressed his lips together in frustration.

"Oh shit!" Maybe she'd had enough gin. That wasn't supposed to be out loud. "It sounds like you're in the right place."

He huffed a humorless laugh.

"He didn't even ask for the car. Just waited for me to be here so he could clean me out," Gin Man said in a quiet voice, talking to himself more than to her. His knuckles were white around the bottle as he took another pull. "What did he think I'd do?"

Giving the stranger some privacy, she finally checked her own phone. Her lawyer had texted her with a new date and time in two weeks and profuse apologies. Apparently, they had been on the phone with Jehudin's legal team trying to prevent the reschedule. But with Maxine getting literally everything in the settlement, there weren't additional concessions to threaten Jehudin with.

She didn't *want* to threaten Jehudin. He could ask her for anything, and right now he was asking her to come back later and go through all this again.

Watching Gin Man, she saw him internalize his situation. His face slowly hardened into a stoic mask while he stared at his phone, forgetting she was sitting there. He looked a few years younger than she was, maybe early thirties. His shirt was several sizes too large for him and still creased from the package, probably purchased from a department store right before coming here. A few days' worth of stubble and dark bags under his eyes hinted at his own personal drama that led him there.

He could also use a distraction and some kindness. Maybe if coming here meant that she helped someone else, she could pretend that it was meant to be. That made for a better story than spending her day suffering without purpose.

"Do you need to do anything else here?" she asked him, gently nudging his foot so he'd know she was talking to him. She startled him, but he took the question in stride.

"Nah. It's kinda out of my hands at this point." He turned off his phone and slipped it into a pocket.

"Come on then, I'll buy you lunch. And, uh... I can give you a ride home if you need it, Mr...?"

His smile was weak, but genuine.

"Tom. And I'll take you up on that."

The thought of coming back here was a raw nerve she couldn't touch. But now she knew to bring gin next time, so that was something. He'd helped her; maybe she could help him too.

Counting your chickens

L unch with Tom was going poorly. Maxine was losing.

"How about that one?" She indicated an older couple being seated at a booth across the room. They had both clearly dressed with care, looking a shade too classy for an Italian restaurant with all-you-can-eat bread. "I say they're celebrating an anniversary."

With a contemplative pinch to his forehead, he shrugged one shoulder and took a bite of his jalapeño-topped pizza.

"I think you're right. How about... them?" He subtly indicated another table. Two young women were on a date. One of them, with dyed-red hair pulled back into a ponytail, was leaning her elbow on the table and smiling at the other, who was eating lasagna. "They're on their third or fourth date." Tom murmured. "The redhead thinks it's going well, but the lady in blue is going to break up with her."

Maxine studied them, taking a sip of her water.

"Noooo..." Adjusting in her chair for a better view without being creepy, she watched another minute while the strangers talked. "No. They've been together at least six months. Redhead is overcompensating. She did something that blue still doesn't know about."

They ate quietly for several minutes while politely stalking the other table.

"They're both too awkward around each other to have been together long," Tom said quietly behind his soda. "Look, every time red leans forward, blue leans back."

"That's because blue knows something is wrong, but doesn't know what. She's annoyed. See how red is trying too hard?"

Tom looked smug. "It's your turn to check."

They'd have to stop playing this game soon or the waiter was going to kick them out for being a nuisance. There were only so many excuses she could think of for why she needed to interrupt other diners' meals.

"Pretend you're distracted on your phone. I'll be back to tell you I'm right." She plunked her cloth napkin on the table next to her barely-touched fettuccine and tried to look casual as she approached the couple.

They both halted their conversation as she approached.

"Excuse me, I'm so sorry to interrupt, but could you do me a favor?" Maxine smiled apologetically. "I'm on a date and I'm not... I'm not sure about him." Both of the women immediately straightened, glancing behind Maxine. He was poking dutifully on his phone, facing the other direction like a boor ignoring his date. "Is it a red flag if he, um, admits he takes steroids?"

She listened to them debate this for a moment, nodding politely. They both agreed it wasn't necessarily a dealbreaker, but definitely a potential for concern.

"Hah, thanks, I really appreciate another opinion." Maxine rubbed her hands on the fronts of her pants in a deliberately nervous fidget. "Have you two been together long? You're really good with this."

Returning triumphantly back to Tom, Maxine wiggled her way back into the seat.

"They've been together over a year," Maxine gloated. "They share an apartment on the East Side, and red didn't know how to tell blue she didn't get the promotion they were expecting."

"Hmph." In the time it had taken Maxine to verify their bet, he had finished most of his pizza. "Well, best of luck to them."

"Okay, last one?" Maxine found a challenging one. "They're coming in now. Three draconics."

The draconics were being seated at the next table over. All of them had different shades of blue scales and their small horns indicated they were still adolescent. The chairs here weren't designed for tails, but the draconics turned them backwards and sat straddling the seats, tails tucked underneath to avoid tripping anyone.

Tom froze, stiffened into the set-back posture of someone auditioning for the role of Brick Wall on Broadway.

"Are you okay?"

"Yeah." His teeth gritted slightly. "I'm fine."

Maxine, who had purchased matching earrings and shoes in Jehudin's favorite shade of indigo to wear today on the off chance he'd remember how much he loved her when he saw that attention to detail while at the courthouse to sign their divorce papers, felt qualified to say Tom was not fine.

Maxine, who almost daily thought she saw glimpses of Jehudin out of the corner of her eye but found nothing there when she turned her head, but still felt choked up about it and carefully wrote out the incidents in a journal wondering if Jehudin still cared and followed her like a guardian angel, could recognize when someone else was fine.

It was easy to know what "fine" looked like, because it was off in the distance. Far away from Maxine.

"Bullshit. What's wrong, Tom? If you can't tell a complete stranger your darkest secrets in a mid-tier Italian restaurant, who can you tell?"

"I'm not interested in telling anyone." His voice was flat, eyes lidded in frustration. "That's why I said I'm fine."

She leaned in, lowering her voice to make sure the draconics at the next table couldn't hear them. "Do you have a problem with draconics?"

Tom closed his eyes. He went from "Brick Wall" to "Resigned Brick Wall Accepting His Fate." Progress, maybe? With a wry expression, he flicked his eyes at the draconics so she'd take another look.

All three of them had gone quiet and were staring at Tom. Maxine couldn't read their expressions; draconic faces were essentially scaled-up lizard faces and didn't use facial muscles like humans did. But all three were fixated on Tom, their eyes wide enough that she could see the whites around vertically-slitted pupils.

Tom didn't bother lowering his voice when he responded.

"No, I don't have a problem with draconics. Do I?" Turning his head to address the last part to the other table, the three draconics all scrambled to pick up their menus as if they hadn't been staring. "Hey kids, does the Holding know you're out here?"

The draconics dropped their menus and their act immediately. One of them stammered, the other two shook their heads.

"N-no sir!" the darkest blue stuttered. "We just wanted to try human food, sir!"

"Yeah." Tom shook his head, like a few draconic teens going out for lunch was equivalent to experimenting with illegal drugs. "I think maybe you wanna get takeout instead?"

All three leapt to their feet, chairs scraping on the floor.

"Yesss, of course sir!" dark blue hissed in nervousness. They fell over each other to escape the… human sitting peacefully at a booth… and were quickly out of sight.

"Their hearing is better than humans'." He turned back to Maxine, more comfortable now that the draconics were out of sight. "They coulda heard you whisper that from across the room, just so you know. But to answer your question for real this time, yeah, I'm not a fan of draconics."

"Really? They seem to be fans of you."

"No accounting for taste." He took a bite of his pizza and talked with the food tucked into his cheek. "They were kids playing with fire. The Holding doesn't approve of socializing with humans."

"The Holding?"

"Kinda like a consulate, kinda like a church, mostly like a cult?" His head tilted from side to side, giving each option equal weight. "If a drack spends too much time socializing outside the Holding they get pushed out."

"They're called draconics. That other word is a derogatory slur."

"Oh no." Flat sarcasm. "I'd hate to hurt a drack's feelings."

"Don't be a dick. You're acting racist."

She expected him to argue or get defensive, but he shrugged, unconcerned. "Those kids weren't gonna start shit here, but dracks solve problems by fighting. Maybe other Holdings are different, I don't know. But if you see a drack, avoid it."

"We can't avoid the other species, Tom." Maxine's life work was bringing them together. "There's always a way to create a partnership."

Tom's expression soured. "So why did that celestial divorce you?"

Wow. Not taking any prisoners today; she must have hit a nerve.

"I don't know." She had told him to give his darkest secrets, after all. Fair's fair. "We were dating for a year, then married for the best six months of my life, then he said he... he had to go back to the astral plane."

Tom's voice softened, maybe trying to walk back his harsh topic change.

"Celestials see the future, right? Maybe he saw something?"

She could manage this conversation without face-planting into failure and mental breakdowns.

"Common misconception. They see... sort of prophesies?" There wasn't a good word for it, but prophesy came closest. "Jehudin, he—he used to say that when a celestial chose to come here from the astral plane, they were dedicating themselves to making humanity better. Using their astral visions of potential futures to guide humans towards enlightenment."

Tom didn't look impressed. "What's enlightenment?"

"It's..." Talking about it hurt like dragging out a splinter. When she and Jehudin had fallen in love, she had known that his 'mission' of helping humans would always come first for him. When he separated from her and moved back to the astral plane, it felt like a betrayal of their marriage *and* a betrayal of humanity. "Enlightenment is when a human overcomes their base instincts—their selfishness and pride. Celestials can actually *see* our virtues. They can see when we are compassionate, or generous. Not many celestials come to the astral plane, but the ones that do—they try to guide us toward those virtues."

"Maybe you weren't enlightened enough."

A sudden, cold sweat shocked Maxine. She hadn't expected this near-perfect stranger to expose her biggest insecurity, tearing down what little remained of her feeble mental defenses. Hearing her own fear spoken out loud was a knife jabbed into her chest. His own eyes bulged in surprise at what he'd said, and he clearly immediately regretted the thoughtless comment.

"I mean, uh... no, I'm sorry that's not what I meant."

Mistake or not, heat was rising behind her eyes. She had to change the subject. Quickly.

"I guess I don't have to ask why your partner left you."

Tom nodded, grateful for the opportunity to divert the topic even if he was the target.

"Yeah, being an idiot was part of it. But that whole marriage was a mistake. I was trying to—I was turning my life around and thought it would help. He didn't—" Tom struggled, endearing himself back to her just a little. He was trying to give her emotional vulnerability in exchange for his mistake. It showed more empathy and emotional intelligence than she'd expect from anyone, much less a man as big as two linebackers tied together. He swallowed, shrugging and trying to sound less affected by his divorce than he was. "He wasn't gonna be there for me like I wanted."

"Then you're better off." Maxine kept her voice clinical, giving them both a chance to step back from the heavier emotions. "Every member of a partnership needs to be there for each other. In some way."

Tom smiled widely. With his full focus on her, he seemed to have more gravity; it was hard to tear her eyes away from him as he spoke with intense sincerity.

"And you seem like a really enlightened person, Maxine."

⋆

Tom lived across the city from her in West Crestfield, and they both decided to play it safe and stick to small talk while she drove him home. If she had learned anything about him from their game at the restaurant,

Tom was almost—if not as—good at reading people as she was. He knew exactly how much he'd hurt her with his thoughtless comment.

Even the small talk faltered, and she drove quietly. She was getting close to his address.

Crestfield on the whole was at least twenty percent paranormal, but like other immigrants who shared a culture, they tended to congregate and form their own neighborhoods and communities. Maxine, who worked almost exclusively with paranormal clients, could tell that Tom's neighborhood was mostly human.

Vampires usually marked their front windows with stickers so delivery-people knew no one would answer during the day. Most shifters like werewolves lived in wider-open spaces with fenced yards. Celestials were rare, unfortunately. When they did move to the mortal plane they tended to live in much more well-to-do houses. Infernals were also rare, thank goodness, but she didn't know where they congregated.

Finally arriving and pulling up to the address he'd given her, she glanced over at her passenger to see his face lined with grief and entrenched in his own thoughts. The distraction at the restaurant had helped, but looking at his townhouse she could see several broken windows and glass scattered across the sidewalk.

Maxine and Tom gave each other polite goodbyes and he stepped out of the car. They didn't exchange contacts.

She didn't stick around to watch him walk inside. Without any desire to see him pick up the pieces of his life when she had so many of her own, she pulled out of the parking lot for the twenty minute drive East to her own broken life.

Laid out

Thirteen days until she had to sign the papers to officially divorce Jehudin.

"Ephram, I understand you're here because the two of you are having difficulty talking about your vampiric nature and her desire to be turned. Could you tell me in your words why you hesitate to turn Beth?"

"The moment I first smelled her, I knew we were destined to be together. But I... I want to be with her for the rest of *her* life." He stressed the word carefully. "I love her too much to burden her with this... this curse."

He pressed a fist against his chest, turning his head away in shame. Maxine glanced at the woman, confused. The woman was rolling her eyes.

"Ephram thinks being a vampire is a curse," she explained. As she took a breath to say something else, Ephram cut in quickly.

"Bethy, I am a hideous monster!" His voice wobbled with emotion. "How can you bear to look upon me?"

Maxine worked every professional muscle she had to keep her face neutral. Ephram was gorgeous, the platonic ideal of a handsome man, if pale. He was also clearly wearing eyeliner and a soft, shimmery body glitter. They were one electric guitar, a microphone, and an over-sized wig away from being in a glam band.

"I'm getting older." Beth reached out to hold Ephram's hand while she addressed Maxine. "I thought he would turn me after we got married, but he's still on about this nonsense."

"I'm a killer, a predator!" He scowled at the floor between his knees. "You should never have married me."

Maxine felt her eyes widen despite her goal of staying neutral.

"Maybe we should dig into that statement a little more…" She cleared her throat and gave each of them a therapist's bland smile. "Ephram, would you say you feel violent urges as a condition of your vampirism?"

"All vampires are cursed with the urges to kill and drain their victims," he sobbed.

Ooooh boy. Oh boy oh boy. Beth did not look nearly concerned enough about this. Beth didn't look like she had much emotion at all, really.

"I'm glad to say I have quite a lot of experience working with vampire-human couples." Maxine nodded and kept her tone casual, as if she weren't wishing she had a panic button installed in her clipboard. "And there are several support networks and group therapy options I'd highly recommend for anyone struggling with the transition of being turned."

"Oh, he's been a vampire for over a hundred years," Beth said dismissively, waving a hand with a large sparkling ring on it. "He's just being dramatic."

"And, uh, Beth…" Maxine tried not to fidget, preventing herself from tapping her pen against the clipboard. "Do you feel safe at home?"

"Yes, yes." Beth wrapped a comforting arm around Ephram's shoulders while he shook with private emotion. "He'd never hurt me."

"She smells so delicious!" Ephram sobbed into his knees. "I can't keep living like this! I'm going to start drinking her and I'll never stop!"

"Oh, shut up, you big baby."

Taptaptap tap tap tap taptaptap. Maxine dropped her pen.

"I'm so glad you called me for this session." She was not equipped to handle this couple. "It means a lot that you trust me enough to help you work through your challenges together." They didn't need marriage counseling, they needed several professionals in white coats and two separate locked rooms with soft walls. "Sometimes with new clients I like to work individually for several sessions in order to make sure I understand your unique perspectives separately before we try putting them together."

They were nodding along; okay, they were buying it so far.

"Ephram, only if you don't mind, could I start with Beth for this session? There's a waiting room in the main lobby with a blood pack dispenser and some magazines."

"Oh, of.. of course." He didn't have any tears on his face because his body wouldn't produce any unless he'd recently had blood, but old instincts had him brushing at his cheeks. "I'll wait out there."

Calmly smiling as he stepped out, Maxine waited a few minutes for him to get down the hall of the office building.

Beth started blithely, "I think he needs more vampire friends, he and his family just—"

"Beth, this is very important." Maxine swallowed, waiting for the moment of eye contact to communicate her concern. "I believe you are in an unsafe environment. Murderous tendencies are not typical for vampires, and this could be an indication of a larger issue with anger or lack of self-control. Has Ephram ever hurt you or threatened to hurt you?"

The young woman pressed her lips together, eyes narrowing.

"He's fine." Her voice was curt. "You said you wanted my perspective."

"Have you ever witnessed him losing control, Beth? Being violent?"

"I don't like your implication." Beth was getting defensive. "He loves me. He'd never hurt me."

"I have no doubt the two of you care deeply for each other." It was important that she get through to this woman. Her life could be in danger, and she did not seem inclined towards self-protection. "But ignoring red flags will not protect either of you. It is my professional assessment your physical safety is—"

"This session is over!" Beth stood from the couch, gathering her jacket. "We can find a therapist willing to actually listen."

Following her towards the door, Maxine tried one last time.

"Beth, if you ever feel like—"

"Goodbye!" The door slammed behind her.

Groaning, Maxine pressed her forehead against the wood grain of the door. She had pushed too hard. Should have leaned back, let the woman speak her peace and worked more slowly to get past her defenses.

She'd be reliving this for years if that woman's body ever turned up on the news.

<hr>

After parking at her apartment complex, Maxine climbed two stories to unlock her door and bask in the relief of being inside. Inside was the magical place where she could wear pajamas and order Chinese delivery through a pre-set on her phone. Chicken and lo mein delivered with a couple button pushes. She *would* cook, but Noodle Palace was a local business which deserved her financial support. She was helping support locals, not rationalizing her complete disinterest in preparing food for herself. Yeah, that worked.

The apartment was so quiet. It would be nice if there were children upstairs so she could hear them stomp around. She put some music on so she wouldn't have to listen to herself chew. She could still hear herself chew. Even with music, the apartment felt so empty. She had been separated from her now-ex for over a year—she should be used to this by now!

She should be kind to herself, but the thought felt sarcastic, which defeated the point. Grief was a process, and she was still grieving the loss of her marriage. It did no good to beat herself up or to keep dredging up memories to try and discern what might have gone wrong. She had already chewed over this enough; there was no meat left on that bone.

Despite knowing that, her mind refused to let go of the bone. Obsessing about her loss was a well trodden path down, and she found herself wandering down that path all over again.

Jehudin had been so sympathetic about it. So caring. Because of course he was going to be absolutely perfect while he tore out her heart. She had barely a chance to enjoy the marriage. He couldn't or wouldn't explain why he had to return to the astral plane, and he wouldn't consider a long-distance inter-dimensional relationship.

But for that year and a half he had been perfect. Devoted, attentive, considerate, passionate, the body of a god, and every orgasm was a connection to the astral plane.

She wasn't aroused, but she wanted to feel something different and get some relief. Slipping her fingers down between her legs, she gave herself some gentle pressure... She deepened the pressure... She shifted her weight, adjusting to toy with herself a little first...

Nothing. She might as well have been rubbing her elbow. Jehudin had left and took that kind of pleasure with him.

But Kung Pao chicken would never leave her. She hugged the warm carton and kept eating.

It turns out Kung Pao chicken does leave you if you eat all of it. Staring at the empty container she had expected to also provide lunch the next day, Maxine debated ordering more. But if the same delivery person arrived again, to hand over the exact same order from one hour ago to the single woman in an empty apartment, she'd never be able to order from the place again. She went ahead and placed the order again anyway. Pride wasn't a virtue, and they had thin profit margins; they could use the business.

Egg on her face

"**N**ame, age, and species?"

The question was a formality, and needed to be asked to everyone regardless of how obvious their species was. This kind of regulation was necessary to avoid assumptions, but at times Maxine just felt ridiculous.

The giantess peered down at her with watery eyes, already having braved quite a lot to come to the shelter and ask for help. She answered the questions in a dull voice, probably disassociating a little.

The chipped and faded vomit-hued halls of Planar Parenthood catered to all species and served everyone regardless of their ability to pay, making it consistently overworked and understaffed. Government grants helped keep the lights on, but volunteers like Maxine were necessary as well. It didn't help that many of the people emigrating from other planes didn't have family or social networks on the mortal plane, and most medical schools offered only cursory workshops on the most common paranormal species.

Jehudin had praised her for her selfless work here. When she got home from a shift he used to tell her that her compassion and patience were effervescent. She would stretch her aching feet on the couch, eating a quickly assembled peanut butter sandwich while he basked in her. He used to say it was like watching infinite colors spark in a nebula around her. She'd never felt more beautiful than when she was an exhausted mess.

After the initial intake was completed, Maxine filed the form and gently guided the woman to one of their few "extra-large species" rooms. She hovered a hand up to not-quite-touch the woman's elbow, at approximately her own shoulder height.

"I'm sorry..." The woman spoke as softly as she could, but there was still a booming quality to her voice. It was deep and rumbly, more so because of her attempts at whispering. "...if this is breaking the treaty I'll leave, I don't—I don't want to be in violation."

"Asking for help is not breaking the treaty," Maxine reassured her, directing her towards a reinforced chair and sitting down opposite on a similarly large and reinforced chair, her feet swinging above the floor. "And being in a relationship with a native of this plane also does not break the treaty."

That fucking treaty. How many visitors to their plane had been told, "If you break the Mortal Treaty you'll be arrested and sent back to face whatever prosecution looks like on your plane" without actually being told what it was?

"He said I'd be breaking the treaty if I bothered anyone with—"

"Let me please stop you there." The giantess was unspooling, her anxiety palpable. "The official wording of the treaty is that visitors to our plane will 'take responsibility for their effect on humanity.'" And what shitty, vague wording it was. There were very few situations where Maxine would have said *more* lawyers were necessary, but this was one of them. Most of the decisions regarding what "responsibility" meant were made by legal precedent when someone was sued for violations. "The spirit of the treaty was to protect humanity from species with powers. I don't know what you were told, but because giants do not have special abilities beyond enhanced size and strength, there is very little you can do that would break the treaty."

The woman's eyes widened.

"In fact," Maxine continued, "the treaty does not apply at all when someone from another plane commits a crime or does something a native of the mortal plane could have done themselves. So if, for example, you stole something, you would be arrested and prosecuted by our own law enforcement."

"I haven't broken *any* laws!" The woman's voice raised, then lowered as she realized she had lost control of her volume.

"Even if you had," Maxine said, smiling up at her, "you deserve assistance and medical care, like everyone else. Do you want to request a specialist physician? Giant and human physiology are similar enough I'd recommend one of our PAs or the GP, but I'm happy to put in the request if you prefer to wait."

After arranging the physician for the giantess, Maxine stood in the main office to flip through the current waitlist. She was a talk therapist, and most of the visitors here needed physicians, but she'd never had a day that wasn't chaotically busy with people who needed someone to talk to.

"Maxine? Can you help?" The day manager looked frazzled. She was working double-duty on front desk because the regular intake clerk was out with blood poisoning from a poorly refrigerated blood pack. "Someone is in acute distress."

The someone in question was a pregnant human. She had been admitted immediately with heavy bleeding and was speaking rapidly in a foreign language Maxine didn't recognize. The human physician was trying to slow her down, but the woman was frantic. She was wearing a hospital gown, but not one of the gowns Planar Parenthood provided.

Blood could make a situation look worse than it actually was, but this still looked awful.

"Excuse me?" Maxine stepped in. "I'm here to help." She used her "calming" voice. It was intended to communicate through tone that she was in charge, and if *she* wasn't worried, no one else should be worried either.

Ignoring the physician working to diagnose the woman's medical issue, Maxine focused on the woman herself. Young, maybe mid-twenties. Of Asian descent, but it didn't sound like she was speaking Japanese, Chinese, Korean, or Hindi. Which were the only languages Maxine felt she might be able to identify by sound.

After a brief, useless attempt at pantomime of the "me Tarzan, you Jane" variety, Maxine chewed her lip in frustration. The woman's name was Sophia, and she had clearly tried to specify her language, but Maxine didn't understand her.

Her whole life was about communication. How was it Maxine hadn't bothered to learn any more than a lazy tourist's amount of Spanish and a few random phrases in American Sign Language? This poor woman needed someone who could say more than "excuse me, where is the library?"

With a brief flash of inspiration, Maxine opened a map on her phone and zoomed all the way out, so the woman could select her country. It took several painstaking seconds. The woman's hands were shaking, but together they zoomed and tapped until she landed on Cambodia, and victory sparked in Maxine's head.

"I might know someone who can help." It was a fortuitous coincidence; she had a pro-bono client who worked as a translator, and had mentioned she worked with Cambodians. Maxine had a sliding scale payment system, so that people wouldn't feel financially pressured to stop beneficial therapy. In special circumstances, the low end of that sliding scale was zero. Amanda didn't owe Maxine any favors for the free service, but she would probably be overjoyed to be able to help.

When Maxine switched from the map to make a call, Sophia's eyes widened in fear, and she held out her hand with an obvious *No don't!* gesture. She spoke rapidly, voice rising in anxiety.

"It's going to be all right." Maxine said slowly in the "calm" voice. "I'm sorry, none of us can understand you, but we're going to find someone who can."

Tears were smearing the sides of Sophia's face. She was going through physical and mental turmoil, in a place she couldn't communicate and without any of her friends and family. Maxine pulled a chair next to her and held her hand. It was cold and clammy. Maxine squeezed it tighter.

With the phone in her other hand, she looked down to find her client's number and dialed it, giving Sophia a reassuring smile.

"Hi Amanda, I'm so sorry to bother you, but if you have a moment I need language help. Sophia, would you be able to say something? Amanda might understand." Maxine knew Sophia didn't understand the request, but surely holding out a phone was universally understood?

Sophia's face was a mask of... betrayal? Lying bloody in the hospital bed, the woman looked at her as if Maxine had danced on her mother's grave.

"Miss? Um, Miss... Sophia?" Amanda's voice was hesitant. And then Amanda cycled through a couple different languages. One of them was an obvious hit, with recognition flashing behind Sophia's enraged eyes.

She said something in return, pointed edges to her words.

Amanda's voice remained hesitant, but maybe sounded... bargaining?

There was a conversation happening between the patient and Maxine's phone, and Maxine was performing the vital role of phone-holder.

After a relatively brief exchange, Sophia's body language shifted from anger to resignation. She sank back into the bed, her shoulders slumped forward, eyes wet and her voice became softer. Pleading. Maxine was missing something important, a drama within this woman's life that had led her here, where people like Maxine were supposed to help. Anxiety churned in her stomach. Something was off, but she didn't know what.

Finally, Amanda spoke again in English, pulling Maxine's thoughts back.

"She said she has friends nearby." A smile came through in Amanda's voice. "She gave me their phone number, if you're ready to take it down?"

Maxine dutifully took down the number, still confused at the defeat in Sophia's posture. Amanda had sounded happy, where was the disconnect? Well, Sophia was going through physical and emotional trauma; sometimes people in extreme situations reacted oddly.

Sophia was refusing to look at or speak with Maxine, so the medical team took over at that point.

It was a busy day, as always, rushing back and forth and never getting a chance to breathe or get off her feet. Despite that, Maxine still checked in on Sophia throughout the day, and saw some new people had come to help, at least one of whom was a vampire. They were standing next to Sophia's bed, smiling encouragingly at the sullen patient, and helping with translation.

Back at home later that night, Maxine still felt a churning of... unease. Like she'd eaten something on the wrong side of ripe. It was never a pleasant feeling to have someone angry at her, but she still didn't know why. Her peanut butter sandwich tasted like glue and no one was there to praise her good work. She'd never done the volunteer work to get Jehudin's praise, but... well, it had been nice.

Her reward was knowing she'd done everything in her power to help people that needed help. That reward felt oddly hollow today.

Mother hen

Twelve days until she had to sign the papers to officially divorce Jehudin.

A werewolf/human couple who had been married for several years had approached her for sexual incompatibility. But unlike some of her clients, they had the capability to communicate respectfully. They looked at each other with love. They had agreed to get therapy to work through challenges they weren't sure how to resolve on their own to strengthen their partnership.

Her eyes itched. What a blessing, to have something so minor and resolvable.

"I don't want to hurt you!"

"A little pain isn't a bad thing. I want it, Charles. I'm not made of glass, you know."

"You don't understand, this could damage you. I'm happy to tie you up, spank you, bite you a little, all that would be fine."

"I don't want to be spanked, I want to be fucked!'

Maxine allowed the two to go back and forth, taking the occasional note when she thought there was something worth bringing up again later. Charles was a typical werewolf, although apparently larger than average in all meaningful ways. Most werewolf/human relationships like this one could be consummated in any combination of forms, but he was refusing to be intimate while shifted. When the conversation hit a natural pause, Maxine cut in.

"Elaine, if this is a limit for Charles, let's discuss other ways to make sure your needs are met. It isn't respectful to pressure your partner for sexual acts they aren't comfortable with. Have you explored other options?"

"Ugh, there are toys, but they aren't the same. They're cold and smooth, and I need hot and hairy." She gave Charles an exaggerated wink. For his part, he smiled weakly back at her, but he had the expression a lot of her supernatural clients would get after a few sessions. The expression said he suddenly wondered how much of the relationship that he thought was built on mutual respect and appreciation was actually just a fetish for his species.

"Let's all take a breath. This can be a sensitive topic when one or both partners aren't getting their needs met, but we should remember you're here because you do care for each other and you want to make this work. Charles, can you use an 'I feel' statement to tell Elaine how this conversation affects you?"

"I do love you, Elaine." Charles' voice was plaintive as he tried to assuage her hurt feelings. "But I feel as though you're only attracted to the wolf, and I'm so much more than that. I want you to love my human side too."

"I love you too, Charles." Elaine's eyes were large and wet, and she continued with a gentle prompting gesture from Maxine. "Both sides of you, of course! And... I feel like you're holding back when I want all of you."

"Very well done!" Maxine knew her smile was wooden. She should have stopped there, but something in her kept going. "Your problems may seem insurmountable, but you two are so lucky. You don't have a real problem here, just a communication barrier."

"What do you mean we don't have a real problem?" Charles' face was scrunched as he was distracted by her phrasing. "She says she wants 'all' of me, but apparently not the part that says no." His voice was ramping up. "She never wants the human."

"Of course I want the human!" Elaine cut in. "I just don't want *only* the human!"

"Why not?" Turning to his wife, Charles was done with "I feel" statements, apparently. "The human is the one with thoughts and opinions, and you don't want those. If all you want is fur and muscles, you should... you should marry a bear!"

He was working himself up, and Elaine wasn't doing anything to de-escalate. Maxine leaned forward to interject, but didn't make it in time.

"You've always got to make it about you." Elaine, what the fuck? This had been going so well. "I can't get off on your tiny human dick, so now it's a—"

"This is not a helpful pattern," Maxine interrupted, leaning forward and trying to balance a professional but firm voice to counteract their escalation. "But you were starting from a space of mutual appreciation. Let's get back to solid ground so we can address—"

"It's not all about her!" Charles yelled, suddenly snapping under an avalanche of suppressed anger. "She always makes it about her and her needs, like all I am is a big fur rug she's got to drag around."

"Charles, I think we need to—"

Maxine was going to say something like "we need to make a plan to ensure you are both feeling heard and valued" and then do some writing exercises to give them the tools to visualize an equitable therapeutic environment. That would have been a productive use of her expertise.

"It's always the man's job!" He wasn't listening to words, he could only hear his own pent-up shower arguments. "It's always the wolf who has to be the hunter!"

His anger was burning out quickly as his outraged yelling devolved into wounded pain.

"Elaine, I fell in love with you because I thought you were pursuing me. You were always the animal. Not me."

"Now you're just being dramatic," Elaine huffed.

"You never listen to me." He wasn't yelling anymore, but his voice was heavy with emotion. "You've never really listened to me."

"You love her!" Maxine's voice was raised, she belatedly realized, but it felt like the only way to be heard. She turned pleading eyes towards Charles, who was on his feet and lashing out like a cornered animal. "You can't leave her just because of a stupid misunderstanding."

Everything stilled as Maxine realized what she'd said. Charles and Elaine were staring, finally quiet. Her face went numb with shock. She had never... that wasn't supposed to happen.

Standing and tucking her arm into Charles' elbow, cold rage simmered in Elaine's eyes.

"No one said anything about leaving each other," she growled, indeed sounding more animalistic than Charles had this whole session. "And maybe someone who scared away a celestial shouldn't be giving us advice."

The sound of the door slamming behind them was muffled by the static in her ears. She hadn't really registered Elaine's parting jab because the failure of maintaining her own professional distance was a more immediate threat.

If she couldn't separate her own failed relationship from her therapy, she couldn't work. If she couldn't work, she couldn't help people. If she couldn't help people, she wasn't doing the one thing she had always been good at. She would be utterly worthless, instead of just worthless to Jehudin.

Glancing at her schedule, her vision blurred behind unshed tears, she still had two clients to get through today.

She had less than an hour to cry, splash some cold water on her face to bring down the puffiness, eat a granola bar, and plaster another fake smile on her face before her next clients came in. Helping others was all she had left. She couldn't lose it.

Egg timer

Somehow, Maxine got through the last sessions of the day. There weren't any brilliant moments of revelation where she fixed anyone's problems, but she provided a safe space for listening, and that would have to be enough.

After her final clients left, Maxine sat alone in her chair with a clipboard hanging from numb fingers. If she wasn't careful she'd wallow in depression; she'd sink into despair and then she wouldn't be good for *anybody*. But if she kept repressing this it would get worse... so she set a ten-minute timer and just... let herself feel it.

She knew, logically, the walls were cream and the carpet was a mix of light browns scientifically designed to hide dirt from hundreds of shoes scuffing past. But she couldn't see the colors; her vision darkened into a tunnel and she sat lost and disconnected from the world around her.

Her timer beeped. Ten minutes were over, but she was still trapped in the tunnel.

She had to move anyway.

Most of the rented offices in her building kept to banking hours, but Maxine worked later. Leaving the office and locking her door, she was alone with the buzzing of fluorescent lights. She was used to empty hallways, but the silence felt more oppressive this time. Going down the stairs with feet as heavy as lead, she opened the door to the underground parking garage and stepped out into a concrete hallway.

The clicking of her heels echoed back to her as she made her way towards her car, head down, waiting for colors to come back into her life.

Then she saw one.

In the corner of her eye, Jehudin's golden glow was a beacon coming from the parking garage. She looked up, but saw nothing. Nothing except the end of the hallway and a little sign on the wall next to her that said "fire exit" with a cartoon person running to the stairs behind her.

Was this the start of her descent into madness? But... maybe Jehudin would be just around the corner, somehow knowing she needed him. Maybe he'd received a vision in the astral plane and came to make sure she wasn't murdered in this underground garage where she'd leave a difficult stain for facilities to remove.

Then someone *did* come around the corner, approaching her. It wasn't a celestial, though, it was the opposite. An infernal, obvious from his dusky red skin and small black horns over his temples, had stepped into the hallway.

While celestials could see humans' virtues, and guided people towards those virtues, infernals saw and *fed* on humans' darkest emotions like fear, hate, and anger. Lingering at the edges of funerals or loitering in hospitals, infernals tended to congregate in places where humans suffered. She wouldn't have been surprised to see one in the waiting room of the courthouse, sitting quietly in the corner to enjoy humans' grief.

They weren't... technically... hurting humans. At least, it was rare to hear about an infernal getting *caught* hurting a human. They absorbed emotional energy by simply standing nearby, making them the emotional scavengers of the paranormal world. But there were many kinds of infernals. Most fed on fear. Some fed on grief or anger. It was illegal, but many of them could enhance those emotions, and depending on the strength of the infernal this could amount to mind control.

The man in the mouth of the hallway could have passed for human if not for his red skin and horns, around which he'd artfully gelled his hair. He was clean-shaven, a little shorter than an average human male, but the most notable thing about him was his blue jacket with the shiny yellow letters *FBI* visible across both arms.

He looked up from a small notepad in his red hand, and startled when he saw her.

There were three things wrong with this picture. The first was that her workday was *done*. She had a long evening of self-delusion and moping planned and this did not fit into the schedule.

The second was that there were laws against hiring infernals into law enforcement. No one in their right mind trusted an infernal, and several high-profile legal cases had been thrown out because the lawyer successfully argued that an infernal arresting officer might have mind controlled the defendant.

The third wrong thing, and this was the big one: she was staring point blank at an infernal potentially capable of mental manipulation and mind control. Not a great place to be. Start polite, scream later? Scream now while she still could?

She was effectively trapped. He stood between her and the cars, and there would be nothing stopping him from following if she ran to the stairs behind her. She should probably try to run anyway, but what was he doing here?

"Can I help you?" Her voice sounded hollow, and echoed in the hallway.

His eyes sparked with recognition, which jangled her nerves even more. But he also seemed to realize she was scared. Taking a step back and flipping a badge off his belt to show her an official-looking ID, the man pasted a bland smile on his face to try to look nonthreatening.

"Agent Samzen Maliel, special investigator with the paranormal unit."

He was using a curated customer service voice and sounded like those robotic menus that repeat "Your call is important to us. Press one to keep waiting" until you hang up.

"My partner and I were on our way to your office, ma'am. Are you Ms. Maxine Hallis?"

Worse and worse.

"That's me. What do you want?"

His bland smile became strained, but he plowed boldly forward with the absurd premise of being an FBI agent with an apparently invisible partner. Without knowing what kind of infernal he was, she didn't know what sort of emotions he could read off her. But most of them could detect fear or anger.

"I apologize for the interruption, ma'am, but I was hoping to ask you a few questions regarding someone I believe to be a client of yours."

The badge looked real enough, which meant nothing. As long as nobody actually wrote *Female Body Inspector* on there, she couldn't tell the difference.

"Do you have a warrant? Or a court order?"

From the way he tensed his jaw she guessed he was really hoping she wouldn't ask that question.

He took another small step back, as if trying to put her at ease. Fat chance of that. She'd never actually met an infernal before, but Jehudin had described all their abilities as violations of the human mind. An infernal might say they benefited harmlessly from the emotions a human would feel anyway, but what's to stop them from tormenting humans to get more of their desired emotional energy?

Maybe there was some poetic irony here: her life had been ruined by a celestial, and now she'd be killed by an infernal.

"No, ma'am, this ain't that kind of visit, I'm just pursuing my investigation. Her name is Amanda Havelka." His customer service voice dropped slightly, revealing a bit of twang. He was still maintaining the polite exterior to try to get her to lower her guard. "I have reason to believe she's in some trouble and I'm trying to find her."

That was... an odd coincidence. Had he talked to other people at Planar Parenthood? This required more investigation, but *not* by an infernal.

"I think you know I'm bound by client confidentiality, Agent... Maliel, was it? Can you please give me your ID number?"

Sighing and dropping his head in frustration, he obviously knew he wasn't getting anything out of her through polite conversation. This would be when he turned on the mind control, robbing her of free will and taking whatever he wanted out of her head. She should have screamed first—damn her socially ingrained politeness!

Taking a step back and starting to draw a breath for that belated scream, Maxine paused when he jerked away from her like he'd been slapped. He could definitely detect fear, then. He raised his hands, palms out, his own eyes wide.

"Lady, calm down. Whatever you're thinking, it ain't about to happen."

With a creased brow and frustrated edge to his voice, his attempt to stay blandly professional faltered. Perversely, Maxine found herself mirroring his frustration. Why the hell was *he* upset? He was the one ambushing her!

"How often has telling someone to calm down worked for you, 'Agent'?"

He dropped his hands from their position of surrender. "I keep hoping one of these days I'll get lucky. Here, this has my contact information and my agent ID."

She wasn't sure what she expected him to pull out of his pocket, but it wasn't a business card. He extended it with two fingers barely touching the edge, so she wouldn't be at risk of brushing his hand when she took it. His whole body was leaning away from her. If he were anything *other* than an infernal, she'd think he was trying to be considerate of her fear. She looked down at the card he'd given her.

It was thick card stock and official looking with an embossed FBI logo. But if he'd gone to this much effort to impersonate an FBI agent he might as well splurge on good business cards.

"Ma'am, Amanda Havelka could be in real trouble, and if she's willing to talk with me, I would be able to help her. Please tell her that. I could help."

He didn't look hopeful that Maxine would relay the message. That was perceptive. She had no intention of helping him get in touch with anyone, much less a client. She watched him coldly, waiting to see what he'd do next. Maxine was aware he might be able to get information based on her emotional reactions, but at the moment all she felt was fear. It quivered at the base of her spine, making her shivery and weak, but even though she knew he could see the emotion in her aura, she still glared with as much defiance as she could. He might be getting a nice meal from her fear, but he wouldn't get anything else out of her.

"Well, thanks for your time, ma'am." His customer service voice was now tainted with sarcasm, but didn't sound like he was about to take over her mind and tell her to jump into traffic. "Have a good evening."

And then he... turned around and walked back into the parking garage. Huh. She didn't think she'd been mind controlled... but how would she know? Would she feel a blank spot in her memory? The clock on her phone showed only a few minutes had passed, which matched the short conversation.

Peeking around the hallway corner she saw him walk towards an unmarked sedan with his phone held to one ear while he pulled keys from a pocket. He still looked frustrated, but he didn't take off the FBI jacket to reveal a smaller jacket underneath with "Serial Killer" written on it, so she had no idea what he actually wanted.

Amanda's last name wasn't Havelka, it was Havlik. It was possible the infernal was wrong, but it felt more likely that Amanda had given Maxine a fake name. The infernal had said she was in trouble. If an infernal was after her, that could only be true.

Walking on Eggshells

"Thank you for coming to see me, Amanda, I'm sorry if my call worried you."

Sitting across from Maxine in a small coffee shop, Amanda was wearing a featureless brown dress that succeeded in making her look like she'd gotten mixed up and was storing a bunch of potatoes back home in a nicer dress. It bulged weirdly over her pregnancy, stretched over what looked like a late second trimester pregnancy. She was in her early twenties, but a hard life and worry lines made her appear twenty years older. Chewing at her chapped lip, Amanda's hands clutched around her tea and trembled any time they left the cup.

"It's okay, thank you for calling me." Her voice was quiet. "You said… you said it was an infernal? Pretending to be in the FBI?"

Maxine described the encounter. "And he didn't say your name, but it was close enough I wanted to make sure. Is Havelka a maiden name, or is he looking for someone else maybe?"

"…Maybe."

There weren't many things Maxine could say with absolute certainty, but now she was positive that this was the Amanda the infernal had been looking for. Amanda probably hadn't even remembered she'd given Maxine a false name.

"Are you in trouble?" Maxine leaned in. "I will help in any way I can."

The other woman gave a weak smile, winning the Worst Actress of the Day award.

"It's all a big mistake, I'm sure."

It wasn't a mistake.

"He... he was looking for someone else."

Nope, he wanted her.

"Don't worry about it, I'm fine."

Her life was in danger.

"That's a relief to hear."

How did people smile again? This was probably too many teeth. Maxine tried to narrow her mouth to look more natural.

"I know you're fine, but just in case, I wanted to give you this." Maxine passed her a small notecard. "I've got separate phones for work and home, and this has both numbers and my address. Throw it out if you like, but it would make me feel better knowing you have it. So, how are things going with Validus?" Maxine quickly changed subjects and tucked her hands back around her own coffee so Amanda couldn't easily reject the note.

Amanda had been a pro-bono client for just over a year. It was a lot longer than Maxine would ordinarily work with someone for free, but this was one of her last connections to Jehudin. She wasn't sure how Jehudin had met Amanda, but he had introduced them, and Amanda asked for help managing a verbally abusive draconic boyfriend. If nothing else, meeting Amanda was a comforting reminder of how Jehudin had valued her work.

Amanda hadn't been interested in leaving the relationship, but was always looking for new ways to "manage up" and placate his moods. Maxine had been using their time together to work on Amanda's sense of self-worth and help her come to her own conclusion that she had other options. She had told Amanda that therapy couldn't "fix" anyone who wasn't willing to change, and had done her best to leave the breadcrumbs to lead Amanda towards realizing that Validus was *not* interested in changing.

Maxine's personal opinion was that Validus was a piece of shit. Her professional opinion was that he "would benefit from doing the difficult, internal work to take ownership of his own emotions." Which was a fancy way of saying he's a piece of shit.

"It... it's fine." Amanda's weak smile weakened even more. "We're getting close... closer to the due date, and I'm— we're both so excited."

"And he's still in the Holding?"

Since meeting Tom, Maxine had done a little more research into draconic culture. She wasn't an expert yet, but he'd been right about a few things when he'd shooed those adolescent draconics out of the restaurant. Most draconics lived in the Holding. It was essentially its own sovereign land with its own government, like an embassy in a foreign country. They had their own laws and caste system, although they were secretive with their customs, and rumors about draconics were a lot easier to find than facts.

With very few exceptions, the Holding did not want draconics socializing with humans. If a draconic got too involved in human society, they were kicked out—excommunicated—exiled—Maxine wasn't sure of the correct terminology. If Validus was still in the Holding, it was because they didn't know he had a human girlfriend.

Amanda's eyes widened a little, not expecting the question. She was prepared to defend and prevaricate around Validus' behavior in their relationship, but she hadn't expected Maxine to figure out how strange the relationship was to begin with. Maxine was reading her differently than she usually would. This wasn't a therapy session, and for the first time she was seeing the tense shoulders, flushed skin, and difficulty holding eye contact as signs that Amanda was hiding something. Before, she would have thought Amanda was just experiencing anxiety—which was normal for her, but asking about the Holding had thrown Amanda off balance.

"Yes. Yes, of course he—he's still in the Holding."

"That hasn't been a problem for him? Being with a human?"

Buying time with a slow sip of tea, Amanda's eyes roved the café, probably looking for inspiration for a believable lie. Remembering not to push too hard, to let Amanda come to her like a wild bird towards a hand of seeds, Maxine waited for the woman to come up with something.

"Not everyone approves..." The woman's eyes landed on a human kid across the café, sipping on a box of apple juice. "...but when—when we have our child Validus will be happy. He wants to teach him to be strong."

Humans and draconics couldn't breed any more than monkeys and alligators could. Amanda had always staunchly refused to discuss the details of her pregnancy. All she had been willing to say was that she and Validus were going to co-parent the child, and that Validus didn't care it would be a human child. The more Maxine had learned about draconics in general, the stranger that seemed. But Maxine also knew that no society or culture was a monolith; people would always have contradictory beliefs and behave outside the norm.

Maxine carefully studied Amanda's body language for the things she was trying *not* to say. The woman was hiding something important; she was scared, but didn't trust Maxine enough to say what was wrong. Maxine would need to push more. Infernals were dangerous. If one was after Amanda for some reason, they didn't have months to slowly build trust.

"Validus is comfortable raising a human child? The Holding won't push him out for claiming a human?"

"The Holding isn't everything." Amanda's voice got a little stronger with defensiveness. Good, but the balance was important. Couldn't push too hard. "We have other—we're together. He loves me."

Heaven save her from people who thought love fixed everything.

"I'm so glad you have such a strong relationship." Keep her voice warm, try to make the smile reach her eyes. "Do you know what the infernal wanted?"

Amanda's eyes shuttered. Not good, but she wasn't completely closed off yet, they still had a chance to—

A large draconic stood at the door of the café. He had to duck down to clear his horns, towering over everyone inside. With brilliant blue scales covering a seven-foot frame, made even taller with the horns that curved up and behind his head, he looked magnificently powerful. And dangerous.

He didn't spare a glance for anyone other than Amanda and Maxine, walking through the café with the swagger of someone who didn't care if the smaller beings got out of his way or not.

"Are you done here?" His voice was deep, and he spoke in a quiet tone. Cold anger instead of hot. He had the distinctive draconic accent that came from their adaptation to speak without the same kind of lips as humans.

Amanda shrank into her potato sack, a turtle holding a cup of tea.

"Yes. I was just leaving," she said quickly, standing and pretending Maxine wasn't there.

"Wait," Maxine stood, trying to follow Amanda. "I want to help however I—"

Validus didn't push her so much as repel her with his sheer presence. He sneered down, showing large fangs in an obvious display. Amanda wasn't even visible behind him.

"You've done enough."

The draconic didn't back up as she tried to get closer to Amanda. His breath was warm and smelled metallic. Maxine could see the tiny little scales at the corners of his eyes, which were set at the sides of his head like the predator he was. His hands ended in claws the length of her thumb.

"Amanda," Maxine spoke through the draconic standing between them. "I'm here for you, whatever you need. Call me anytime you—"

"Do not talk to my woman!"

Validus was stuck trying to intimidate her without doing anything to make witnesses whip out their camera phones. Which several café patrons had already done. Maxine bit down her prey instincts, ignoring the adrenaline spiking her heart rate as she glared up at him.

"She's her own person. She's not yours." This close, she could see his slitted pupils dilate.

"She is mine." Just like a narcissist who only saw the world in terms of how it affected him. "And we are leaving."

He turned fast enough that his tail knocked her back, hitting below her ribcage and forcing the wind out of her like a gut punch. There were a few exclamations from some other people in the café, but no one got in his way or challenged him on his way out. His clawed hand was on Amanda's shoulder, guiding her. Controlling her.

Wheezing slightly and waving off a kind person who came over to check if she was okay, Maxine watched as Amanda willingly stepped into a van and Validus got into the driver's seat.

Big draconic man—he went out of his way to intimidate *her*, arguably the least threatening human being in the city. Amanda wasn't the only one in trouble. He was afraid of something, too.

Runny egg

axine had come into the office early so she could review session notes from Amanda's file for clues. Having added too much milk and sugar into a too-strong cup of coffee, Maxine felt mildly nauseated and jittery from the mix of caffeine and anxiety. She paced back and forth in front of her "couples couch," glaring at the loose papers stacked on the low table between the couch and her usual "therapist" chair.

The question was, what could an infernal want with Amanda? He had been posing as an FBI agent, despite laws that prohibited infernal employees in law enforcement, so he was either desperate or he thought Maxine was stupid. Having done her best to avoid infernals in general, with success until recently, Maxine had to admit she didn't know much about them.

Two kinds of beings came from the infernal plane, infernals and demons. Technically they were both "infernals", but there were important distinctions. Demons didn't have a physical form on the mortal plane, and had to possess a human to exist here. Infernals like that fake FBI agent—they could come to the mortal plane in their own bodies just fine and were much less dangerous than demons. But, thanks to centuries of misunderstandings, superstitions, and religious iconography, there was widespread confusion conflating infernals and demons. Images of demons were painted with red skin and horns, when *real* demons actually looked like the humans they had possessed.

Infernals, on the other hand, were little more than opportunists. They enjoyed human misery and suffering on different emotional spectrums. The way humans included redheads and blondes, infernals included types that could feed on fear, anger, grief, etc.

So what kind of infernal had this "FBI" one been? He could definitely sense fear, but hadn't seemed to *like* it.

Pulling all her session notes from conversations with Amanda, Maxine tried to find patterns she might not have caught before. She consolidated the questions Amanda had brought into their sessions.

How to manage Validus' moods. How to manage Validus' refusal to listen to her opinions or desires. How to recognize the signs of anger so she could defuse the situation early.

This was so depressing. Maxine rested her head in her hands. She had been trying to give Amanda the tools and self-esteem to leave Validus, but it looked like she had only entrenched herself further into the relationship. Amanda was taking responsibility for his moods, trying to prevent him from getting upset. She might as well take responsibility for preventing the rain.

Something caught her eye as she flipped through months of session notes.

The situations Amanda described made Validus oddly inconsistent. It was more of a gut instinct borne from years of experience than any concrete detail that could be highlighted, but sometimes Amanda described Validus as overbearing and harsh, and sometimes she described him as passive aggressive and manipulative. Both were certainly possible but... looking at them again Maxine suspected Amanda was describing two different draconics.

While they'd rarely discussed Amanda's job, there were a few notes about work stress. Amanda did translation and interpretation. She struggled with how she could reconcile translating something she didn't like, when it was a necessary part of the job.

These were pieces of a bigger picture. Based on how Amanda was lying and hiding something at the coffee shop, Maxine would bet that she was involved in something unsavory with draconics.

It was the infernal that didn't fit.

Jehudin had said celestials and infernals were at war... sort of in the way neighbors trying to out-do each other's yard decorations were at war. Celestials received insights from the astral plan to guide more humans towards their virtues. They tilted the scales towards "enlightenment" versus hedonism or indulgence in baser instincts, which in contrast infernals encouraged and fed on.

At the time Maxine had thought Jehudin sounded selfless, wanting to help more humans push towards enlightenment. Now, looking at the mess of notes reducing Amanda's life to pain points and struggles, she wondered how often humans became collateral damage in a celestial/infernal tug-of-war.

When the session notes failed to produce any new insights, Maxine turned to the internet. But Amanda was a ghost. No social media, no records in local schools, unemployment records, news articles, obituaries (just in case she was using the name of a deceased person,) or prisons. Having never charged Amanda for therapy, Maxine didn't even have any documents to show her full name.

But whatever she was involved in, she was in danger and needed help. The silver lining was if Maxine couldn't find her, maybe the infernal couldn't find her either.

When someone was at a complete loss and not sure what they should do, there was a one-in-a-million chance a celestial could help. Not long ago Maxine would have said *her* chances were better, with an actual celestial husband by her side. But she wasn't confident of her odds anymore.

For banal mortal concerns there was Craigslist, a website where strangers could find lost connections, sell their unwanted crap, look for prostitutes, and risk getting murdered to buy a cheap, used motorcycle. For celestial prophesies, there was Astralist.

On the astral plane, celestials had access to divine insight and could see potential futures. The future was never set in stone, but when a probability became strong enough, a celestial might be able to offer guidance to a human to help them make the right choice. Astralist provided a place where celestials could describe their insights and offer guidance in the hopes the correct human would find it.

The added bonus of this method was that it became nigh impossible to hold a celestial legally responsible for the results of any prophesy they may have listed. The mortal treaty made it legally dangerous to use special powers in any way that might harm humans—when the human didn't agree to it. That was an important detail for vampires, who maintained meticulous records of signed consent forms. Celestials eager to guide a human might find themselves the target of a human who didn't like the outcome. This made helping humanity a quagmire of potential complications and dangers, which had frustrated Jehudin to no end.

Astralist didn't count as direct intervention, just an anonymous data dump for anyone who might recognize the details and act on the information.

As Maxine navigated the outdated user interface and entered her name and location, she took a sip of her now-cold coffee and tried to avoid looking at the celestial names she was scrolling past. The coffee must have been from yesterday; it had a skin that left a disgusting film on her tongue.

Like all good things, a worthwhile concept was overrun with scams and vaguely worded or useless suggestions. Jehudin once complained that as a free service, nobody bothered confirming that the person posting was actually a celestial, so finding a real post was nearly impossible. Maxine felt embarrassed even to be on the site, but desperate times called for stupid measures. And after all, if a woman divorced by a celestial and stalked by an infernal wasn't worth some divine insight, who was?

Well, probably not all these horny single moms who needed some help to cover their tuition payments while they put themselves through medical school.

Or this suggestion a human named either Mike, John, or David should purchase a home security system. Their life was vaguely in danger, but they would "only" be safe if they purchased a top-of-the-line *MortaLife Magic Detector* system.

Nothing.

This was a familiar disappointment. Maxine would never admit, under pain of having to read her middle school poetry out loud, that she had this website bookmarked. She could recognize the familiar scams at this point, and she hadn't seen *anything* that looked like an actual celestial had posted in months.

So much for this idea.

Her phone was in her hand. She stared at it like a mushroom hunter trying to determine if a particular mushroom was a tasty treat or deadly poison. He was on the astral plane; there was no way she could reach him. If she actually *did* reach him, it meant he returned to the mortal plane and hadn't contacted her, which was a new level of devastation she didn't need in her life right now.

Several months ago, she had deleted his number in a desperate attempt to remove the temptation to call him, but she still had it memorized.

She put the phone to her ear, imagining the sound of his voice and—

"We're sorry. The number you have dialed has been disconnected."

Nope. She couldn't even pretend it had been worth a try. This was another scab she should have known better than to pick.

⸺◆⸺

Several days had passed with no updates or breakthroughs, so when Maxine saw Amanda's phone number on her caller ID she scrambled across the office to pick up.

"Amanda! Hi! Um... I'm sorry one moment—" Maxine smiled apologetically at the middle-aged man in the middle of his talk therapy session. He was understandably affronted; this was very unprofessional. But he'd also been venting about work stress for the last twenty minutes, ignoring her attempts to redirect to the source of his problems, and Maxine had stopped caring about ten minutes ago. "I'm sorry this is a—a family emergency, just a minute." Stepping just outside the office, Maxine returned to the receiver.

"Amanda?"

"Ms. Hallis, could I... I, um..." her voice was muffled. "I need the number for that infernal."

There were few things Maxine thought Amanda needed *less*.

"Are you in trouble, Amanda?" If she could prevent infernals from getting involved in this poor woman's life, that would be *one* good thing accomplished. "I'd like to help you."

"I'm not... it's... it might be dangerous."

"That's fine."

"I think... I mean... I *will* be breaking up with Validus." Her voice increased in confidence while she talked.

Maxine barely bit back a cheer. At least Amanda couldn't see the fist-pump.

"I'm so proud of you, Amanda." Maxine bounced on the balls of her feet. "And you're right, this can be the most dangerous part of leaving an—a problematic relationship. But I'm here for you."

"You can't—I mean, I'm sorry Ms. Hallis, but if Validus comes after you, what are you doing to do?"

"I don't want you to worry about me, Amanda. This is about you. Are you in a safe place right now?"

"No, I'm..." That was her instinctive, honest reaction, and she followed it up with the lie. "I mean, I'm in my office. I'm quitting my job too."

That was a lot of major life changes.

"Validus works—he works with me," Amanda continued. "And I need a clean break. Can I come to your house?"

"Yes!" She said it too quickly. Play it cool, Maxine, don't scare her away. "Any time. Come over right now. Can you come over right now?"

Very cool. Good job. After a quick confirmation of the address, Amanda said she'd be there soon and disconnected the call. Well, now she had to go home. Maxine hustled back into the office where her client was waiting.

"I apologize, but something urgent has come up and I need to reschedule our session. Would you be available next week to continue talking about your fear of abandonment and insecurities about being a nameless background character in your own life? Fantastic, thank you. Have a great week!"

Poached

By the time she got home, she had driven through a restaurant and counterbalanced a hamburger with a diet soda to make sure she was still maintaining a healthy diet. There was another bag with a meal for Amanda, who deserved a whole pile of treats to celebrate her good life decisions.

She was pulling closer to her building, French fries hanging out of her mouth, when she saw several police cars with their lights flashing out front.

That wasn't good.

She parked and stepped out, not sure if she should approach her building. Her mind spun through disaster scenarios, trying to analyze the way officers were standing and moving around their vehicles to get a read on the situation.

No one was screaming, running, or brandishing weapons, so there wasn't an immediate threat—that they knew about, anyway. Maxine was intimately aware that when someone left an abusive relationship, they were at the greatest risk. This was when the abuser would be most likely to use violence, gaslighting, emotional manipulation, or any tool they had in their toxic playbook to make sure they stayed in control.

Amanda might have come to her apartment, been caught by Validus, and the ensuing violence had prompted neighbors to call the police. But just looking at the bored expressions of the officers standing around their cars, Maxine could tell that wasn't likely.

Amanda wouldn't have broken in, would she? And if she had, this better not be the typical police response to a pregnant woman seeking safety.

Maybe this had nothing to do with her, a small optimistic voice whispered in the back of her mind. But whatever was happening, the goal was to protect Amanda. She didn't know what Amanda was involved in, or what kind of secrets the woman had, but that didn't matter. She needed a safe place to land, so Maxine needed to make sure her apartment was safe. If Amanda showed up to see this, she might be scared away.

Maxine looked for the one with the tell-tale posture of being in charge. She could typically pick the boss by looking for which one was annoyed with the colleagues around them.

"Excuse me, officer?" He was a sturdily built Hispanic man in his late forties or early fifties. He had been looking down at a tablet, typing in a report with a furrowed brow, but looked up when she approached him. "This is my building, did something happen?"

The officer, a "Detective Ramirez" according to the badge on his chest, maintained a cool professional tone. "Could I see some ID, ma'am?"

She showed her license, and he compared the picture to her face. "I'm very sorry to inform you, Ms. Hallis, but your neighbors called to report a break-in to apartment 355. Can you confirm you live in that apartment?"

"Yes, that's mine. What—"

The man looked a little uncomfortable and glanced over at his colleagues. Another two cops walked out of the apartment building and joined the group. How many police did it take to inspect one break-in?

"Ms. Hallis, I'm sure this is a shock. I've got a few questions here but then we can drive you to the station to give a statement."

"What *is* this?" she finally asked, nerves jangling enough her voice shook a little. "I'll need to see my apartment to know if anything was stolen. Was... is anyone hurt?"

"I can escort you to your apartment, ma'am, but the purpose of the break in does not seem to be theft."

She walked up the stairs with Detective Ramirez. When they got to her apartment, the door was hanging from one hinge and there was police tape across the opening. She looked inside to see... chaos. The contents of her bookshelves were scattered across the floor. Her kitchen drawers had been pulled out and dumped. Her fridge was knocked over, leaning against the side wall with the door hanging open and several takeout containers spilled.

Standing outside the police tape, Maxine's mouth gaped open. Her eyes bounced around the room. A potted plant was dumped on the couch, dirt scattered. The couch cushions were torn up, stuffing all over the floor. It didn't look like anything had been left undisturbed. But most obvious were the bright red letters painted across the back wall.

GIVE IT BACK

She read it several times, confused. She pointed at the dripping red letters.

"That isn't..."

"No," he said immediately, knowing what she was thinking. "It's just paint." He consulted his notes. "Do you know anyone who might have a motive for this?"

There were obvious claw marks in her apartment, violence and destruction, and she'd recently had a confrontation with a draconic. But this didn't fit her expectation around an abuser lashing out. For one thing, it had clearly happened *without* Amanda. And there was nothing for Maxine to "give back" to anyone.

"I don't—I'm not sure." She wasn't even feeling upset about the destruction, the situation was so bizarre. She had to wonder if this was all a big mistake, and the perpetrator had gotten the wrong address.

He shut down the notes on his tablet and tucked it under his arm. "If you're willing, I'd like to take you back to the station for a full statement. And I'd recommend you stay somewhere else tonight in case whoever it was comes back."

Snapping her head over to look at him, she stared for a moment. "Comes back?" she repeated, not having even considered that. She still thought it must be a case of mistaken identity, getting caught up in someone else's domestic drama.

Nodding, he grimaced a little. "Until you know more about who did this or why, it might not be safe here." Some small voice in the back of her head whispered potential headlines. *Single Woman Found Murdered, Killer Says "Whoops!"* or maybe *Local Chinese Business Closes—Blames Loss of Lonely Mein Noodle Lady for Financial Ruin.*

Amanda's phone number sent her straight to voicemail. She left a message and texted anyway.

Maxine drove behind Detective Ramirez to the station to make sure she had her car afterwards, and she gave a full statement. There was a lot of waiting, a lot of little Styrofoam cups of bad coffee, and a lot of repetitions of "I don't know, I really don't." She gave details about her interaction with Validus, but there was no reason for him to break in, and she certainly didn't have anything of his, so it got added to the file and they moved on.

She kept the call with Amanda private. If it was related, she didn't want Amanda to have to deal with the police. It might scare her away, putting her in a more dangerous situation without Maxine to help.

The fact Maxine was going through a divorce was interesting to the police, and just... so fun to talk about while giving her statement. The majority of her time was spent repeating herself to the point of exhaustion. This had nothing to do with Jehudin. He didn't want anything from her. Nothing at all.

After so many repetitions, she was starting to internalize the exhaustion, anger, and violation of the attack against her apartment. She reviewed pictures the police had taken as evidence, confirming it didn't look like anything was taken. Finally, after it seemed they were done being useless and filling out paperwork that wouldn't help, she was told to go to a hotel for the night.

⸺◆⸺

The parking lot of the police station was well-lit, and there were several people standing around outside the doors despite how late it was. She glanced at her watch. Almost midnight now. Her car was parked under a streetlight to make it easier to find, and she slowly trudged towards it through the mostly empty lot.

Still no word from Amanda. Where was she?

Hotel for the night... maybe for the week. See if there were any neighbors with those doorbell cameras, or if the police would see anything on the street cameras nearby. But all that would take time and legal paperwork to access anything. Instead of any real answers, she was more likely to have weeks of tedious non-updates and paperwork to get insurance to recover the damages.

She unlocked her car and sat down, rubbing her eyes until the overhead lights fragmented into rainbow shapes behind her eyelids. Then she leaned her head back against the headrest.

It wasn't until she turned her head to back out of the parking spot that she saw Amanda in the backseat. She was curled up under a blanket, completely still, and apparently asleep. Hopefully asleep, oh god.

"Amanda?" Her voice was shrill and surprised, waking the other woman.

"Ms. Hallis!" Her voice was weak, she clutched the blanket closer around herself, but didn't try to sit up. "I'm... I'm so sorry, I thought I could get out."

Immediately Maxine shut off the car and got out, opening the back door to get closer to Amanda. She put a gentle hand on her shoulder. The woman was ice cold, but she wasn't shivering.

"Amanda, are you okay? Are you hurt?"

"You have to help, it's... it's..." Amanda struggled with something under the blanket. When she pulled her arms out, she was cradling a large egg. It was maybe the size of an ostrich egg, but dark gray with an opalescent sheen to it. "They didn't want me to leave, but... but I got it away," Amanda finally said. "He was angry. He tried to... take it back."

Realizing with dismay Amanda's voice was getting softer, Maxine tamped down rising panic. She lifted a corner of the blanket to see blood. Far... far too much blood had been slowly seeping from an incision on her abdomen. How long had Amanda been bleeding in her car? She must have sneaked in while Maxine was viewing her apartment invasion, but it had been hours since then.

"Oh... oh no. Amanda, I'm going to get you to the hospital. Hold tight, we can—"

"No!" With one arm still cradling the egg, Amanda's other arm grabbed onto Maxine with surprising strength. "They can't find the egg! I need it to be free!"

Maxine wasn't about to let someone bleed out. But she couldn't run and leave Amanda there, so she pulled out her phone and dialed 911, ignoring Amanda's protests.

"Hello, 911? Please help! I'm with an injured woman, I don't know what's wrong but there's a lot of blood." She gave the address, clarifying "Yes, I know that's the police station. I don't *need* the police, I need an ambulance!"

Amanda was crying quietly, curving her body around the egg. Staying with her, Maxine also called the goddamn police station and waved at them frantically, but she got an automated message saying if it was an emergency she should hang up and dial 911. Very helpful.

"He lied to me." Amanda was whispering over and over again. "Said he wanted... a strong boy..."

It should only take minutes for an ambulance to get there, but every second stretched for an eternity. Maxine stared at the woman, gently brushing damp hair off her brow. She was so pale, skin chilled from blood loss.

The world was full of magics and mysteries, but human women didn't lay eggs. Amanda had been pregnant, and now she *wasn't* pregnant and had an egg, which meant—there was a draconic somewhere with a baby? That would need to be its own emergency as soon as Amanda's immediate, life-threatening injury was addressed.

"What happened, Amanda?" She asked the question as much to try to keep her awake as to get an answer. "Stay with me, everything is going to be okay. What happened? You had the baby? Why—why do you have a draconic egg?"

"I was wrong. We had to hurry and... I thought he wanted it, but... he got angry." Her voice was soft as she rested the egg against her chest, petting it with a loving hand. "Never wanted... human baby... wanted egg. They break everything, just like... it's mine. I need it to be free," she repeated. Amanda wasn't crying anymore, but the remains of dried tear tracks were highlighted from the overhead streetlight.

Maxine heard a siren approaching. Oh, thank god!

"Hold on, Amanda, they're almost here."

"Sorry... sorry... don't let them get it back..."

Her words were slurring now, almost too soft to hear.

The ambulance came barreling in, siren painfully loud, and Maxine stood by her car to wave both arms frantically. Someone jumped out and rushed over, leaning into the car and immediately lifting the blanket to assess the damage.

Amanda wasn't unconscious, but she wasn't responding coherently to stimuli anymore. Her eyes were unfocused and glassy, and she was moving her head as if she was looking for something. Without noticing how it happened, Maxine was handed the egg while two paramedics transferred Amanda to a stretcher. They hustled her into the ambulance, where Maxine heard them yelling back and forth about fluids and stimulants. She was watching the paramedics frantically checking over the bloody woman to make sure they found the injuries, but it looked like all the blood was coming from a recent cesarean section scar. She must have just come *from* a hospital.

Maxine couldn't travel in the ambulance with Amanda as they rushed her to the hospital. The driver didn't say much, just specified which hospital they were going to and sped away with the sirens blaring. Which left Maxine standing there in the well-lit parking lot of the police station in the middle of the night... holding a draconic egg.

You can't make an omelet without...

Maxine looked down at the draconic egg she had instinctively cupped against her chest as if it were a baby. Which... it was, but... also an egg. Dull thumps of her heels against pavement punctuated her slow march back into the police station.

The sirens of the ambulance had brought several people outside to see what was going on. Maxine went back to the officer she had hoped never to see again only minutes prior.

"I need to modify my report." Her voice was monotone, emotions numb as her panic ebbed.

Describing the interaction with her client, Maxine reviewed the conversation and confirmed what she knew about Amanda's boyfriend, Validus. What had Amanda said? *"They break everything."*

There weren't many details she could add. Maxine hadn't been invoicing her, so she didn't have any payment information, and they communicated by email and phone. She didn't know where her client lived. The only description she could give for Validus was "draconic male, blue scales." They noted her description of the infernal claiming to be an FBI agent, but even that seemed to be entered into the report in the spirit of "just write it down and she'll go away eventually."

"What... what do I do with the egg?" Maxine finally asked. The officer glared at the vulnerable egg for a moment. It would take such a small amount of pressure to break it.

"Eggs from sentient races fall into a gray area, I'm afraid." He looked like he really wished she hadn't asked the question. "Technically, until it hatches it's not considered born. And in this state we don't have abortion laws that cover... this situation." He grimaced. "If the father of the egg wants to destroy it, he wouldn't be breaking any laws."

"How is that possible?" She watched as his face twisted a little further into "please don't make me talk about this" territory. She waited out his discomfort. She needed to know.

"If the child inside the egg is viable, then breaking the egg doesn't kill it. It's just an early hatching. It might be a case for child abuse depending on the situation. If the child isn't viable, then it's an abortion, which is legal."

"But... it's not. It's not in her body anymore. Abortions are a medical procedure on a pregnant person." Uselessly gesturing at the egg, as if looking at it again would help, Maxine willed the law enforcement officer to magically make the law make sense. "I'm holding it, see? It's been born."

"The legal maternal parent or guardian can bring these details to a lawyer if she wants to sue or claim punitive damages."

She shifted her weight, feeling the heft of the egg much more all of a sudden. It was slightly warm, but completely still. She couldn't feel the baby shifting or wiggling at all, which... she wasn't an expert... but it made it seem like the kid wasn't ready for hatching yet.

"But what do I do with it?" she asked again. "Can I leave it here, in an... evidence locker or something?"

From his expression he did not appreciate her idea, and he thought she was a gibbering idiot for asking. Maybe he was right; she certainly didn't know what the egg needed to survive.

"Legally speaking, your client left you with property jointly owned between herself and her... partner." The officer didn't seem to approve of inter-species relationships. Or maybe just not this one. "If you left it here and he demanded it, we would give it back to him. Same if you bring it to the hospital to leave with your client. If she can't stop him from taking it, he has a legal claim to the egg, and it would not be considered theft or kidnapping."

Privately, Maxine doubted Amanda was the legal joint owner of the egg. She still didn't know why or how she'd shown up with a draconic egg. But she wasn't about to start arguing this point.

"I can't go back to my apartment." Maxine reminded him. "And I... don't feel safe going to a hotel alone right now. What if Validus comes for the egg?"

"I'm very sorry." He didn't sound very sorry, but it was the middle of the night and she was a complete stranger holding another complete stranger's egg. He was generous for giving half a shit. "The station is open twenty-four hours. You're welcome to wait in the lobby until you have another plan or hear back from the mother."

She did end up sitting in the lobby for a couple hours. After another cup of lousy coffee on an empty stomach, she felt queasy. Or maybe that was from the stress.

Amanda had been pregnant, and now she definitely had an injury that looked like a cesarean section incision had reopened. She must have had a human baby sometime between meeting at the coffee shop and calling for help, but where was it? Why was she carrying an egg? What did that infernal have to do with this?

Maxine called the hospital. She asked about Amanda's status and was relieved to hear she had been admitted and was in fair condition, but due to privacy regulations they couldn't give her any details. That was fine; the important thing was that Amanda was receiving care.

She leaned her head back against the wall. Anxiety warred with exhaustion to keep her awake.

She couldn't go home. She couldn't leave the egg here. She didn't want to take it to the hospital, because Validus could go there and take it anyway. If she got a hotel and he found her, she... she didn't know what he'd do, and that was scary by itself.

This cheap plastic seat in the lobby of the police station was identical to the ones at the courthouse. Her butt was going numb and she felt pins and needles starting to prickle her feet.

She blinked up at the ceiling. She had a bad idea. But it was her only idea.

⬤

Ten? Yes, ten days until she had to sign the papers to officially divorce Jehudin.

She had been awake all night, mostly at the police station and then for a few hours at a twenty-four hour diner where she ate pancakes she was too stressed to taste. Converting an old exercise shirt into a sling allowed her to wear the egg hands-free over her chest.

At least she wasn't worried about being stylish. She looked like she was one tin foil hat away from saying she laid it herself.

She remembered where she'd dropped Tom off—it had only been a handful of days since they'd met. After waiting at the diner long enough that it could be considered "early" instead of "late night the previous day," she pulled into his parking lot.

The lights were out. His window had been repaired and curtains drawn. A car was in the spot designated for his townhouse, so he either got it back from the thieving ex or got a new one. Hands shaking a little from the mix of exhaustion and overcaffeinating, she stepped outside and tied on her egg sling.

What was she even doing? This is absolutely insane. But she had been trusted with something that would become someone's child. Regardless of what the law said about treating eggs like property until the child was viable, she couldn't rationalize doing anything that would put it in harm's way.

She stood in front of the door for a full minute, working up the nerve to ring the bell.

She rang the bell.

After several anxious minutes trying to remember the protocol for how long to wait before ringing the bell again, he opened the door.

Tom had clearly just woken up. He had bed head hair, and he was wearing a loose t-shirt and low-slung sweatpants. The physique that had been hidden under an ill-fitting button-down was now clearly on display. Having forgotten how big he was, Maxine gaped up for a moment, then belatedly closed her mouth and tried to look like a woman who hadn't been awake all night babysitting an egg.

For his part, he was gaping down at her, the last person he expected.

"Maxine?" he asked after a pause to remember her name. He looked behind and around her, as if there would be a camera crew filming the world's weirdest prank show.

"Hi Tom. I really hate to ask for a favor, but... I need a favor."

His face scrunched in confusion, but he stepped back and waved her in. He lived in an obvious bachelor pad. The place was messy, but not dirty, which was an important distinction. There were some stacks of books and papers covering countertops, boxes of things in some state of either packing or unpacking, and the dryer rack was full of bone-dry dishes that needed to be put away. She looked around curiously, and when he pointed her towards the sole couch in the living room she nodded and sat down.

He pulled a stool from the kitchen bar top counter and dragged it over to sit across from her.

"Are you okay?" he asked first, which warmed her heart a little.

"Yeah, kind of." Trying to act more casual about it than she felt, she adjusted her sling and carefully pulled out the egg. They both stared at it for a few seconds. He raised his eyebrows at her with a doubtful expression.

"I'm... not the father, am I?"

"Hah!" She had been wound so tight, even a small joke felt like a pressure valve releasing. "No. Someone broke into my apartment looking for it, and the police won't help. The mother is in the hospital and I... I don't have anywhere safe to keep it."

They both went back to staring at the egg. He frowned as though he wasn't sure he wanted to know, but still asked, "What happened?"

So she gave a summary of the situation with her client. Although she tried to keep the story clinical and as objective as possible, it was a traumatic evening, and she felt her voice shake at various points, like when she described watching Amanda get weaker while waiting for an ambulance. Or when she was numbly sitting in a diner with a shitty breakfast trying to figure out how to tie up a spare shirt to hold the egg securely so she wouldn't break it.

Tom listened attentively the whole time. Sitting on his barstool with his feet tucked into the rungs and his elbows braced against his knees, he nodded and kept glancing between her and the egg while she talked.

"And... that's it," she said, finally. "I know it's really sad, but I don't have any close friends right now, and it seemed like you knew about draconics. I don't want to put you out; I just need a safe place to hide it until I figure out what's going on."

Tom didn't move or acknowledge the end of her story. He stared at the egg again for a painfully long period of silence before he looked back up at her with an inexplicable expression of fear.

"Were you followed here?"

"N-no?" She hadn't been checking; she had been driving one-handed while cradling the egg. "I don't think so."

His face darkened with anxiety, and he ducked over to the window to look out through the curtains. After a tense several seconds, he squinted against the sunlight and stepped away from the window, looking down self-consciously as though suddenly realizing he was still wearing his sleep clothes. He wiped his hands against his shirt in a nervous fidget.

"I don't want anything to do with dracks. I'm sorry, Maxine, I can't help you."

Another dead end. Except this time it wasn't some officer trying to half-ass his job. The rejection felt personal.

"What... you can't even hold onto it? Validus knows I have it."

He swallowed, looking like the tight, sweaty, anxiety-riddled version of him she'd seen when they were at the restaurant. "No. Find somewhere else to hide it."

Standing from his couch, Maxine's stomach sank deeper into the ground.

"O-okay."

He didn't ask for any of this, she had just shown up. He didn't owe her anything. But what was she going to do now? Tom opened the door to show her out, still casting a paranoid eye outside.

"Dracks..." His voice stopped her as she was stepping out the doorway. She saw his hands clench at nothing, and he looked away from her towards the parking lot again. "They're vicious bastards, especially the men. It's all about who's the toughest for them. This guy who wants the egg? He doesn't get anything from attacking you, it doesn't prove anything. If you give it to him, he'll leave you alone."

Maxine gasped, whipping her head around to stare at him and cupping her hands protectively over the egg as if he was about to go after it. The suggestion was obscene. Just give the egg to someone who was going to destroy it?

"It's basically a child! And I'm going to do whatever I can to save it, with or without your help." She curved herself around it. "And one violent draconic doesn't mean they all are, whatever your history is. They're people, just like us."

His face twisted in ugly hatred, lips curled in disgust. She took another few steps out the door, for the first time getting the gut feeling this man was dangerous.

"You haven't seen them like I have, Maxine. If you don't forfeit the egg, leave it somewhere he'll know to find it, he'll... Well, he probably won't kill you. But he'll hurt you." His eyes were dark, and there was urgency in his voice. "Don't risk yourself for a fucking egg."

This was a dead end. Tom was a bigot, and she was worse off than when she arrived.

"Goodbye, Tom." She didn't have any more time to waste.

She would make some phone calls, talk to people who knew more about draconics. If there was a... a draconic child protective services agency or something... they could help.

She left without a backward glance. What kind of person would give up a child who needed help?

...breaking a few eggs

Maxine sat in her car trying to figure out her next steps.

Validus had gotten both of her numbers, either from Amanda or somewhere else, and had been calling and texting nonstop. Threats, demands, and insults poured in with sickening frequency.

Draconic body language was different from humans'. Maxine couldn't read them the same way, but without real facts and information, she'd have to rely on instinct and jump to a few conclusions: Validus was scared, and he was used to bullying humans. Bullies who pushed around weaker people tended to be cowards, but that didn't really help Maxine. Validus could be as cowardly as he liked, it wouldn't stop him from ripping her arms and legs off if he caught her.

Every notification chime spiked her heart rate, and there were only so many breathing exercises she could try before breathing itself got stressful. Maxine canceled her next week of clients, then she took the battery out of her work phone and put her personal phone on Do Not Disturb, trying to ignore incoming calls. Validus' threats would still be piling up in the background, but it would help her compartmentalize and think about what to do next.

Amanda was reportedly stable in the hospital, but wouldn't be able to answer any questions. The hospital was doing the best they could, but there was a blood shortage. There was always a blood shortage; vampire blood banks paid top dollar and medical supplies tended to rely on volunteers. Until Amanda was in better condition, she wouldn't be allowed visitors, which was probably for the best right now. She'd be safer under the constant surveillance and security cameras of the hospital.

The infernal was the one who started all this—kind of. He wanted Amanda for something, and Maxine still didn't know what. He'd claimed he could help Amanda, but infernals didn't help humans. Why would they? They fed on human suffering.

Running out of ideas, she looked at the business card he'd given her. It still looked real enough. Doing her best not to look at the notification alerts on her phone, Maxine dialed the number. He answered the phone after a couple of rings.

"Agent Maliel speaking." It was his voice, anyway. She might get more information by pretending she believed him at first.

"You said someone named Amanda Havelka was in danger. Do you have any other details you can give me?"

"What do you mean, lady?" His voice was a familiar mixture of sarcasm and frustration. "Details like she's five-foot-three and allergic to peanuts, or details like how someone matching her description has been admitted to Mercy General hospital and the recorded 911 call was initiated by a Ms. Maxine Hallis?"

He was a well-informed fake FBI agent, anyway.

"I was hoping for details like what happened to her pregnancy, actually." The egg was its own problem, but a c-section meant there was a human baby somewhere too.

"She was pregnant?"

The surprised squawk in his voice sounded real, but maybe he was just a good actor. She shouldn't have made this call; she wasn't trying to give him information. And she certainly wasn't going to ask him for help with the egg. A violent draconic was enough of a problem; she could only hope the infernal wouldn't add to it.

"I'm sorry, this was a mistake. I shouldn't have called."

"No, wait—"

She hung up and blocked his number.

If she were a draconic mother who had lost an egg, what would she do? Go to the Holding for help? Maxine didn't know what sort of social services were provided by a Holding, or where to find it. Ask a draconic? They mostly avoided humans and she wasn't about to start walking down the street looking for a random draconic. Besides, Validus was presumably looking for her, so she had to keep moving.

What she needed was someone knowledgeable about the local Holding whom she could find with an internet search, and who would be close enough to visit. Maxine did a local area search while carefully avoiding looking at the increasing number of missed calls and texts counting up at the top of her screen.

Professor Frederick Jiminez was a researcher at Crestfield Western, only a short drive away. Maxine read through his publicly available research, which specialized in extremist organizations and cults, but he had written one notable paper about the Crestfield Holding.

Feeling the pressure of a vise closing around her chest and planting her feet to suppress restless jitters, she skimmed through the publication for the major details. The paper itself looked like sensationalist click-bait. Even researchers liked to get views every now and then. The paper gave a horrifying image of the internal political structure of the Holding, as witnessed by a human whose identity was kept anonymous. The anonymous human witness described how legal precedent was set by arena combat and overseen by a draconic leader known as a Premier.

Professor Jiminez didn't have a phone number listed, but she had all day to avoid Validus pulling her arms off, and the university was close enough that Maxine could go there and try to find him.

------◆------

Finding Professor Jiminez's office was the easy part.

Maxine stood in the doorway of an office with hardly any floor showing through stacks of papers and books. The back wall was a conspiracy theorists' dream of notes and pictures connected with string. Several cheap folding tables, bent under the weight of their own stacks of books, started the obstacle course just inside the door.

He must not get many visitors.

"Um... hello?" Maxine half expected the professor wouldn't answer because he was already dead, buried in his own paperwork and eaten by rats, but she didn't smell a dead body, just dust and the old paper aroma of a library.

"Hello?" a disembodied male voice answered from within the office, sounding as confused as she was. Maxine bit her tongue to prevent herself from yelling "Marco!"

A man in his early-to-mid-thirties did a meerkat impersonation from behind what must have been his desk. He wore thick glasses with one of those safety strings so they could hang like a necklace if they fell off his nose. As he navigated his office like a ballerino scarecrow, his skinny legs knew exactly where to place his feet to land on tiny clear spaces of floor between the paper stacks. He was wearing running shoes, incongruous against his jeans and button-down shirt.

Surprisingly quickly, Maxine was faced with his large eyes, framed within the lenses of his glasses. The folding tables were still between them, but he was now close enough for a conversation.

"Are you a student?" He spoke quickly, the words tumbling out of his mouth like they were racing each other. He focused on the egg she wore on her chest. "Oh. Please tell me that's an ostrich egg in a strange lunchbox."

"It's a draconic egg." Maxine felt her eyebrows lift to her hairline and fought to bring them back down to neutral. A specialist in cults and extremist organizations being a crackpot shouldn't be a surprise. "I need to protect it from its father."

He didn't take his eyes off the egg sling. And even though she knew he was staring at the egg, it still gave the effect of him fixating on her breasts.

"My eyes are up here, professor."

He startled slightly, looking back up at her. "You're here to ask about draconics?"

"Yes."

"Are you being threatened by one or more draconics?"

"Yes."

"Do you have a gun?"

"What?" she yelped. "No!"

"Were you followed here?"

This time she had been checking her rear view mirror on the way to the university.

"I don't think so."

He nodded. "You'd better come in." Stepping backwards, he gestured as though there was a way she could possibly walk into the office.

She was up to date on her tetanus booster. She'd probably be fine.

Sharing a chair with printouts of eyewitness reports of demon possessions in the 1800s, Maxine explained her situation to Professor Jiminez.

He listened carefully and asked intelligent questions. He didn't glare at the egg as if he hoped it would magically disappear, and he didn't tell her to drop it or give it back to Validus, which so far made him the most helpful person she'd met.

But then he tried to give advice.

"A handgun would probably work best for you." He was nodding to himself. "Something you can open carry so he knows you have it. They respect strength and don't really care if it comes from weapons. Also, you can access it easily if you see him."

"I'm not going to shoot anyone!" Maxine could hardly believe this conversation. "Professor Jiminez, do you have any advice about how I could find the egg's mother? Is there someone at the Holding I could talk to?"

"Hmm." He chewed on his lip as he thought. "Draconics are isolationist. They typically eschew contact with humans except when absolutely necessary, but even within the Holding they do not discuss their eggs until viable. Do you know if your egg is viable?"

"No, I... how can you tell?"

"It needs to mature enough to hear a heartbeat. How long since the egg was laid?"

"I don't know, I got it yesterday."

He frowned. "Without knowing the laying date, lack of a heartbeat could either mean it is unviable or viable and immature."

"Do you have any contacts within the Holding I could call?"

He gave an immediate nervous laugh, fidgeting with his glasses.

"No. No no no, they don't like me there." Shocking. "And you shouldn't go there, either. If you're keeping the egg from its father, you're making an implicit statement that you're strong enough to keep it from him. They consider that a challenge."

"But that's insane!" Maxine realized as soon as she said it this man might not be the best person to argue rationality with. "Professor, you published a paper about the Holding's Premier setting some kind of legal precedent with a human. Who was that human? Do you think they could help me?"

Alarmed, the professor looked around as if the anonymous human was about to pop out of his messy papers.

"His deal with the Premier carried the requirement he never get involved or associate with draconics in any capacity." He gave his nervous laugh again. "If he breaks that agreement, it could be construed as a challenge against the Premier himself."

"And that's bad?"

"It—it's a death sentence." He swallowed. "I think... I think you may have more luck with avoidance if you want to avoid physical conflict. There are—"

A familiar voice called out from the door. Suddenly Maxine had a strong suspicion about the identity of the anonymous human in Professor Jiminez's paper.

"Fez! You're not answering your phone. You dead?"

The professor's eyes bulged behind his glasses. "Uh... excuse me for one moment."

He popped up and somehow managed to dash through his office without knocking anything over.

Where she was positioned behind the stacks of papers and books, she knew Tom couldn't see her from the doorway. She put her head in her hands and groaned softly. No wonder he had refused to help. Getting involved or associating with draconics could be a death sentence. Thank goodness they hadn't—

"I'm fucked, Fez." Tom's voice carried clearly; he was talking over the professor's hushed attempts to warn him not to say anything. "A drack saw me talking to someone who stole a goddamn egg, and now I'm back in the hierarchy."

"You don't—no, we can—stop, wait!" The professor, or "Fez," apparently, couldn't stop Tom from picking his way into the office. Maxine stood up and put the professor out of his misery.

"I did *not* steal it."

She started to work her way through the mess, then decided to just kick papers out of her way. Tom didn't even look surprised. He glared at her from across the turbulent ocean of printouts.

"It was given to me." With a somewhat sheepish shrug, Maxine added, "By someone else who probably stole it."

Over easy

"**S**o now they think I'm back in the hierarchy, and I've got dracks popping out of every goddamn shadow thinking they're gonna get lucky."

Tom and Maxine successfully cleared a couple chairs and a corner in the back of Fez's office, ignoring his complaints about ruining his "system."

"I'm so sorry, Tom. I never meant to put you into danger."

"Well, as long as you didn't *mean* to do it."

Maxine knew she wasn't winning any fashion shows, but Tom's outfit made her look halfway normal in comparison. On top of a skintight, long-sleeved black turtleneck, he wore a tactical vest and some kind of armor over his forearms. It reminded her of what an archer might wear, except it covered both sides of his arms and the backs of his hands. He also had on thick canvas pants and steel-toed ankle boots.

He looked like he'd lost the rest of his backyard militia at the mall food court.

"What do you want me to do, Tom?" Maxine threw her hands in the air. "Give me the number for the Premier. I'll tell him you're not involved."

Both Tom and Fez's faces fell in dismay at the idea.

"No!" Tom said at the same time Fez exclaimed, "Bad plan!"

"Well you're the two draconic experts here, you tell me." Maxine looked between the two of them. "Any ideas?"

Fez opened his mouth.

Whatever he was about to say was interrupted as a gravelly draconic voice yelled from the doorway, "Thomas Morgan! You will face me! ...Uh... sir?"

Tom's face darkened into an exhausted scowl. Maxine was barely on her feet before Fez, in a lightning-fast lunge, grabbed at her elbow and pulled them both down to their knees behind a stack of books.

"Kid, I am in the middle of something!" Tom called back, even as he pushed his way to the door. Just before he stepped out of Maxine's line of sight, she watched as he rolled his shoulders back and cracked his neck from side to side.

From her vantage point, Maxine couldn't see the draconic at the door. Fez was still holding her arm and ducking down out of sight.

"We'd only get in the way. Quick, follow me." Going in the wrong direction, further towards the back of the office, the professor led her into a utility closet.

"This isn't... Tom needs help!" Maxine hissed, still craning her neck to try to see what was going on, but Tom and the draconic were out of sight in the hallway. She could only hear some faint thumping sounds filtering through the office detritus.

"Tom needs help, alright," Fez grumbled, pushing through the closet door to reveal a cramped alcove with another door. "This is how it was the first time I met him. Come on, we can get out through here."

The door led to the back of the building. An unremarkable concrete pad lined the edge of a shipping entrance where delivery trucks could back up. Standing on the stained concrete and breathing in the putrid rot of a nearby dumpster, Maxine watched as Fez closed the door behind himself and gestured for her to follow him down the ramp and around the building.

Did the university build him an escape route, or did he cut his own door into the back of the building? His entire office was a fire safety violation. It was easy enough to picture the professor gleefully cutting into a load bearing wall.

"Tom showed up like you did, asking for help. He couldn't walk five steps without a draconic challenging him to a duel. I wasn't even a professor back then, I was still doing my postdoc. We figured out how to stop them coming after him, but... it wasn't easy."

"Duels? You said they were isolationist—why would—"

Rounding a corner of the building, Maxine could see several more draconics milling around the entryway. She and Fez watched as the small group of adolescent draconics postured and pushed each other around playfully. It looked like they were waiting for something.

"Draconics gain status by winning duels, and Tom's a holy grail. Human *and* high status in the Holding hierarchy." Fez's face was drawn and serious. "Any draconic who beats him wins the jackpot. And a lot of them think they're going to be the one do it."

"I don't understand. Can't he reject the challenges?"

"I've tried." Tom's voice was right behind her, inches from her ear.

Maxine's shriek of surprise was quickly muffled when his calloused hand clamped over her mouth. He pulled her back tight against the hard armor on his chest, and hauled them both around the corner, out of view of the entryway. He let go as soon as they were around the bend.

"Don't ring the goddamn dinner bell!" Tom's voice was hushed, and his eyes scanned their surroundings to make sure none of the draconics heard them.

Tom looked fine, other than his man-bun having become disheveled. No loss there. His face was flushed and he was breathing faster than usual, but otherwise Maxine would never have guessed something was wrong.

"Follow me." Fez darted off in the direction they'd come from. "I've got a secondary office space."

They gave him *two*?

The university had winding paths separated by landscaped bushes and beds of grass trampled in places where students made their own shortcuts. Based on the odor in the air, someone was smoking marijuana nearby, getting the most out of their college education.

"The ones that come for me, they're desperate," Tom explained, hunching a little as they walked as quickly as possible without actively running. "And they think humans are easy prey. When I've tried forfeiting before a fight, they don't accept it. They keep coming after me."

"Are you okay?" Maxine looked him over again. He was walking with his left arm tucked into his side. "Did you get hurt?"

Tom didn't respond immediately. His left hand flexed.

"It's a battle of attrition," he said, finally. "They never give me time to recover."

"Here we are!" Fez was unlocking a door of his "secondary office" space, which turned out to be a large garden shed. It was shaded by trees and well hidden from the road.

In one of the few mercies of the day, he had not redecorated the interior. There were some disorganized boxes, mowers, and lawn equipment, but also a few folding chairs Fez set out. The shed was dimly lit by sunlight filtering through ventilation windows close to the roof.

When Tom sat heavily on a chair, a small cloud of dust motes surrounded him.

"I can't do this again." His voice was soft enough Maxine wasn't sure if he was talking to them or himself.

"What exactly *is* 'this?' Are the draconics actually trying to kill you?" She asked, watching as Tom twitched, suddenly shifting his shoulders down and back slightly. Taking her own folding chair, she sat and studied Tom while her heart rate settled. If he were anyone else, she'd have thought he was angry. His faced was hardened, mouth pressed thin, and eyebrows furrowed.

But she had seen fear before he deliberately changed his expression and body language to hide it. He glared at her, and she looked calmly back, waiting for him to remember she could *also* read people at least as well as he could. Sighing, he rolled his eyes and gave up trying to fool her, leaning back in his chair.

"Dracks don't try to kill during duels... usually." Tom's voice was quiet. "The Premier is the only one who kills his challengers in the arena. But they don't need to *try*, Maxine. A drack's claw is about this long," he spaced his index finger and thumb several inches apart, "and they aren't trained to fight humans. If I get hit in the wrong spot, I'll bleed out before they have a chance to say 'oops.'"

"How did you stop them last time?" She watched as Fez and Tom exchanged a glance. Neither of them looked happy. "What deal did you make with the Premier?"

"Didn't you read my paper about it?" Fez was wiping dust and dirt off his glasses. "I assumed that's why you came to me."

"I... I skimmed it." Maxine tried not to sound defensive. "I wanted to keep moving in case Validus was stalking me."

"That was one of my best publications," the professor moped, looking hurt as he put his glasses back on.

"It doesn't matter because the deal is broken, as far as they're concerned. I need to prove I didn't get involved with dracks, and who's gonna believe it when the egg thief went straight to my house?" Tom complained bitterly. "I'm going to have to skip town for good this time."

Probably not worth arguing that she wasn't a thief. Maxine didn't know the law around receiving stolen objects, but she knew it wasn't "finders keepers."

She didn't have any response for Tom. She didn't know how to handle one draconic stalking her. Tom had a never-ending stream of them.

"If no one has any ideas, I'm taking the next flight to Hawaii. You should join me, Maxine. It's warm there; perfect climate for the egg."

For a moment, it was a tempting idea. Just fly somewhere else. Leave behind the miserable life of Maxine Hallis, failed wife and therapist, and become someone better. Someone blonde, maybe.

"It's a shame you're married." Fez sighed, looking at Tom. "If you could claim Maxine as your woman, then any threats Validus makes to her are also threats to you. You could argue you never broke the agreement with the Premier, you're just responding to *his* attack."

Maxine felt every muscle freeze, and she saw Tom similarly turn into a statue. Tom recovered first, uncoiling from his hunched position.

"All I'd have to do is fight Validus." Tom was actually considering the idea. Maxine watched in horror as his face lifted, as though this were a lifeline instead of an anchor.

Maxine thought back to her encounter in the coffee shop, staring up at Validus' seven-foot-tall, scaled, fanged, and clawed body. The adolescent and desperate draconics like the ones she saw play-fighting outside Fez's building were one thing, but no human could fight *that*.

"That's ridiculous," Maxine interjected before this line of thought could go too far. "You can't challenge Validus."

Fez agreed with her, but for the wrong reason. "They know you're married, Tom, and only committed couples are allowed to fight on each other's behalf. They won't believe—"

"We broke up," Tom interrupted Fez. "And if I've got dracks stalking me close enough to report Maxine's visit, they definitely know that asshole is out of the picture."

Tom's whole posture had changed. He was opening up and smiling. Jehudin's celestial glow had always brightened when he was excited. A full body throb of grief shook Maxine.

"I'm not your woman, Tom."

This was possibly the least vital issue to start with. She didn't want to let on how much it hurt to even consider. The only person she wanted to "claim" her was no longer on the mortal plane.

"Don't worry, it doesn't mean anything."

"It sounds like it means something."

"Well sure, to the *dracks* it means something!" His voice became sharp, and his fists clenched against his legs as he visibly fought to rein in his reaction. Startled by his outburst, Maxine watched as he hauled backwards on his self-control and hunched his shoulders again to look less threatening. "Dracks fight duels to steal eggs and think being able to tear out your throat means they're better than you. They're monsters, Maxine. And if I hadn't gotten lucky, I'd have died to the sound of hundreds of them cheering."

Maxine could hear her own blood rushing in her ears through the ensuing silence. Fez looked mournfully at Tom.

"What happened?" She was too loud in the small space, so she softened her voice. "How did you get involved, and how did you make a deal with the Premier?"

"Like I said, it doesn't—"

"It matters because I don't believe you can win against Validus." Bluntness seemed to work best with Tom. "And I won't risk the egg for your ego."

The two men exchanged another look. The professor shrugged helplessly, but Tom just looked resigned. He stood from his folding chair, ducking slightly thanks to the low ceiling in the shed. He put a hand on the doorknob, but he paused to raise an eyebrow at Maxine.

"You coming? If I'm gonna prove this to you, you'll have to see it."

And then he was out the door, walking back the way they'd come.

Bad egg

Maxine hurried to catch up with Tom, but Fez got there first.

"Tom, you—you know fighting on campus is against the rules." The professor's words caught in his throat. "We have strict codes of conduct here."

"Tell that to the dracks, Fez." Tom's eyes were scanning the grounds until he found what he was looking for. A young draconic wearing a hoodie and sweatpants like he was Rocky Balboa prowled the footworn grass paths. "Hey you!" Tom bellowed, startling them. "What, do you think I've got all goddamn day? Find your buddies and figure out which one's gonna challenge me today."

The draconic gasped in excitement and dashed off, pulling a phone from his pocket. Tom's mouth was pursed in thought as he looked around.

"This is a decent spot. No obstacles and the ground's flat."

"*Tom!* You cannot fight here!" Fez squeaked. "Take it off campus!"

"The lady needs a show, Fez."

"I don't want to see you fight *anywhere*!" Maxine snapped at him, walking in front of him in case he'd forgotten she was there. "Watching you get your face chewed off isn't going to help me."

"Hey Fez, you can report it to security if you want, but..." Tom was entirely ignoring Maxine while delivering a vicious smirk towards Fez. "...you could also get rare live footage of a human/draconic duel."

The professor's eyes widened and his mouth dropped open. For a moment, Maxine wondered if he'd start drooling. Fez's agony of indecision was obvious as he glanced around and chewed his lower lip. He fumbled a phone out of his coat pocket and looked around again.

"I'll be right back." Without another word, he turned and...

"Wow, he's fast." Her eyes tracked his flapping lab coat as he disappeared behind a building. "But Tom, you should leave before they get back. You don't have to prove anything to me."

"Oh?" The man was bouncing on the balls of his feet and loosening his arms. "You think I can challenge Validus?"

"No, of course not, but you're better off leaving town than getting yourself killed."

"I like it here." He wasn't looking at her while he talked, eyes darting around for potential threats. "And these scaly assholes won't drive me away if I can help it."

"But—"

"Too late now." His smile was grim. "Here they are."

A small cluster of draconics rounded the bend, immediately fixated on Tom. He called out to them as they got closer.

"Who've you picked? You can tussle it out yourselves first, but I'm only taking the strongest."

There was harsh snarling and posturing between the draconics. Maxine backed away several steps automatically, seeing claws swipe at each other and tails lash in a small circle too tight and fast for her to follow what they were doing. A victor emerged quickly.

He was the largest of the group, several inches taller than Tom. Brown scales with a few crackled areas indicating scars decorated his face. Sharp fangs grinned at Tom, and the draconic pulled off his t-shirt to reveal the perfect tessellated scales of his chest and belly. The draconic postured for his friends, baring long claws and striking what Maxine could only assume was a combat-ready pose. It looked to her like he was waiting to catch a football.

"Okay, make this fast, please." Fez's voice startled Maxine, who had been so focused on the draconic challenger that she hadn't heard him return. He was setting up a tripod on the soft loam, camera already recording as he positioned it towards Tom. "Security will be here soon." And then Fez walked several paces to the side, closer to Maxine. He pulled out his phone to take video from a different angle, mumbling date and location details quietly for the recording.

She wasn't sure if she should do something... or what she *could* do. Watching from the sidelines, Tom stepped forward against an opponent no human could possibly take in hand-to-hand combat.

Looking towards the professor, it was obvious he would not be a voice of reason. He was ducked with his eye glued to his phone, not only unconcerned for his friend, but apparently eager to record Tom's grotesque maiming.

"Pay attention!" Tom's voice snapped. He wasn't looking at her, but she could feel his words aimed towards her. "Think of my precious fucking ego, Maxine!"

Before she could respond—not that she knew what to say—Tom lunged under the draconic's claws and drove a shoulder just under his ribcage. She watched as the draconic tried to slash down at the—human who wasn't there anymore. Tom had stepped forward at a forty-five-degree angle and spun a kick connecting the middle of his shin against the connection between the draconic's tail and spine.

Pushed forward, the draconic was lined up perfectly for Tom's steel-toed boot to drive into where the kidneys would be on a human.

Tom knew every move the draconic was about to make. Nothing connected—Tom was too fast—and each of the draconic's attacks somehow helped position Tom for another strike against his opponent. The draconic snarled and snapped his teeth, but it quickly started to look less like intimidation and more like desperation.

"Do you forfeit?" Tom didn't even sound out of breath yet.

His only response was another bloodthirsty snarl, so Tom closed in again with another strike that drove the side of his hand against the draconic's neck before sidestepping an attack clumsier and slower than the last.

"How—" The word fell out of Maxine's mouth, and she cut herself off, unable to tear her eyes away from the horrifying display.

"They never bother to learn humans," Fez answered her faltered question, his eyes still focused on his phone as he made minute adjustments to follow the action. "But Tom has learned them. He's probably the preeminent human expert in draconic anatomy and body language."

The professor quieted, tracking the combatants as they circled each other. The draconic was moving oddly after Tom kicked the side of his knee; his leg wasn't taking the draconic's full weight.

"I don't normally work for free, you know!" Tom called towards her again, giving the draconic a few jabs that only served to position it for driving a heel kick into its gut. It wheezed, bending over and lining itself up for an immediate snapping shin-kick to the side of its head. She winced in empathetic pain, jaw clenched with her own mix of anxiety and horror while Tom kept talking. "This kind of show comes with a cover charge."

"I thought you got out of that, Tom." Fez's voice was disapproving.

"Yeah, me too." Tom was huffing now, but still able to carry on a conversation while whittling away at an increasingly desperate draconic. "But my ego, Fez! I've got to defend my *ego*!"

"And showboating is going to do that?"

"Eh... you've got a point."

The two men stopped talking while Tom focused more intently on his opponent. Maxine only had to hold her breath for a few more brutal crunching attacks before the draconic dropped to his knees and held up his claws.

"Stop! I forfeit!" His voice ragged with humiliation. He had no visible injuries, but Tom had clearly done some real damage to his knee, and one of the draconic's arms wasn't able to lift as high as the other. "I... I forfeit," the draconic repeated, in a pained defeat that had his friends murmuring nearby.

Tom stopped, nodding and stepping back with a few heavy breaths. As if the draconic had just disappeared, Tom ignored him and his friends, turning back to Maxine.

"When I defeat a draconic..." His voice was soft, and he was gently massaging the knuckles of one hand. "It increases my status. And because of the fucking *transitive* property, every time I win, I'm higher status than everyone my opponent has defeated."

She absorbed that for a moment. A "holy grail," Fez had called him. A jackpot of status in a soft, skin-covered human.

"How did you stop them from coming after you?"

"Just like that." He nodded back at the scuffed ground where he'd fought the draconic. "I made my own challenge to the entire Holding. The Premier didn't want me in their fucking hierarchy any more than I did, and he declared it valid. As long as I stayed out of their business, the fights I won during that challenge meant they weren't allowed to go after me."

"You—you didn't fight the entire Holding—"

"Hah, I might as well have! C'mon, I want to sit down." Tom started walking back towards the shed, with Maxine and the professor trailing behind. Fez was stumbling slightly as he tried to adjust camera settings and carry the tripod while moving. "No. They narrowed it down to five." His eyes darkened and his voice deepened. "Five fights in five weeks. It was... hard."

"He almost died," Fez interjected. "If the last one hadn't forfeited, he would have."

"What, but... couldn't *you* forfeit?"

"Forfeit wouldn'ta helped me." He pushed open the sticky door of the garden shed. "*They* could forfeit. But my challenge was "fight me now or fight me never." If *I* tried to forfeit, they could still come after me any time." With a strained creak of plastic, Tom dropped on a folding chair as it held on for dear life beneath him. "So without any broken bones or torn ligaments, I'm pretty damn sure I can take this asshole Validus. Satisfied?"

⚬

Maxine sat in miserable silence for several minutes while Tom waited for her answer and Fez fiddled with his camera. She was unsatisfied with a lot in her life right now, but he had successfully shown her how well he could back up his boasting. Still reeling from the violence she'd just witnessed, she ran against a mental barrier trying to acknowledge his solution. What kind of person would she be if she were accomplice to this... barbaric challenge?

"It's not about you, Tom. If you fail, he gets the egg."

"The egg is the most important thing, right?" Still sitting back and recovering, he clasped one wrist with his opposite hand, his fingers tapping against the black armor protecting his hands. "Not you? It might not even be viable. But you're alive right now, and you're in danger too."

"Correct." The tightness in her chest constricted further.

The garden shed had become uncomfortably hot and muggy with their body heat warming the small space. Both Tom and Fez were looking at her in silence.

"Please tell me you want to live, Maxine," Tom spoke in an angry hush.

"I took responsibility for the egg, Tom. It can't defend itself."

"Neither can you!"

Accurate, but rude. She might not have biceps that could crush coconuts, or abs that could grate cheese, or pecs the size of watermelons... when was the last time she ate?

"Violence isn't going to fix anything. I need to find its mother or someone who will care for it."

Tom's eyes followed the line of her body where it curled around the egg, down to her feet, then back. It looked like he was measuring her. Maxine curled a little more before she realized she was doing it. He wasn't making any threatening moves, but he was still someone the size of a refrigerator wearing tactical gear, and she had just seen how dangerous he could be.

"I need you to agree to this," he said suddenly. "If you don't, I'll be dead in a week."

"I'm sorry, Tom, but—"

"You. Got. Me. Involved." His voice became harsh, edging away from reasonable towards angry, but physically he stayed perfectly still in the cramped, claustrophobic space. "And the answer is easy, for you, anyway.

If I claim you and convince them *Validus* broke the deal with the Premier, I can defeat Validus and the egg will be yours before sunset."

Bile rose in her throat as she considered it. Saying she was "Tom's woman" would be an uncomfortable lie, but ultimately harmless.

She didn't have any other brilliant ideas.

"Fine!" she snapped. "But I want it stated for the record, I *hate* this. Violence does nothing but create more violence."

"Fez, update the record," Tom's voice drawled, but the professor responded with complete sincerity.

"My report will make it abundantly clear it was not your preferred solution," Fez spoke in a preoccupied rush. He was scribbling furiously on a little notepad. "And of course you will have an opportunity to review the accuracy of my representation before—"

Tom stood, hauling Fez in for an actual hug, not one of those manly back-slapping hugs that looked painful. Instead of returning the hug, Fez held his notepad and pen extended behind Tom, still trying to write ideas while they were fresh.

"If this works, you've saved my life twice." Tom backed up, grasping Fez by the shoulders. "And I'll be coming back to your office with matches. You've got a problem, Fez."

"There is a sophisticated system of—"

"Get a fucking filing cabinet!"

"My budget has—"

Maxine had to jam her shoulder into the shed door to open it from the inside.

"Let's go, Tom."

Eggs in a basket

T hey made it back to the parking lot and stood outside Tom's car. Tom had visibly relaxed his hypervigilance, trusting implicitly in the nearby draconics to honor the challenge he'd won, which was interesting. Despite his dislike of draconics, he seemed to believe they were honorable enough to respect a spoken-word agreement before a duel. Maxine wished she knew more about their culture. As the guardian of a draconic egg, she needed to know more about them.

Tom's voice cut into her thoughts.

"I have to make the challenge to Validus before we go to the Holding. Let me see your phone."

Wordlessly, she handed it over. Tapping through her messages, his expression was disdainful as he read through the threatening texts Validus had been sending her.

"Charming." He winked as he pressed the call button. The other end of the call picked up to the sound of Validus' angry voice.

"Shut up, lizard."

Tom spoke with a tone that wasn't quite anger or arrogance; it was vocal posturing that evoked both while implying the person he was talking to wasn't worth the breath. The other end fell silent in surprise.

"You want the egg? I have it. And I'll be making a pair of shoes out of you to wear when I walk away with it."

Validus was yelling something that made Tom's face split into a bloodthirsty smile.

"You're not dealing with a nice young lady anymore, rot-scale. Thomas Morgan. Do you need to look it up?"

Silence, followed by a much more polite sounding voice.

"Yeah, I didn't think so. I'll see you at the Holding. You can forfeit anytime, but now? Now I'm hoping you don't."

He ended the call, handing back her phone.

"That's the first step."

He looked calmer, happier, now that his plan was in motion. His plan that tied the egg's life to Tom's challenge.

"What happens next?" The familiar nausea of anxiety was building in the back of Maxine's throat. "Because that ticket to Hawaii wasn't the worst idea."

"C'mon." Tom opened the passenger door for her. "Next we go to the Holding. We need the Premier to oversee this challenge."

Tom's car was cleaner than hers usually was. A pack of gum had been warming on the dashboard, suffusing the interior with mint. She sat down, buckled herself in, and watched through the side mirror as her own car, left in the university's parking lot, receded behind them.

Never go to a second location.

The intrusive thought was unwelcome. This was her second time alone in a car with him. The first time, he had been grieving a failed marriage and seemed like a completely different person. She realized now that he must have been wearing ill-fitting clothes to hide his muscles—as much as possible, anyway. At the courthouse he had been a large man hunching and using expert control of his body language to convey as much harmlessness as possible.

Now *he* was driving the car. And he was wearing strange combat gear, with abraded knuckles from fist-fighting an actual *draconic*. She felt the weight of the egg where it lay against her chest, trying to look calm even while her heartrate spiked. She had thoroughly lost control of the situation. She trusted Tom... mostly. Sure, she barely knew the guy, but they'd had a whole lunch together and he hadn't murdered her. That had to count for something! If nothing else, he seemed to have his own best interests at heart. So far, they aligned with hers.

He glanced briefly in her direction.

"Do you—do you think I'm kidnapping you?" His voice raised with incredulity at the end. "I'm not kidnapping you, Maxine."

Damn. She wasn't used to being around someone else who read people the same way she did. Maxine frowned with frustration, not used to the taste of her own medicine.

"Sorry." She shrugged, trying to relax the tension in her neck. "I'm not used to... any of this."

"Yeah, I should hope not." He turned back towards the road, huffing air through his nose. "This'll all be over soon, and you can roost on your egg... or whatever you wanna do with it."

"I need to find out where it belongs. Make sure it's safe."

"Isn't Validus the dad?"

"I'm not sure about that, actually." Maxine leaned back in the seat. She let her eyes unfocus, making the world blur outside the window. "But Amanda made it sound like—she said something about him breaking it." At the time, Maxine had been panicked about the woman bleeding to death; now she desperately wished she could remember exactly what Amanda had said. "But all I know about him is that he's violent; he was abusing Amanda and sent me threats. I won't give the egg to an abuser."

"Fair enough." From his tone, Tom couldn't care less what she did with the egg.

"What should I expect at the Holding?" They had left city limits, and were cruising down a highway lined with tall pine trees.

"Dracks." He sounded grim. "A *lot* of dracks."

⸻

The Holding was a large compound of buildings a twenty minute drive outside of town, settled in a lush, landscaped area of shady trees giving the illusion they were much further from civilization than they actually were. The largest and most impressive building looked like a modern skyscraper had a baby with a Gothic cathedral. Pillars decorated marble steps leading to the main entrance and lemon trees lined the walkway. It was gorgeous; she'd had no idea anything like it existed so close to Crestfield.

The parking lot was oddly circular, built around the main building and shaded by closely spaced trees. Tom walked around to open Maxine's door, but she was already out and staring at the carved marble of the main Holding entrance. He didn't give her time to admire it, walking ahead with a determined expression and set-back shoulders.

"This is where they conduct their business and host all the official challenges."

"It's beautiful."

The building was designed to draw people in. Clean, curved lines of marble flowed up a staircase narrow at the top, giving the impression of a frozen waterfall. Carvings too intricate to see from the bottom made her want to climb closer for the details. Light from the afternoon sun turned into brilliant colors as it scattered against stained glass.

"Yeah. So's a cobra."

It was a quiet building. A few draconics were walking with purpose from one place to another, and a semi-circular welcome desk was positioned to greet anyone who entered. Other than herself and Tom, there were no humans. A female draconic with emerald green scales that nicely complemented her lavender blouse was sitting at the desk, reading something on her computer. She looked up and did an honest-to-goodness double take when she saw Tom and Maxine walking in.

"Do you... have an appointment?" she asked hesitantly, glancing between the two of them. Tom positioned himself in front of Maxine, shoulders back and hands loose at his sides.

"I don't need one." His voice was cold. "Tom Morgan; I've got a fight. Please call Rex Invictus and tell him we're here."

"Oh wow," the receptionist whispered, apparently not caring he could hear her. His face scrunched in mild discomfort, but he didn't otherwise react. "You're not what I pictured."

"I get that a lot," he said, dryly. "Can you make that call?"

"What message do you want me to give the Premier?" She reached for the phone without looking at it. Her voice was breathy and she hadn't taken her eyes off him, making Tom look even more constipated and uncomfortable.

"The message," Tom said slowly in the same professional tone as before, "is that I'm here. What he wants to do from that point depends on how busy he is, I guess."

She pushed a couple buttons and the phone connected almost immediately. Another female voice could barely be heard on the other line.

"Hey Callidus," the receptionist effused, "is Rex in a meeting? He needs to know that the human Tom Morgan is here."

The responding chatter of words was unintelligible.

"No, he's smaller than I thought!" the receptionist gushed, apparently unashamed to gossip right in front of Tom. Maxine couldn't help but look up at him. He was over six feet of muscle, by a wide margin one of the largest humans she'd met in person. "Okay, yes, please give Rex the message. Thank you!"

She hung up, still staring at Tom. "Someone should be down in a minute."

"Thank you." He did not sound thankful, but he guided Maxine over to the side where they could wait. The receptionist took out her phone and was obviously taking selfies with him in the background. He turned his back to keep his face out of frame.

It only took a few minutes for a gray-scaled draconic in a matching gray suit to come out of the elevator, hurrying into the lobby as if his tail was on fire. His eyes latched onto Tom and Maxine as he hustled towards them.

"Mr. Thomas Morgan?"

"That's me." He started walking towards the elevator before the draconic could ask. Tom put a gentle hand on Maxine's elbow to keep her close by his side. "This way, right?"

If the gray draconic was upset that Tom took the lead, he didn't show it.

"Yes, yes, please, this way!" Scrambling ahead of them to the elevator, the eager draconic held the door open and pressed the second from the top button. "Could I get a selfie?" the draconic asked hopefully, reaching for his phone.

"No."

Sagging in disappointment, the gray draconic nodded and dropped his hand. Maxine couldn't help but feel bad for him. But it also hadn't escaped her attention that neither the receptionist nor this guide had given her or the egg she was carrying a first—much less a second—glance. She didn't say anything about it but glanced quizzically at Tom. Was this normal? How high status was Tom that he could show up and demand an immediate audience with the Premier by name?

The elevator opened into a large hallway with what must be the female draconic who had been on the phone earlier standing eagerly nearby to get a glimpse of Tom. Other, older draconics were in the process of squeezing themselves along the wall to avoid confrontation.

With the Premier towering over Tom and Maxine in the hallway, confrontation wasn't trying to avoid them.

Into the nest

The largest draconic Maxine had ever seen was taking up the middle of the hallway. His scales were pitch black and he wore a navy suit with gold trim. His horns were capped with gold. He was looming outside the elevator, waiting for Tom to step into the hallway. The tips of his horns had to be nine feet high, nearly scraping the ceiling. Maxine couldn't help but clutch the egg a little tighter to her chest as she craned her neck to see her own reflection shining back by the hundreds from each of the little scales on the large draconic's face.

When he spoke, his voice was deep enough to vibrate the floor.

"Why?"

That was all he said, his arms crossed over his chest as he stepped forward to tower over Tom, who, for his part, stepped forward without any evidence of being intimidated.

"Asshole named Validus attacked my woman," Tom said smoothly. He indicated Maxine with his thumb. "He broke into her place, got me involved. I want his egg as punishment, no more of your draconics fucking around with my stuff. Then I'm out again."

Maxine felt chills, freezing like a mouse caught in a trap, as the large draconic pinned her down with his eyes then looked back at Tom.

"It seems you already have his egg."

"I haven't paid for it yet."

"Ah." Now the large draconic nodded, uncrossing his arms. "Validus is in violation. Confirm the arena." He turned to the female draconic standing by the wall, hanging onto every word. "Assign them a room and guard until the fight."

She nodded, and that seemed to be the conclusion of their business. The large black draconic turned and ducked his horns under the door frame to his office, closing the door behind him.

Squeezing her elbow, Tom murmured softly, "Almost there, hold tight."

The female draconic gripped a tablet and smiled at them. "We've got a free room upstairs, and we can text you when Validus arrives. All I need is your number to—"

"You don't need my number," Tom said, cutting her off. "Just have the guard knock when it's all settled."

"Oh—oh, of course. Um, please follow me!" Her smile faded. She glanced quickly at Maxine then back at Tom as though she didn't know if she were allowed to look at "his" woman.

She led them back inside the elevator, where she clicked the top level button with a manicured claw. In moments the doors were opening again, and she gestured them down a hallway that looked like it belonged in an expensive hotel.

Instead of generic carpet and fluorescent lights, this level was appointed with dark, rich colors. None of the doors had numbers, but they were all fitted with electronic keycard locks. Worryingly, they each had a heavy deadbolt on the outside of the door. They followed the woman around several corners, until she stopped at a seemingly random door and waved her badge in front of the lock mechanism.

It blipped green, and she turned the handle to open it for them, standing welcomingly to the side as she pushed the door open. The woman lingered in the doorway for a moment too long. She smiled at Tom, continuing to ignore Maxine. "Call and place an order if you need food. The guard will be here shortly."

He nodded, barely looking at her.

"O-okay," she stammered. "Good luck!"

And when she closed the door behind them there was an audible *click* and the sound of the deadbolt locking into place.

It took a moment for Maxine to unstick her tongue from the roof of her mouth. This was a luxurious hotel room on the top level of the Holding. There was a kitchenette, a small sitting area with two couches facing each other, a door that presumably led into the bathroom, and a king-sized bed piled high with pillows.

Grimacing, Tom walked to a side table where he proceeded to unravel any attempt to put her at ease by laying out a wicked-looking combat knife in a sheath and a retractable baton from where they had been hidden inside the waistband of his pants. A set of brass knuckles landed next to them with a heavy *thunk*.

Feeling entirely out of her depth, Maxine struggled to think of something to say.

"So, what happens now?"

"It's pretty simple from this point. I issued an official challenge, and Validus needs to respond or he forfeits by default. That's basically a one-way ticket out of the Holding." He laughed without any real humor. "Forfeit just lowers status, but getting kicked out of the Holding is worse. This is where nearly all of the dracks live and work."

Tom leaned back on the couch, gesturing broadly at the well-appointed room.

"A guard will be outside to make sure we stay put. They want to stop cowards from killing their challenger before the official fight. When Validus comes in, he can either forfeit in person, witnessed by the Premier, or be stuck in a different room and have his own guard until our spot's available."

Wow. There were a lot of business processes designed around brutal fighting.

Maxine walked to the window and twitched open the curtains. They were looking out over the meticulously landscaped winding gardens and trees. From this high up, the patterns of the paths and trees became obvious. They all interlocked in complex concentric rings around the building, forming a labyrinth with the draconic Holding in the center.

Squinting at the patterns of the garden, she saw a second node in the maze. Fractals of trees and carved bushes connected it to the main Holding. It was much smaller though; a marble and stone edifice surrounding—

"They have their own planar gate?"

"Hm?" Tom loomed over her shoulder to see what she was looking at. "Yeah, I guess. Is that bad?"

"No, not... not bad." Controlling a planar gate was like having your own airport, expensive and politically advantageous. Even more than the Premier's imposing appearance, this was their real flex of strength.

She sat down in one of the soft chairs, sinking into a seat designed for someone with a tail.

"Tom... how much danger are you in right now?"

He removed his body armor and carefully placed it all in some strangely specific order on the kitchenette table. Once he was left in a turtleneck, canvas pants, and socks, he finally looked back up to make eye contact with her again. Without the armor and combat boots, with his hair loose around his shoulders, he didn't look like a soldier anymore. He just looked tired.

"On a scale of one to ten? Eh, this is a six or seven." His voice was dismissive. "These fights aren't typically to the death, but... draconics don't know how to fight humans. They don't even need to be trying. Their claws will go this deep if I don't stop them." He held his fingers several inches apart— easily enough depth to kill him depending on where it was. "But Validus didn't sound high status, I'm not worried."

"And... he'll actually stop harassing me if you win?"

"When." Tom smirked. "When I win, yeah he'll let it go. There's no do-overs. If he steps into the arena, loses, and still tries to go after you, that's a challenge to Rex Invictus' authority."

No more questions were needed about that. After one look at the Premier, Maxine knew he wasn't a draconic who would allow a challenge to his authority.

"And what if you lose?"

"I won't."

"Humor me."

"If I lose," he said with good-natured sarcasm as if she was being unreasonable to think a six-foot-tall squishy human could possibly fail to defeat a seven-foot-tall scaled draconic in hand to hand combat, "then it's the best possible outcome. I'll be dead, and Validus will take the egg. All your problems solved."

"That's not funny, Tom."

"It's called gallows humor for a reason." The lines around his eyes crinkled, and he pushed himself off the couch. "Hey, hey, it'll be okay."

Coming closer, he perched his butt on the arm of her chair to give her an unexpected side hug. She hadn't been hugged in… a long time, and the contact startled her out of her doom spiral. He pulled her close against him in a gentle squeeze, warmth suffusing her side.

"Relax, it'll be fine. Look on the bright side."

He waited for her to say something like "and what's that?" but she sat there quietly suffering, so he continued anyway.

"You're a couple's therapist, right? How often do you get to fix a relationship by getting someone to beat up a shitty boyfriend?"

Blinking, Maxine stared into middle space while his words sank in. How many sessions with Amanda had she spent holding onto professionalism with a vise grip? But she'd never wish *harm* on anyone, that wouldn't—

"C'mooooon," he cajoled, shaking her gently. "Enjoy this. Got any requests? Want me to make him eat his own teeth?"

"That's horrible!" She tried to make her voice sound horrified. She didn't succeed. He shook her a little harder, laughing again as he saw her mouth twist in an attempt to hold back a smile.

"Give horrible a try," he said cheerfully, having successfully lightened the mood. "It's a lot more fun."

⋅•◦•⋅

Maxine was pretending to play on her phone while Tom worked off some excess energy.

He was on the ground doing push-ups. A lot of push-ups. Wow… how many… Maxine found herself transfixed, watching for far too long. He was still going! Not trying to be a creep, she couldn't help but stare as he smoothly lowered himself to the ground and back up with perfect form.

His back was flat as a plank, his butt was... taut... she needed to keep her eyes moving. Don't stare! He moved smoothly, faster on the up and a bit more slowly down.

He didn't even look tired. His face wasn't red or sweaty.

"See something you like?"

She jumped at his voice breaking into her lack of thoughts while she'd be staring. She had somehow forgotten that if she could see him, he could see her.

"Ah, oh, I'm sorry!" Blushing, Maxine turned away, looking anywhere else around the room to find some dignity. Nope. Maybe they could order some from room service. "I—I didn't mean to stare."

"You can stare." He popped up to his feet and brushed his hands down the front of his shirt, briefly outlining his abs in the process. He moved closer, shifting into a flirty tone. "We might be waiting a long time; it's the hardest part. If you want to play with more than your phone, I'm down."

The way he said the word *down* sent a jolt of adrenaline through her body. The invitation was obvious and... forthright. An opportunistic suggestion made by someone who had no emotional connection to the outcome.

Would it be wrong to have casual sex for once? She wanted Jehudin back, but logically she also knew that was a fantasy born of desperation. He'd left her a year ago and she had to admit she was... pent up.

Even if she could ignore that their current circumstances amounted to being in a comfortable prison cell, the fact of her own inability to have "fun" with him weighed in her mind. He didn't deserve to be saddled with her dysfunctions.

All this went through her mind, having no idea how to respond to him. She stared for an uncomfortable minute clutching her hands around figurative pearls. Meanwhile, he stood on display, studying her lack of reaction with his particular brand of telepathy.

"Didn't mean to make you uncomfortable." He smiled casually, raising both hands in an exaggerated shrug. "You're sexy and I'd be happy to kill some time with you, but that's all I—"

"I can't have sex anymore!" she blurted out, saying the first thing she was thinking without a goddamn mental filter to be found. "I'm sorry."

His casual expression intensified into sharp attention at her phrasing. If her goal was to move away from this conversation, it backfired. He looked like a dog catching the smell of bacon.

"You *can't* have sex anymore?" he repeated, sounding like a therapist digging into an interesting topic. Or he would have, if there weren't so much unprofessional fascination in his voice. "What does that mean?"

"There just, uh..." Based on the heat in her cheeks, her face must be beet red. As her heart hammered, she wished she hadn't put herself in this hole, but maybe if she kept digging, she'd find a way out. "There isn't really a point. After Jehudin left, nothing... nothing works."

His eyes widened, but before he had a chance to say anything she kept going, a glutton for embarrassment. Maybe she could somehow make it sound better than it was, whispered the dumbest part of her brain. The one that was currently in charge.

"It's fine!" she continued. "I'm sorry, I didn't mean to imply— but, no, I just... after being with a celestial, there isn't... nothing else is going to be... you know what, forget I said anything, I'm sorry."

"Max*ine*." He stressed the second syllable of her name, leaning even closer until she could feel his heat radiating out. "I'm bored. You can't say something interesting and then say 'never mind.'"

"Well... clearly I can, so..."

"What's sex with a celestial like, anyway?"

There she was again staring at him for completely different reasons. He stared right back, a slow grin starting across his face.

"It can't be *that* good," he scoffed.

"I barely know you, Tom!" Maxine couldn't help but defensively cross her arms, despite knowing the more she tried to close herself off, the more he could read her like an open book. "That's personal."

"I like personal." He was not deterred, an impish grin on his face. "Did his dick glow?" His grin widened. "Did he vibrate, or something?"

"No!" Maxine defeated her own attempts to change the subject by immediately following up with, "It did glow, a little. But that's not, he just..." She gave in to the embarrassment. "He was a direct connection to the astral plane, okay? When we had sex, it was bliss that just— it overwhelmed everything. Everywhere."

She had never actually talked to anyone about this, and he looked so interested and nonjudgmental she kept going.

"Normal stimulation just doesn't do anything for me, after that. I mean, sure it feels nice sometimes, but so does a massage. It's like... friction by itself doesn't do enough anymore. It's fine. I'm fine. It's just one of those— one of those things now." One of those things she lived with, no matter how unfair it was. One of those things she tried not to think about. One of those things she'd lost in the separation.

"Hmmm." He didn't look sympathetic, which she appreciated, but he looked like he was evaluating a puzzle, which wasn't much better. "Since the separation, have you tried with anyone else?"

"N-No, that wouldn't... be fair to me or them."

"Why not?"

"It's not fair to compare someone else to him." Why did he care so much? It's not like her sex life was any of his business anyway. "And anyone I'm with, I'm going to compare to— Look, I said it's fine. Let's drop it."

"Do you really want me to drop it?" His voice got deeper. He was close enough to smell the last twenty-four hours that she'd been unable to shower. "Because I see this as a perfect opportunity."

A sharp knock at the door had her jumping in surprise. Tom scowled and turned.

"What?" he yelled curtly at the closed door.

"Your guy came in," a gravelly voice answered. "You've got a meeting."

Tom didn't respond, but glowered at the door before rolling his shoulders and stepping back to restore her personal space. Smirking down at Maxine for a moment, he walked back to where he had organized all his equipment and began the process of armoring himself. "Don't worry, I'm gonna ask more questions later."

Yolking around

After Tom put all his gear back on, ate an energy bar, and fixed his bun back in place, a large, brown-scaled draconic guard opened the door for them. The lighthearted mood from before was gone, but Tom didn't seem quite as grim as when they first entered the building.

The guard led them through a series of twists and turns in the hallways, ending up at a large glass door which opened automatically. This opened into a VIP stadium box designed to look down over the arena. Tom barely glanced at their surroundings, focused on the several other draconics in the room, but Maxine craned her neck trying to take it all in.

She had been picturing something like a Roman coliseum, but this was closer to a pay-per-view fighting stage. Everything was sleek and modern, made of nonporous materials capable of being wiped clean. Or hosed down. She could smell bleach, which turned her stomach for the implication of what it had been used for. There were spotlights trained on a large stage, with doorways on either side for dramatic entrances. All the surfaces were matte black with brilliant accents of red and gold. All the seats were designed for draconics, with a c-shaped cut-out in the back which would allow for their tails to easily slide in from the side. The stadium contained at least a thousand seats—how many draconics lived here? If this place were packed full, the roar would be deafening.

Maxine shifted her gaze to the other draconics. Rex was the most recognizable. He towered over what appeared to be a few guards... and Validus. In direct contrast to how Validus had behaved with her in the café, she saw him hunched in an obsequious posture next to Rex Invictus.

Validus was glancing between Tom and Rex the moment they walked in, and even backed up a couple steps. Rex, meanwhile, glowered with the attitude of someone who considered everything they were doing to be a waste of time.

Before they had walked far into the room, Rex called out in his deep voice, "Validus contests your right of challenge."

Tom's steps faltered in surprise. Maxine's constant anxiety spiked even higher than before. What did that mean? Approximately thirty doomsday-scenarios-per-second rotated through Maxine's head.

"I did not break the agreement," Validus snarled. "The human Thomas Morgan has not claimed this woman. And she is the one with my egg."

Tom squared off a few feet away from Validus, sneering up at him.

"You sure about that?"

"This has nothing to do with you!" Validus' voice had a hint of whine to it. "She stole the egg, and I will take it back."

Maxine had one hand protectively cupped over the egg and two eyes locked on Validus. He was stuck in the uncomfortable attempt to both cower in front of Rex Invictus and posture in front of Tom. The effect made him look like he should be ringing a giant bell in the tower of Notre Dame.

If Validus had been scared in the café when she first met him, this was what he looked like terrified. Here was a bully finally forced to face a real opponent instead of picking on people who couldn't fight back. But there was something else there.

If she had to guess—and until those mind reading powers came in, guessing was all she had—he was terrified that someone would discover his relationship with a human and force him to leave the Holding. He probably never wanted any kind of attention from the Premier, and when a famous human like Thomas Morgan got involved, Validus didn't know what to do.

"Maxine is mine." Tom put a possessive hand on her shoulder, giving her what he probably intended to be an apologetic squeeze. "And I'm going to pull out a scale for every text and voicemail you left her."

Validus' blue scales paled as he blanched. He swallowed, desperate not to lose any further face in front of Rex Invictus, but cowed by Tom's reputation.

"Lies! You human filth always lie!"

"We've been seen together." Maxine stepped into the conversation. "A few young draconics saw us on a date days before I was given the egg."

"That is not proof." Rex's voice commanded the room. "And it is common knowledge the human Thomas Morgan has until recently been in a committed relationship with someone else. I will not permit our rituals to be cheapened into champion fighting. He may not claim the egg."

Feverish sweat chilled her body as Maxine realized how tenuous their lifeline was. Without the acknowledgment she was "Tom's woman," she had walked the egg right to Validus and Tom couldn't stop the draconic from taking it.

If she conferred with Tom, would it look too much like they were trying to get their story straight? It wasn't until this moment she realized she didn't have a strong enough grasp on what draconic partnerships looked like to convince them she and Tom had the kind of relationship which would allow one to fight a challenge on behalf of the other.

"Give me my egg now, human." Validus saw his victory in sight, and he was starting to look more confident. "If you do, I will not tear it from your lifeless body."

Tom's hand was still clamped on her shoulder. He was tense, probably unsure of the best way to proceed, but started pulling Maxine back to stand behind him. Taking an involuntary step back as Tom pulled her off balance, she saw the difference in Tom and Validus' postures.

Tom was leaning forward, concerned for her wellbeing. Validus was also leaning forward, but in the same looming way as from the coffee shop when he tried to intimidate her the first time.

He was trying to scare her... because he was scared. No, he was panicking! He never wanted this to go in front of the Premier. With a flash of inspiration and recklessness born from a dearth of options, Maxine stepped forward in front of Tom, shaking his hand off her shoulder.

"Validus." She looked up at the draconic's snarling face, the egg a warm and comforting weight against her chest. "I've got a challenge of my own. But first, let's talk, you and me."

The draconic was about to sneer something insulting, but she headed him off.

"If you don't admit this egg isn't yours after five minutes talking with me, *I* will fight you for it."

Maxine was still trying to get the hang of draconic facial expressions, but between Validus, Rex, and the nearby guards, she was pretty sure she got a good sampling of disbelief. Or maybe pity.

"Maxine," Tom hissed, limited by what he could say with so many listening ears. "That is a very bad plan."

"Five minutes in private." Maxine repeated, staring up into Validus' eyes. Her heart was racing against her ribcage, and a burst of adrenaline lit up her nerves. "And after that, if you still want, I will walk into that arena with you."

"Why would I waste my time?" Validus sneered. "I can take it from you without the challenge."

"Maybe." She shrugged, and then she took a shot in the dark. "But I don't think that's what Amanda had in mind when she gave me the egg."

Validus' eyes widened as her gamble paid off. He didn't want the other draconics to know about Amanda. He had been associating with humans too much, and it risked his position.

"Make a decision," Rex Invictus' deep voice rumbled.

———◄O►———

Ignoring the desperate anxiety on Tom's face as the door to her small private room clicked shut, Maxine grinned at Validus, who straightened as soon as he didn't have Rex Invictus to show deference towards.

Maxine wasn't going to waste precious time finding out what unimaginative threats he would dredge up. The texts he'd been spamming her with had given her enough of a picture of his idea of what he thought was frightening, and it was all descriptions of how her weak human flesh could be maimed.

Maxine was filling in a few blanks with a mix of intuition and guesswork. She had no idea what Amanda was involved in with draconics, but she was doing something with Validus that wasn't sanctioned by the Holding. She stole the egg, and now he was stuck trying to get it back and the only thing he knew how to do was scare human women.

Which was what he was trying to do now. Standing as tall as he could, puffing out his chest, and showing all his fangs. He snarled, "I will—"

"You need to stay in the Holding for some reason," Maxine interrupted. "And I don't know what that reason is yet, but the draconics here probably don't know you've been dating a human for months. Or that this isn't your egg."

That last bit was a guess, but her shot in the dark paid off. Validus took a step backwards, surprised into silence. Maxine advanced.

"Who are you working for, Validus?"

"You know nothing about—"

"I know you don't want attention. And I know the story of the mighty Validus tearing apart Thomas Morgan's woman in an official challenge overseen by Rex Invictus... that would get you a lot of attention, wouldn't it?"

Validus swallowed, lashing his tail.

"What would the Holding discover about you if they were paying attention?"

His claws flexed in the air and he bared his fangs even more. But he didn't say anything. Time was tight; she talked fast.

"If you rescind your challenge when we leave this room, neither of us need to forfeit anything. You can keep your status in the Holding. You can say this was a mistake, wrong egg, whatever you like. I don't care." She took a deep breath. "But you're going to tell me who wants this egg. And why."

"Or else what?"

"Or else..." Maxine paused briefly for emphasis. "I'll challenge you for it. I'll get in that ring with you, and you'll have to beat me while everyone watches. How many draconics would show up to watch the fight against Thomas Morgan's woman?"

She took another step closer, reveling in his continued retreat. It was a small room. His tail bumped the back wall.

"You'll get all the status and glory you deserve for beating up a helpless human woman. And as a bonus, every draconic in the Holding will crawl up your tail to figure out what you're up to."

Maxine held up her phone to show ninety seconds remaining from their five-minute countdown. He was a coward and he was in hiding. Now he was under pressure.

"Hurry up, Validus. Who do you work for?"

"Exalt." His furious growl held stark contrast against the defeated hang of his head. "And they will not stop chasing you for that egg. If you don't give it back, you will never know a moment's—"

"What is Exalt?"

"We are seeding a new future for draconics, nourished with your blood!" Validus snarled. "Humans will finally be useful as our fertilizer, you whimpering apes!"

"I can't wait." Maxine hadn't gotten all the answers she wanted, but the timer was down to a couple seconds. "Pleasure working with you, Validus."

He burst out of the room with an outraged roar, but he stopped in his tracks at the sight of Rex Invictus and several guards waiting.

"I withdraw my challenge!" Validus' voice was harsh, but he seemed unsure of how much to cower, or to whom. He had lost. "It was... it was not mine. An error. She has the right of ownership."

Stepping out of the room with a little more dignity, Maxine got to enjoy the variety of expressions and tried to memorize them. Was this what draconic shock looked like? Admiration? It was getting close to dinnertime, maybe they were just hungry.

Rex nodded, grateful for nothing so much as completing this task he considered beneath him.

"Observed." The draconic leader turned his terrifying gaze to Maxine. "Given the circumstances, I will acknowledge your partnership with Thomas Morgan. In future challenges, he may claim you and fight on your behalf." There might have been a twinkle of amusement in his slitted eyes. "Or you may claim him. Now leave. You have no business with the Holding."

Egghead

Walking with Tom back to the car, Maxine cleared the sting of bleach and the metallic taste of draconic breath from the back of her throat.

She still had the egg, and now she also had a name. Exalt.

"What did you say to him?"

Tom had been silent during the entire walk out of the Holding. She wanted to think it was in quiet admiration of her non-violent diplomacy, but she suspected he didn't want to start screaming until they were out of the Holding.

As she finished relating her mostly one-sided conversation with Validus, Maxine was energized with victory. "I still don't know what is so special about this egg, but now I have something to go on. Maybe Professor Jiminez knows something about Exalt, or... or maybe Amanda will be able to tell me more when she wakes up."

Tom was nodding along with her, unlocking his car. He looked... disappointed?

"Tom, this is the best-case scenario! The draconics won't be after you anymore."

"The word still needs to spread, but yeah." He looked at her sideways. "But you don't know who's coming after *you*."

"True." Maxine started buckling up, ready to get back to her research. "Whatever Exalt is, Validus failed, and they might send someone else." It didn't feel real enough to worry about yet. "I'll figure it out."

He drove carefully, still checking his mirrors for anyone following. The silence was starting to feel sullen.

"Please don't tell me you're disappointed this ended peacefully." Was this where his machismo would finally win out, and he'd complain about being saved by the woman? "I hope I didn't damage your—"

"Using your weakness against Validus was stupid," Tom interrupted. "But if something is stupid and works…" He shrugged. "It won't work against someone who isn't draconic. Or if there aren't witnesses."

"I'll have to be careful." It was true that her ability to threaten Validus with being able to beat her up was a very specific circumstance. Don't try this at home kids; she was a professional. "But you can relax, at least. You're in the clear."

She wasn't sure how to interpret the look he gave her.

⸻ ◆ ⸻

By the time they got back to campus, the sun was low in the sky and the silence in Tom's car had become oppressive. He hadn't given up his paranoia, still checking all the mirrors for anyone following them. It was true, Maxine mused, that he still needed to worry about any draconics who hadn't heard Tom was back out of the hierarchy.

Tom parked his car all the way on the other side of the lot from hers. He had been through a lot, and Maxine was sympathetic, but this felt like the pettiest revenge on his part. Making her walk the length of the parking lot was an annoyance, but not a problem.

"Well, Tom, thank you for—"

"Your life is in danger."

"Maybe. But this isn't your problem." She pushed as much sincerity into her voice as she could. "I knocked on your door after meeting you once, and I thought all I needed was a safe place to stash the egg for a while. I never meant to put you at risk."

"Now *you're* at risk."

"I'll be fine. You didn't even want to be involved!"

"Yeah." He nodded, but didn't look like he was agreeing. "But you're gonna get yourself killed, Maxine. You can't protect yourself."

"Fuck you!" She snapped it without thinking. "I mean, thanks for all your help, but also, fuck you! I may not be able to fight off draconics, but if Amanda can't take the egg back, I'll figure out whatever kind of foster system exists that can find it a home. This is an awful, shitty situation but it's my responsibility."

"You're not prepared for anything Validus is afraid of."

"And you're not going to help me get answers, Tom. You're going to look for violence until you find it, and that puts the egg at risk."

"What's your plan if Amanda doesn't know what's going on? What if she's unconscious or dead?"

"I—" The idea Amanda might be dead hadn't occurred to her. She was safe at the hospital receiving care. But the thought of showing up to ask her questions and getting no good information about the egg was unnerving. Maxine didn't have any other resource to learn about it.

"Will you leave the egg at the hospital? If she's not able to take control of it, what will you do?"

Anxiety and frustration gnawed at her. She didn't know what she would do, but she also didn't want Tom's presence to make peaceful solutions impossible. If she was carrying a hammer with her everywhere, people would worry they looked like nails.

Maxine pulled the door handle, but Tom reached across her and closed the door before she could do more than open it a crack. His arm was an iron bar blocking her in the car.

"Wait." His voice was pleading in response to her outraged expression. He let go and leaned back. "Please wait. It's not safe."

Tom was struggling with something internal. She couldn't read the thoughts passing over his face, but she could tell he was fighting for the right words.

"I'm not going to solve anything with violence, Tom." She didn't think he'd understand, but it was still worth trying to get through to him.

"You've got a blind spot. Not everything can be solved by talking."

"So far talking has worked well for me."

"Okay." He looked through the windshield towards her car, sitting alone at the far side of the parking lot. "There's somebody waiting for you in your car. What do you think they want to talk about?"

⚬

She hadn't noticed, because she didn't have Tom's paranoid hypervigilance... which she may need to reclassify as justifiable hypervigilance... but the chassis of her car was sinking lower to the ground than it would if it were empty. It was a detail she would never have noticed on her own, and she still wasn't entirely sure it didn't always look like that.

"Stay back." Tom got out of the car, taking a circuitous route across the parking lot.

Watching from the passenger side of his car, she could now see the subtle shifting of her rear bumper as whoever it was hiding moved around slightly. Not sure what to expect, she was still surprised when the back door of her car burst open and a wolf exploded towards Tom in the middle of transforming into its primal form.

A werewolf typically had three forms. Human, which looked human, wolf, which looked wolf, and primal, which looked like a nightmare creature designed for no other purpose than ripping bones from flesh and cracking them to splinters in its jaws. Standing approximately seven feet tall on its two legs, its arms were freakishly long, ending in blackened claws. Its maw, gnashing towards Tom's face, could crush skulls.

The primal form was a pants-shittingly terrifying monster. It was also, completely coincidentally, the same approximate size and shape as a draconic. Tom, an expert at fighting draconics, lunged forward to meet the attacker without a moment of hesitation. He was still wearing the tactical gear Maxine had once considered ridiculous. It looked much less ridiculous now.

Tom grappled against the primal in a chaotic tsunami of fur. It gave a snarl so ferocious that Maxine froze in her seat from across the parking lot and squeezed her eyes shut. She couldn't watch. The wolf was going to tear Tom apart in—

The ferocious snarl turned into a high-pitched yelp of pain and surprise—like someone had just stepped on a puppy's tail. Her eyes shot open again, blinking against the blur of movement.

Tom closed in on the werewolf, holding his combat knife in one hand and those brass knuckles wrapped around his other hand. She would have expected him to look angry, but his face was set in a mask of intense concentration. A chess master planning out the next ten moves. Watching him move now, it was obvious that when he'd fought the draconic, he'd been showing off.

The primal backed up to reevaluate his opponent. Tom looked unhurt so far, although she could see a score of white across his body armor where the werewolf had scratched him. That would have disemboweled an unarmored man.

Riveted by the fight, Maxine was too surprised to react when her own car door opened and a hand gripped her by the hair, pulling her out.

She shrieked, scrabbling her heels on the pavement as she was dragged several feet away from Tom's car. Instinctively grabbing the wrist holding onto her, she tried to turn to look at her attacker, but she could only hear his harsh chuckle.

"Take the egg off, slowly." His voice had a distinctive vampire lisp. "We don't want to crack it, do we?"

This was her moment to use that three-hour self-defense seminar she'd taken in college. She could try to throw some elbows back, or stomp on his foot, or... or do nothing.

Maxine had never been attacked before, and the combination of inexperience with her own ingrained hesitation to hurt anybody resulted in a freeze reaction. The vampire shook her head with his grip on her hair.

"Are you stupid?" he hissed. "Give me the egg!"

She couldn't move her hands. It felt like he was going to rip off her scalp. Every time she tried to get her feet under her, she was pulled further back and off balance again.

Tom was fully occupied by the werewolf. They were circling each other, keeping out of reach but not letting the other one get too far. If Tom knew Maxine was in trouble, there was nothing he could do about it.

"Useless human!" The vampire holding her was losing patience. Her limbs came back to life as soon as she felt him groping for the egg.

"No!" She grabbed at it desperately, crossing her arms to prevent him from pulling it out of her sling.

The sound of rapidly approaching footsteps clattered to a halt nearby.

Professor Jiminez stepped into Maxine's view. He was training his small portable camcorder on Tom's fight, but was looking at the man holding Maxine. His voice cut in.

"Excuse me sir, can you confirm your affiliation?"

"What? Turn that camera off!"

"Oh no, this footage will be invaluable for my grant proposal on paranormal conflict. However it would help if I knew your organization or societal affiliation."

Professor Jiminez looked like a hungry—no, like a starving man at a buffet. He was staring over Maxine's head with the fascinated focus of someone memorizing details.

"I assure you," Fez continued, "my characterization will be very respectful."

"I'll break her neck if you don't drop that camera."

The vampire sounded serious, shaking Maxine slightly for emphasis. Still trapped, Maxine watched as Fez turned the camera to focus on her captor.

"I have permission to film on this campus."

Find a career you love, and you'll never work a day in your life. Professor Jiminez clearly loved his work.

With a hiss, Maxine was thrown to the side and the vampire snatched the camera out of the professor's hands, smashing it down onto the pavement.

Signaling the werewolf with a piercing whistle, the vampire retreated.

Tom allowed the werewolf to disengage. The primal form shifted to a comparatively gorgeous wolf and bounded past them, allowing the vampire to grasp his fur and cling to his back as they fled the scene.

Everything had happened so quickly, Maxine registered the action like the still-frame flashes of a strobe light. Frozen as if in a blue-screen brain failure, Maxine felt nothing. Not scared, not angry, just... stuck.

Watching as they fled, the professor hardly looked put out at losing his camera. His hands were planted on his hips, an expression of consternation on his face as he lost his interview subject.

"I'd like to ride a werewolf someday."

Maxine sat down to enjoy the solidity of the cracked pavement, barely aware of the plastic and glass from the broken camera.

⚬

"Excuse me, are you injured?" She felt Fez gently probing her head where the vampire had grabbed her. Tom called out as he came closer.

"Maxine, you okay? Did he bite you?"

When she failed to respond, Fez answered for her. "I believe she is in shock, but unharmed."

"Thanks for the assist, Fez." Tom was now next to her. The streetlights lining the parking lot illuminated the dark stain of blood on his left leg. "Hey, you ever heard of a group called Exalt?"

"Of course." They talked like this was a normal conversation, their voices casual and relaxed. "It's a multi-chapter and international paranormal society, but each chapter operates independently. I don't know much about the local chapter, but they're all anti-human."

"Shocking." Tom's voice was sarcastic. "And here I was hoping they'd invite us to the cookout."

"They still might." Fez crouched to look through the pieces of broken camera. "You do have quite a lot of blood to go around. Oh, careful where you step! I should be able to salvage the data card."

"Maxine, you with us?" Tom was squinting at her face.

"Am I... Tom, you're bleeding!" This was suddenly a more pertinent issue than her own mental crisis.

"Yeah, that asshole got a shallow slice, it's fine."

"Pr-Professor Jiminez, are you okay? What were you—"

"Oh, yes. You won't catch me wrestling a werewolf, but an obvious camera has saved my life several times. Never go anywhere without it!"

"No one ever catches this slippery bastard." Tom's voice was warm with affection. He nudged the kneeling professor with his bleeding leg. "Is there a species you can't outrun, Fez?"

"Several!" Fez laughed. "But I try not to get close to giants, and the Fae are rare. I don't think any of them hate me yet."

Maxine started to feel her limbs coming back online. Her fingers were shaking, but she only knew this because she was looking at them. She couldn't feel her hands.

"Hey, hey." Tom knelt close by, but hovered his hands as if unsure of whether she'd welcome his touch. "It's okay. They were expecting to ambush you, not planning on an actual fight."

"Ambush me." The werewolf had been in the back seat of her car. If she had ignored Tom and gotten into her car alone, what would have happened? All of this fit nicely into a box she could repress and unpack later. First Amanda and now this. Was her car *that* easy to break into?

"Acute stress is normal after violence, especially if it is a new experience. You may be feeling numbness, difficulty focusing, out-of-body perception, or any number of post-traumatic symptoms."

Thankfully, Professor Jiminez's eagerness to mansplain psychology to Maxine awoke her from her shock.

"Yes, I know." A quick examination of the egg showed it was unharmed. "I don't have time for PTSD right now; I need to get to Amanda."

She was exhausted, but this latest encounter was a reminder that there were other people in danger. Amanda was either safe in the hospital, or she was an easy target.

"Are you gonna let me go with you?" Tom had his lips pressed tightly together, probably barely preventing the "I told you so" from bursting out.

Did she want backup for the insanity that seemed to be coming at her from every direction? Yes, of course. But he was already bleeding. She couldn't put anyone else at risk.

"This... this still isn't your problem, Tom."

"Not my—!" After pausing to rephrase what was not likely to be productive, Tom tried again. "You're right. But you don't know what they want with the egg, right? And it's basically a child to you—you're going to do whatever you can to save it, with or without my help." It was close to what she had said to him; he was using her own words against her. His face was pleading, fear of... something behind his eyes. "I can help you. If you don't care about yourself, don't risk a kid for your own pride."

He was wrong. This wasn't about her pride. He was also right. She didn't know what Exalt wanted with the egg, and she was not going to hand over a child to a mysterious, anti-human organization. She had no arguments left.

"Yes. Yes, okay. And thank you."

"Finally!" Tom turned to his friend. "Fez, you good?"

The professor was using his phone flashlight to sift through the scattered camera fragments.

"Aha!" He triumphantly held up a memory card that might still have footage of the werewolf fight and of the vampire holding Maxine. "But you need to give me details about Exalt. Don't make me chase you down like last time; I want a full report."

Cracking up

While Maxine made the phone call confirming that Amanda could receive visitors, Tom bandaged his leg using a worryingly comprehensive first-aid kit he kept in his trunk. He also had a go-bag with several changes of clothes, making Maxine think about his escape plan to Hawaii. His preparations could easily have been sufficient to go to an airport and get on the next plane to anywhere.

It wasn't until they were parked in the hospital's visitor lot that he pulled off his body armor and weapons. When he closed the trunk and straightened up he looked more like a fashionable gym rat than a fighter after a battle.

Maxine, meanwhile, looked like any average businesswoman wearing a large egg on her chest in a handmade t-shirt sling.

She was more conspicuous than she wanted to be.

They walked side by side to the visitor desk, ignoring and being ignored by the crowds milling around. Tom was in what Maxine began to think of as "bodyguard mode." His posture was relaxed, but his eyes were alert and he kept his hands loose and available at his sides. He always had her in his sightline and tended to position himself between her and the greatest number of people.

After getting the room number and directions from the visitor's desk, they navigated the maze-like halls of the hospital. The walls were an ugly shade of green, the hallways smelled like antiseptic, and the background murmur of voices was somber.

The pallor of the walls and muted sounds made the halls seem longer than they were. Maxine hadn't spent much time in a hospital. She was hoping to get out of this one soon.

When they arrived at the appropriate area, the nursing station was empty. Maxine walked down the hallway, her eyes up to track the room numbers. When she came to the right one, she knocked on the door, but didn't wait before stepping inside.

There was Amanda, sleeping. Her skin ghastly pale from blood loss as she lay in a hospital bed with an oxygen cannula in her nose., the monitors beeping at a slow but steady rate. An IV bag of what looked like saline was hooked up to her arm. The cheap hospital gown she wore had a faded pattern that might have once been pretty blue and white checkers. Amanda was so young, and looked younger in her sleep, face relaxed instead of set in its usual anxious expression. Her body looked small and frail surrounded by medical equipment.

She wasn't alone.

Maxine didn't look at Amanda for more than a moment, her attention immediately drawn to a draconic woman with green scales wearing a lab coat sitting beside Amanda's bed. The fading in her scales indicated that this woman was older, but Maxine didn't know enough to estimate age in draconics.

Held in the draconic woman's claws was a human newborn. It had been carefully swaddled and was sleeping, as delicate as a soap bubble. A small, wooden crib, the kind that rocked back and forth, was carefully positioned amongst the medical equipment.

As soon as Maxine and Tom had walked in, the draconic woman looked up, movements jerky with surprise. She stood from the chair, her claws curled over the human infant.

"Please... please don't hurt it!" The draconic's voice pleaded. She lowered her head, hunching her shoulders to look smaller. "We never meant to challenge you, Mr. Morgan. Please do not punish the egg, it is innocent."

Tom looked at Maxine for help.

"It's okay, no one is going to hurt you." Maxine stepped forward, but this was the wrong tactic. The woman's eyes widened with fear. She held up the human infant as though it were an offering.

"My egg. Please do not hurt my egg!"

The pain in the draconic's voice ripped through Maxine's chest, but at the same time, a euphoric rush of air filled her lungs. This was the best-case scenario: they had found the true owner of the egg who wanted it to be safe.

"I've been protecting it." Maxine reassured her, shifting herself between the draconic and Tom in an attempt to assuage the draconic's fears about him. "It was stolen and given to me. We can..."

Maxine's voice trailed off. Her gut instincts were screaming that something was wrong.

The draconic woman was studying her while she talked, but her eyes kept darting to the egg. The sleeping human baby looked obscenely small in her claws, but she held it with obvious care. It wore a small plastic wristband, the kind hospitals used to identify children in their care.

Maxine had thought at first that the human baby completed the puzzle. There had been a pregnant human, then there was a not-pregnant human with a draconic egg, and now there was a draconic with a human baby. All species and their children accounted for.

But looking more closely it became obvious this infant couldn't be Amanda's; it was too large to have been delivered by c-section in the last couple days. Maxine couldn't begin to guess the age of an egg, but the human infant looked at least a month old.

Maxine cleared her throat, anxiety growing as she wondered if that baby was intended as a hostage. "We can talk. But... can you please put down the baby?"

"Yes." The woman stepped to the side to clear the path towards the crib. "Yes, of course. I will put the baby down, and you will put the egg down?"

Either instinctively or deliberately, the draconic woman cradled the baby against her chest in a mirror image of how Maxine was holding the egg against her chest. The baby squirmed, tiny mouth opening in a yawn as it wiggled in its sleep.

"I don't—why do you have a baby?" Maxine stepped back slightly, looking up at the taller woman's scaled face. Draconic body language was still foreign to her. "I just want to talk. I won't hurt the egg."

"I am not the one holding *your* child," the draconic hissed in outrage. "You admit you have my stolen egg. You... you challenged Validus for it... why?"

"I thought he was going to break it," Maxine answered quickly. "Amanda told me it was in danger."

"Amanda..." They both looked down at the sleeping woman. She was too pale, connected to so many tubes and cables she seemed part machine. The monitoring equipment continued to beep in a slow, steady tempo. "Amanda stole it and injured herself in the process. I will give you whatever you want, pay any price for its safe return."

"I don't want *money*." The concept was vile. Money in exchange for a life?

"What *do* you want?" The draconic's voice was a mixture of desperation and outrage. "You can have this one—a fair trade and your own species."

Once again, she extended the human baby slightly, although her claws still formed a cage around it. The newborn looked like any newborn, squashed and uncooked.

This was a typical hospital room, with tubes and tanks and IV bags all carefully arranged to allow for nurses to move around with efficiency. Everything was plastic, rubber, and metal. Why was there a wooden crib? The hospital would use something more durable and easy to clean.

"Whose baby is that?"

The draconic woman gave a sound of utter frustration, sharp teeth gnashing. "Is this a human conceit? To steal and hold our eggs hostage while demanding answers? What do you want? I will give it to you."

"I want to know it's going where it belongs." Maxine glared up at the draconic. "I can't give it back to someone who won't care for the child that hatches out of it."

"It is *mine*," came the immediate response in a hiss. "And I will care for it with more love and devotion than you can even imagine."

Tom's voice cut into the conversation, startling them both.

"She's lying."

Maxine tore her eyes off the draconic woman briefly to glance backwards. A familiar ugliness was twisting his face, but his voice was clinical. "She's too old to lay."

"He has always hated my kind." In Maxine's distraction, the draconic stepped closer. One clawed hand still supported the human baby against her chest, but the other one snatched out to grasp at the band of the egg sling. "It is mine in every way that matters; give it back."

Despite her obvious desperation, the woman didn't try to take it by force. Her grip on the sling kept Maxine from stepping away; she must be afraid playing a tug-of-war game might damage the egg.

"I want to know what's going on!"

It was difficult to talk this close to a draconic. Her snout was so long that even pressed nose-to-nose, conversation felt like a long-distance call.

The tiny human baby continued to sleep peacefully in the draconic's clutches. Was that normal? Shouldn't it have woken up and started screaming by now? Maxine was only barely competent at caring for an egg; she didn't know how to keep anything complicated alive.

Under no circumstance was Maxine going to start walking around with an egg *and* a human newborn looking for their mothers.

Under no circumstance was Maxine going to hold the egg hostage or threaten its safety in exchange for someone else.

That didn't leave her many circumstances.

The room was quiet. They stood in hushed tension, only broken up by the metronome beeping of Amanda's heart monitor to remind Maxine lives were waiting.

"That egg," hot metallic breath washed over her, "is the hope of future generations. Millions have been spent in research and development."

Research?

"It's a living thing, not an experiment." Maxine felt her voice getting harder, her resolve returning. "Where is its mother?"

"You walk with a murderer and hold our egg hostage!" the draconic growled. "You are risking countless lives with your human stupidity!"

"I'll return it," Maxine said reassuringly, intently studying the reactions on the draconic's face. Was that optimism? Suspicion? "Don't worry, I will give it back."

Maxine leaned a few inches to her left and hit the code blue emergency button.

"To its real mother."

That button was intended for life-threatening medical emergencies. Maxine suspected she might have one in a second. A siren blared immediately, audible in and outside the room, while lights flashed urgently.

The draconic bared her teeth and tightened her grip on the sling, but glanced towards the door, seeing her chance at a clean escape swiftly dwindling.

"We will find you, wherever you go." The draconic's voice was shaky. Oddly, Maxine got the sense this woman was uncomfortable threatening her. She groped for the words. "I will not let you steal our future."

People were already flooding the doorway, nurses and medical staff summoned by the sirens.

With a bitten-off curse, the draconic woman none-too-gently dropped the human baby into the crib and pushed her way out the door. No one tried to stop her.

⸻ ◆ ⸻

The sirens were still blaring and now that the threat was gone, Maxine took several steps back from Amanda's bed and the crib to allow the professionals access. The baby, startled by its sudden drop into the crib, woke and wailed an ear-piercing screech to rival the code blue alarm. Yes, carrying the egg was much better than a human baby.

Cacophonous emergency sounds warred against each other for attention.

A nurse was yelling something, picked up the child and checked its wristband. She walked into the hallway, rocking the screaming infant and removing it from the scene. Trying to be as invisible as possible, Maxine warmed her back against Tom's front while they stood against the wall, watching the chaos and keeping out of everyone's way.

Maxine had expected the alarm to be turned off once the nurses saw that everyone was fine. But they didn't turn off the alarm. Someone next to Amanda was yelling something about vitals.

With horror enhanced by the brief respite and expectation of safety, Maxine looked at Amanda again. She was still hooked up to medical monitoring equipment, but as the hospital staff conferred over her and removed the wires and tubing, the metronome beep of Amanda's heart rate didn't stop. It wasn't until someone unplugged the machine that it went dark and silent.

Amanda had been dead the whole time.

Egg yolks, pecorino, guanciale

It was time to go. They wouldn't get any more information here, and Maxine didn't want to get caught up with hospital security—or the police, for that matter. Maxine didn't bother giving Tom a signal; he was already responding to her body language as soon as she shifted her weight towards the door.

Someone in scrubs confronted them as they tried to slip out of Amanda's room.

"Who are you? Hospital security is—"

"We were visiting a friend." Maxine did not need to fake the shock in her voice. "I thought something was wrong and I hit the button."

Stepping around the nurse to duck through the door Tom was holding open, Maxine grimaced apologetically. No one here would physically try to stop them from leaving, so they had to go now.

"I hope... I hope she's okay."

She obviously wasn't.

Maxine walked quickly with purpose, and no one bothered her. Tom was a shadow somehow staying precisely behind her left shoulder without tripping on her as they made their way back to the car. She had to focus, but the image of Amanda's body kept returning to her mind. Was she dead before they got there? Would it have been possible to save her, if they had realized it sooner?

What—what was she going to do now? She would have to wait to feel the horror of Amanda's death; Maxine was responsible for the egg's life, and she didn't know enough about who was after it—or why.

When they were walking through the parking lot, both of them scanning for anyone who might be following them, Maxine finally spoke.

"This is too public; the egg is exposed." A tight breathlessness made the words feel difficult to push out. She had been in and out of panic mode too much in the last forty-eight hours. Her reserves were gone.

Tom had a hand on her elbow, supporting some of her weight. When had he started doing that?

"You're about to pass out," he murmured, gently.

"I can make it to the car." She swallowed, a rainbow aura flickering like a kaleidoscope in her vision. "Can you... Tom, can we go back to your place for a bit? I need a... a nap. I can't make a good decision right now."

"Yeah." There was relief in his voice. "Yeah, hold tight."

The drive to his place was a blur. She didn't think she'd fallen asleep, but then she was stumbling at the lip of the entryway, his hand at her elbow helping her inside. He was close. Closer than she expected for some reason, his other hand braced behind her.

"You're okay."

It vibrated from his chest through her shoulder. The words didn't make sense, though. Was she okay? No, of course not, but... she had to be.

The constant weight of the egg moved, shooting an icicle in her brain as she jerked her hands up to catch it before it could fall.

"Shhh, I've got it. It's fine."

He was gently removing the egg. That was wrong, right? He didn't care about it. Didn't think it was worth saving. She reached out to take it back, but suddenly her side was cold; he wasn't supporting her weight and she stumbled.

"I've just put it over here." Why was he talking like that? Like she was a child. She tried to see where he'd put it, but her weight swayed and the room was darkening. Arms like steel cables took her weight and the next thing she knew she was sinking into something soft.

"Get some sleep. You're safe, Maxine. You're gonna be okay."

If there was more, she didn't hear it.

Maxine woke up to someone calling her name and the smell of bacon.

She was on the couch with a blanket tucked around her, but it was still dark outside, so she couldn't have slept the whole night. She blinked some of the fog from her eyes, sitting up and pulling the blanket over her shoulders like a cape. Her head felt stuffed with cotton balls, but after a minute to reorient herself, she remembered where she was.

The draconic egg was sitting in a salad bowl on the coffee table, cushioned by a tea towel.

The sound of fat sizzling was accompanied by the vision of Tom moving around his kitchen. He was remarkably quiet while he kept a large pan moving, using tongs to stir whatever was inside. He looked... happy. Peaceful, even. His face was calm and meditative as he moved.

When he pulled two plates from a cupboard and started serving, Maxine stood, gravitationally drawn towards food, and dropped her blanket. Taking the barstool in front of the kitchen counter, she successfully kept the drool inside her mouth while he grated pepper over the dish and pushed it towards her.

It was carbonara. He had made spaghetti carbonara. He had made spaghetti carbonara and then he had plated it as though they were in an expensive Italian restaurant, piled high in the center of the plate with freshly cracked pepper and shaved parmesan on top.

Her mouth was full before she even realized she'd picked up the fork. Under other circumstances she'd be embarrassed, but he didn't seem to mind while she devolved into little more than approving noises. He was eating more slowly, still standing in the kitchen across from her. In the rare breaks from her food fugue state, she would look up to see him watching her as if she were an animal in a nature documentary. Fair enough.

Before her plate was fully empty, he had another serving ready to slide in place in front of her. This one she forced herself to eat like a civilized human being.

"Ahem, ah. This is... really good." She straightened up a little, suddenly noticing how she had been hunching over her food to shorten the distance from plate to mouth. "Thank you!"

"You're good for my ego, Maxine." He was smiling, small wrinkles crinkled in the corners of his eyes as he watched her. "How are you feeling?"

"Better," she admitted. "I'm sorry, that was—"

"Don't apologize," he interrupted. "I had a beautiful woman moaning in my kitchen. I'm not complaining."

This was the right time to change the subject.

"That draconic woman. She called you a murderer."

"She also stole a baby and killed Amanda." He wasn't as excited about this topic as he was about food and moaning. Tough luck; this was important.

"I just need to make sure that having you with me isn't going to escalate conversations into violence." Maxine gently set her fork down, resisting the urge to lick the plate. "I can't get information if everyone is afraid of me."

"She stole. A baby." Tom finally pulled out the matching stool and sat next to her, leaning his elbow on the counter. "And killed. Amanda."

"You think I don't know that?" Maxine exploded. "But is it true? Because I can't claim the moral high ground if I'm also holding a stolen egg and walking around with a killer."

"The moral high ground will do fuck-all to keep you safe." He kept an even tone, which was only more frustrating. If she was going to lose her shit, the least he could do was match her. "And I've only ever killed in self-defense when those dracks forced me into fights."

"Maybe you can bullshit Fez with that, but you could have forfeited those fights."

He watched her coolly, his face blank.

"Maybe not all of them, but when there were witnesses? You would have lost status and eventually they'd have stopped coming for you."

His jaw tensed and he said nothing.

"Why didn't you?"

"I didn't start any of those fights."

"Never said you did," Maxine pushed. "But you didn't have to end them with violence, so why fight? Was it ego?"

"I didn't want—I couldn't let them win." He turned his head away, baring his teeth towards the kitchen counter while he confessed. "Their whole society is based on 'might makes right' bullshit. I couldn't walk away and let them think they were right."

"So you risked your life... and theirs, repeatedly, to prove a point?"

He didn't like that. In the long, tense silence, they both held as still as possible, knowing the others' body reading would catch any twitch.

"I guess. Yeah."

If this were one of her therapy sessions, Maxine would tie it back to his formative years and ask which parent or guardian had used bullying to try to control him. She was tempted, curious about how he'd gotten to this extreme. But that wasn't her priority.

"That draconic woman in the hospital. I couldn't read her, but you could. What did you see?"

"She was faking submission." He closed his eyes while he tried to recall the details. "And she was scared, but not of me."

"She said it was hers. 'In every way that matters.' Was she telling the truth?"

"Yes." He didn't have to think about it. "She wanted that egg more than anything and she thought it was hers."

They sat in silence while Maxine processed that.

"Maxine, you don't have to like it, but you need me."

Celestials help her, he was right. Maybe that woman was the rightful guardian of the egg—but at the moment, all Maxine knew about her was that, as Tom said, she had stolen a baby and killed Amanda.

"What I need is information. About Exalt, about the egg, about that draconic woman."

"Okay."

"I think I met a member of Exalt before all this started. An infernal who was looking for Amanda."

Tom considered this, leaning back on his stool.

"I don't know much about infernals. Where do we find him?"

Digging through her wallet, Maxine found the business card she'd gotten from the infernal looking for Amanda.

"Well Tom, I've got good news and bad news."

Tom's face was blank while he watched her. He didn't know which direction she was going to go with this.

"Gimme the bad news first."

"You've figured out I can be seduced with food."

He brightened, not at all concerned that his motives were obvious.

"And the good news?"

"I definitely need you for backup."

------◆------

Maxine wished she had a better plan than "call the infernal again." But that was the extent of her creativity so far. There was an address on the card an internet search showed to be a local FBI office, displaying admirable attention to detail on his part.

"How are you so sure he's not really FBI?" Tom was doing push-ups nearby while she dithered.

"Infernals can't be hired into law-enforcement. It was sloppy of him to impersonate an FBI agent. If he'd gone for private security I might have believed it."

But probably not. Since they fed on humans' base emotions like fear and anger, infernals weren't known for *helping* humans.

Finally working up her nerve, she dialed the number again.

"Agent Maliel speaking, and do *not* hang up on me again, lady." She heard a chair squeaking and footsteps in the background. "My lead is dead, and I see you on the hospital security footage after her time of death. I've got reports of an attack on a university campus, and traffic cameras show you leaving the area. What the *fuck* are you up to?"

"You can stop the act, I know you aren't FBI."

For several long seconds there was only breathing on the other end of the line. Then she heard his voice calling in another direction.

"Hey Echles, did they finally fire me?"

Another male voice, much more distant but still understandable, replied.

"Not yet, Agent Maliel, despite your best efforts."

"Damn. Well, sorry lady, but I'm not quitting. And I need you to come to my office for a statement before I lose my damn mind."

It's not like she had a script of what to expect from him, but this didn't fit. And a seed of doubt was sprouting in her gut. She turned a confused expression to Tom, who shrugged. She decided to fall back on the basics.

"The government doesn't hire infernals."

"This ain't hard, lady. I showed you my badge. I gave you my card. Look up my name in the goddamn directory of public employees. Don't judge me for the picture; flash cameras wash out my skin and make me look like Pepto-Bismol. And *then*, come and give me a goddamn statement to explain why the *fuck* the woman I was investigating is being fitted for a toe tag right now."

With her stomach sinking, apparently trying to escape downwards, Maxine searched the FBI's website while the infernal impatiently waited on the line. They did indeed have a directory of employees, most of whom didn't share pictures, but the listing for Agent Samzen Maliel had a small image of the man she had met grinning at the camera.

"I... um..."

Nausea churned. Could she have actually saved Amanda if she'd done this incredibly easy search to verify his identity? Tom had said she had a "blind spot." He had been referring to her inability to see a threat, but as she looked into the unblinking eyes of the infernal's overexposed headshot, she thought about how different things might have been if she hadn't immediately written him off.

"But law enforcement doesn't permit—"

"Ugh!" Keys jingled in the background. "How about this: you give me a location and I'll meet you there. Wanna meet in a church? Splash me with holy water? I promise not to get ash on you when I burst into flames."

Nothing could have been more mortifying. The kinds of people who thought infernals came from hell and were repelled by Judeo-Christian religion were the most ignorant kind of bigots who didn't even understand basic interplanar travel. Maybe two hundred years ago it would have been forgivable, but now it was tantamount to thinking an airplane flew using dark magic.

"I can meet you at your office." She forced the words out, hoping she didn't sound as if she were looking around for a trash can to throw up in.

"Lady, I'm trusting you here. If you don't show up, I'm gonna... I'm gonna be sad, alright?"

"I'm on my way now."

Right after she finished dry heaving into the toilet for a few minutes thinking about Amanda's dead body. Then she would be on her way.

Yolks on you

By the time Maxine and Tom pulled into the parking lot of the FBI office building, she had processed some, but not all, of her own guilt and mortification. Tom was blessedly quiet, but the silence only helped her spiral further down a pit of shame. She'd spent the entire drive preventing herself from voicing self-recrimination, knowing she wanted someone to tell her it "wasn't that bad" or that she had behaved rationally.

She *hadn't* behaved rationally. Thinking back to her first interaction with Samzen made her want to pull her own hair out. She had treated the infernal like the bogeyman, and he *knew* it because he could see her fear.

The infernal was waiting for them. Leaning against a pillar at the building's entrance, he wasn't wearing the FBI jacket anymore, but the badge was still visible on his belt over skintight black jeans. A gray shirt and fitted black jacket completed the image of "fashion forward cop, felt cute, might arrest someone later." He didn't waste time on small talk.

"You should know, your office is trashed and someone broke into your apartment a second time. It looks like shit. You're a popular lady."

Good. She could remodel later.

"I'm so sorry about—"

"Nah, none a' that," Samzen interrupted. "It happens a lot, and I ain't interested in why."

Oh no. Now he was the one being magnanimous, while at the same time preventing her from apologizing and feeling better about her mistake. He couldn't have made her feel worse if he were trying.

Was he trying? Did he feed off embarrassment or guilt? A fresh surge of both tormented Maxine when she realized that thought process was part of her own prejudice.

He was still talking. Focus, Maxine. She could at least try to be useful while she was here.

"My partner will be here in a second. We can sit down and—woah!"

Samzen finally noticed Tom, who joined Maxine in his "bodyguard" position behind her left shoulder. He'd probably wanted to check the perimeter, or possibly had lagged behind because he was nervous around law enforcement.

"Oh, um, this is Tom." Maxine smiled weakly up at Tom, who was stone-faced. "Tom, this is Agent Samzen Maliel."

Samzen glanced nervously between them. This was exactly why she hadn't wanted to go everywhere with a walking tank. Now the agent was worried about conflict when all she wanted was to give him all the information she had, beg forgiveness for keeping him away from Amanda, and hopefully also learn about the FBI paranormal investigation unit's secret draconic egg protection program she desperately hoped would exist.

"So, that report about a human fighting off a primal werewolf... that wasn't just high college kids seeing things, huh?" Samzen took a few steps to the side, studying Tom from the new angle.

"He's here because I've been... I've been getting some threats." Maxine wanted Samzen's attention off Tom. "And maybe you can help. Have you heard of Exalt?"

Attention successfully diverted, Samzen arched a judgmental eyebrow at her.

"Have I heard of—yeah, lady, I mighta heard of them. Anti-human hate group." He looked back towards the doors expectantly, still waiting for his partner. "Exalt does a buncha shady shit, but all you gotta know is they think you humans aren't worth more than the blood and meat you're made of."

Lovely. But not exactly surprising or new information.

The doors finally swung open and Samzen's shoulders relaxed. A tall man ducked through, heading towards them. He emitted a familiar golden glow.

Maxine felt her stomach drop when it became obvious that he was a celestial. But despite her initial shock at seeing him, he wasn't *her* celestial.

She should relax. It wasn't as if every celestial knew each other. He probably had no idea who Jehudin was.

Samzen's partner was as tall as Tom and glowed with the shimmering gold celestial light which blessed all their kind. Otherwise, he wore ordinary street clothes, albeit with a badge visible on his belt like the infernal's. His inhuman beauty was different from Jehudin's, but nonetheless breathtaking. While Jehudin had round, soft features, this celestial had sharper features and hawk-like eyes glaring at Samzen.

"Agent Maliel, you are not permitted to speak with humans alone."

His voice was deep and reverberating. Maxine had almost managed to forget how they vibrated through you. The voice was different from Jehudin's but the similarity still made her ache.

"Then be on time, pal," Samzen rebutted cheerfully. "Do our new friends look familiar? They're the witnesses from the hospital we wanted to speak with."

While Samzen made it sound like meeting Tom and Maxine was an early Christmas gift, Echles' face darkened. "You are not following standard operating procedure."

"File a complaint tomorrow, yeah?" Ignoring his partner's disgruntled expression, Samzen gave him a casual clap on the shoulder, his skin brilliantly red against the celestial's glow. "This is that divine providence you're always on about!"

The celestial begrudgingly turned to inspect Tom and Maxine. Giving the man a cursory glance, he did an honest-to-goodness double take when looking at her.

So much for every celestial not knowing each other. Dammit.

Samzen looked between the two of them as the celestial rudely stared and Maxine felt the remaining scraps of her self-esteem shriveling into a raisin. She instinctively crossed her arms in front of herself and hunched a little. It was only a few seconds, but those seconds dragged towards eternity. Finally she snapped out, "What, does every celestial know about it?"

"Yes." His voice was amazed, like she was a celebrity dog doing a trick. "Everyone knows of you and Jehudin. It was the first celestial divorce ever recorded in the mortal plane."

Her eyes bugged out. "What? I'm literally the only human to have ever been divorced by a celestial?"

"Yes," he said again, perhaps not understanding the excruciating long-term damage his honesty was having on Maxine. "Marriage is a blessing and a promise. To turn one's back on those vows is considered sacrilege. None other than Jehudin have ever done so."

Tom put his arm over her shoulder and tucked her into a side hug, turning himself protectively between the two of them. Meanwhile Samzen, who had a much better grasp of human emotion than Echles, apparently, stepped forward with his hands up to try and change the topic.

"Woah, hoo boy, sounds like there's some backstory there!" He chuckled nervously. "But we're not here for personal details; I just want to ask some questions about what you've seen in the last week, Ms. Hallis."

Safely tucked into Tom's side, Maxine fought through mental static. She was here for an important reason. Focus on that.

"Yes, I can…" She swallowed back some bile. "I can tell you about what I've seen."

"Great! Great, we're all gonna help each other, yeah? Tell ya what, how about my partner goes back to the office to do some paperwork…"

Samzen kicked at Echles' ankle, trying to get his celestial partner to stop staring at her.

"…and I'll take you and beefcake here to a Starbucks and get your statement. It'll be more comfortable and we can have cake pops or whatever, my treat."

"You can't be alone with humans, Maliel," Echles repeated, demonstrating his inability to read the room. "I will accompany you to take the statements."

"She's got her bodyguard!" Samzen gestured up—and further up—at Tom. "And I bet she'd prefer not to have you glowing all over the place and drawing attention. We're going to keep a low profile and go over what she knows."

"Her bodyguard…" The celestial managed to stop staring at Maxine by turning his attention over to Tom. He kept openly staring, inspecting him.

"You're being an asshole," Tom said, bluntly, still angling himself in front of Maxine. For his part, the celestial startled like it hadn't occurred to him he was behaving like a child gawking at an animal in the zoo. Or maybe like he hadn't expected the zoo animals to talk back. Tom turned to Samzen. "Can you help her get off this anti-human group's radar?"

"Yeah! Maybe! I mean, no I have no idea. But let's go over what you know, and I'll do what I can."

Tom nodded. He squeezed Maxine a little tighter around the shoulders. "Hey," he said softly, trying to gauge whether she was still with them or if she had successfully dissociated from this latest emotional trauma. "What do you need? Can we go talk with these guys or do you want to take a break?"

"We—" Her voice broke and she had to clear her throat and swallow a few times to get it working again. "We can talk. I'll be okay."

Samzen and Tom both looked skeptical but seemed willing enough to go along with it.

"Okay, good deal!" Samzen was injecting too much false cheer into his voice. "There's a Starbucks down the street. Just follow our car and we'll get some burnt coffee and you can tell me all about the egg... situation..."

His voice trailed off and he kicked Echles' ankle again. He hissed more softly up at his partner, "Move it, you jackass!"

⸺◆⸺

Tom dutifully followed their car but kept glancing nervously at Maxine as if he thought she were about to explode.

She groaned and allowed herself to curl up into a ball in the passenger seat. The egg was safely tucked inside her fetal position and she pulled at her hair with both hands. A silent scream was coming along.

"The only one!" Her voice was muffled into her knees. "A celestial would rather commit sacrilege than be married to me!"

"You can't think like that, Maxine." Tom was trying to make his voice sound reassuring, but he missed by a few miles and landed on condescending.

"Oh, like you're an expert?" She knew it wasn't fair, but she had no targets other than herself and an egg. "At least your ex actually wanted something from you. Mine was so desperate to get away that he left all his mortal possessions behind and committed sacrilege to leave me."

"My ex stole my car and a thousand bucks worth of random shit." Tom seemed eager to talk about his own shitty ex to change the topic. "He was a selfish asshole. You know, he never once gave me head?"

Maxine blinked at the crumbs and smudged dirt on the floor between her feet, successfully delaying her incipient scream. She pushed her elbows against her knees to lift herself up enough to watch Tom's expression while he talked.

"He never reciprocated oral sex?" Tom had once again drawn her out of her own problems by dangling his own dysfunctional relationship in front of her like a carrot on a string. She desperately latched onto this distraction.

"Not once." Tom smiled, already relaxing and smiling a bit as he saw her unfold. "We were together for three years. You'd think he'd at least offer on my birthday or something, right?"

"Well..." She wanted to be fair, but she wasn't actually his therapist and she also wanted to be on Tom's side. "Some people aren't comfortable with certain sexual acts, but that doesn't mean they shouldn't find ways to give their partners pleasure. It's an unhealthy dynamic if one half of a relationship feels like their needs aren't being met."

"Right! Unhealthy dynamic," Tom agreed cheerfully. "Like when he wanted to bring in a third this one time, and we found a lovely lady willing to join us, but I don't even know what the two of them did because she was sitting on my face all night and no one helped *me* get off."

"Oh my god!" Maxine was sitting up now, one hand flying to cover her mouth as if it could shove the words back in her mouth.

Tom was quietly laughing, his eyes crinkled up as he got the reaction he was hoping for. "And don't get me wrong, I'm happy to give a lady a seat, but if I'm making breakfast the morning after I'd like someone to touch my dick the night before."

Maxine couldn't believe she was also laughing alongside Tom, drawn out by his ridiculous story.

"That didn't really happen?" she asked incredulously, hand still hovering over her mouth.

He winked in her direction. "I can hold my breath for a very long time."

They were pulling into the parking lot of a Starbucks before she could try to think of any response to that. Tom found a spot a few spaces away from where Samzen and Echles were parked. Before she could open the door to step out, though, Tom stopped her with a hand on her shoulder. He was still smiling, but more seriously now.

"Just let me know what you need," he said softly. "I'm following your lead, remember?"

She nodded, briefly putting her hand over his. It was a quiet moment that helped center her after an emotional rollercoaster. With that moment to brace herself, she squeezed his hand, turned, and stepped out of the car.

Hard Boiled

S amzen turned out to be correct about many things. There had been a Starbucks not far down the street, their coffee was burnt, and Echles was a jackass. After getting their drinks, the four of them sat around a table and Samzen asked Maxine and Tom to give details about their last couple days.

He took notes, asked questions to glean further details where he could, and made sympathetic noises at all the right times to confirm himself as a supportive listener. Maxine was professionally impressed, even while she spent the whole time tamping down the voice in her head saying "Look! That's a technique designed to manipulate your trust!" Now that she was looking for it, she could clearly see the edges of her own hypocrisy. If Samzen were any other race, she would have appreciated his attempts to make her comfortable.

Echles said very little. He had mostly stopped staring at Maxine but would frequently glance down at his phone under the table. Maxine was pretty sure he was texting every celestial currently on the mortal plane, *Hey everyone, I found her: the most pathetic human! I'm going to get a selfie!*

"Agent Samzen, what happened to Amanda's baby?"

"The one you saw in her room was stolen from the NICU; it's fine and back where it belongs. But there's no record of any other missing newborn. And as a rule, I don't like losing babies." He winced and gave a sheepish look as if he were embarrassed to ask. "You're certain that draconics and humans can't breed?"

"The DNA isn't compatible. Draconics are technically warm-blooded, but they aren't mammals. The eggs are fertilized internally, like ducks." She paused. "Although I recommend you not look up duck reproduction too closely..." She gently cradled the egg on her chest to recenter herself with its comforting weight. "But from there, it's kind of like humans. Our brains get too big to continue development in utero, so we have to be born at nine months to fit through the pelvic bone. A draconic egg has to be laid while the shell is still soft, but the longer it can be incubated internally, the better the odds the egg will be viable."

Samzen did not properly appreciate the biology lesson. He was staring in the middle distance, tapping his pen against his notepad.

Maxine leaned in, aware they were in a public space with lots of people milling around and not sure if that made her feel more or less comfortable having this discussion.

"Who was that draconic woman at the hospital? How did she kill Amanda?"

"Lady, I really wish I knew. Never seen the draconic before, but she wasn't working alone. There was a vamp with her. Looks like he was the one who tampered with the monitoring system and injected something into the victim's IV line." Samzen sighed, blowing air out of his cheeks in resignation. "Allegedly."

"*Allegedly?*"

"Yeah, lady, what do you think this is?" Samzen pulled out his badge to wave for emphasis. "A prop? We got laws, y'know."

"I haven't really noticed lately." Her voice was desert dry. "I need to know where this egg came from, so I can find its mother or a safe home. Do you know anything?"

"Lady, I know so many things that have nothing to do with eggs." Samzen kept tapping his pen. "We got lucky with that vamp accomplice. He's an employee at the hospital and we have an address. We're bringing him in for questioning after sundown."

"Yes!" Finally, some actual good news! "Do you need me to... to identify him in a lineup? I might recognize his voice if—"

"Nah, no need." The infernal held up a hand in unofficial sign language for "calm down." "We've got him on camera. This is all handled."

"What should I do?"

The response she got was a raised eyebrow.

"Nothing," Samzen said, with the hopeless tone of someone who knew their recommendation would not be followed. "You're a civilian."

"But I've got the egg. What do I do to keep it safe?" With a cautious look towards Echles then back, Maxine heard the note of begging in her own voice. "Does the paranormal investigations unit have a... child protection service?"

With an expression uncomfortably mirroring her time at the police station, Samzen glared at the egg, checking to see if he wished hard enough it would miraculously disappear. Not a hopeful sign for that draconic egg protection program.

"The strongest legal claim to ownership we have is that you adopted it using draconic policy overseen by their internal political systems," he said, finally.

Putting down his pen and picking up the coffee he had barely touched during their conversation, Samzen tipped his chair precariously backwards. It made him look more casual than professional. Maxine suspected he was intimately aware of the image he projected, and used it to build rapport. Out of their celestial/infernal partnership, Samzen was the one with all the social skills.

"The egg might be considered evidence in a crime, but my investigation is into human trafficking and I don't see the link yet. We might get more information when we question that vampire." Samzen was about to say something to Tom, but Maxine interrupted with a new and exciting sense of dread.

"Human trafficking?"

"Uh, yeah." Samzen shrugged, trying to act dismissive and walking back from information he probably hadn't intended to share. "But that's not your concern, I've got—"

"That's why you were investigating Amanda." Maxine had a lump in her throat so large it felt like she'd swallowed a frog. Suddenly thinking back over guilt-coded work conversations with Amanda in therapy. Amanda had known she was doing something wrong, but wouldn't discuss it beyond vague rationalizations. Maxine remembered Sophia—a scared, injured woman who couldn't speak English, a woman who hadn't seemed to want help from people that Amanda had claimed were friends. "Amanda was working with them, wasn't she? And that woman—Sophia. She..."

She had spent so much time thinking of Amanda as a victim, it took a mental tow truck to turn the thought around. Was Amanda working with Exalt? The betrayal and anger in Sophia's face suddenly made sense. She must have thought Maxine was working with them too. She might as well *have* been.

Echles was watching her with laser eyes. He saw something in her aura, or her character, or whatever it was they saw. Samzen was similarly alert, although in his case it looked more like he was waiting to see if a toddler was about to fall down the stairs.

"Lady, I talked with the volunteers at Planar Parenthood." He cut into her thoughts, voice gentle. "They all told the same story. You made a call asking for translation assistance. Your whereabouts were well corroborated, I know you ain't part of that."

"I'm not worried you think *I'm* a suspect," Maxine hissed, although maybe she should have been, realizing how suspicious her actions would have looked from the outside. Samzen's chair thumped back down onto four legs as he started to take the conversation seriously again. "I'm worried I returned a victim to a *trafficker!* What happened to Sophia?"

"She was given medical assistance and signed out with her 'friends.'" Samzen confirmed. His grim expression told her everything she didn't want to know.

Numb horror was becoming familiar. She should get a loyalty card. *Free straight jacket after ten stamps.*

The constant weight of the egg recentered her. One thing at a time. She'd failed Sophia... and Amanda... she had to get this one right.

"How do I protect the egg from them?"

Samzen bit his bottom lip as he thought, looking between Maxine and Tom.

"They've been following you. If you agree, I can assign someone to watch your place for the next week, in case anyone tries to—"

"No." The interruption was from Echles, and it surprised Samzen enough he jumped, apparently having forgotten the celestial was there. Echles was glaring at Samzen. "The woman is not to be used as bait. She must be protected."

Samzen leaned an elbow on the table, turning towards his partner. "Technically the egg is the bait. And what are you on about?"

Now everyone was staring at the celestial who, it seemed, had not properly thought through his position before objecting to his partner's plan. He struggled to piece his words together before he said in a voice that indicated the conversation was over, "We cannot do anything to jeopardize the woman's well-being. She should be allocated a safehouse."

"My *name* is Maxine." She stared daggers at the celestial. "And *you're* not putting me at risk. Amanda did that when she gave me the egg."

"Did you know her ex?" Tom cut in. He sounded speculative, studying the celestial while he spoke. "This seems personal for you."

Celestials, for all their many literal and figurative blessings, were universally awful liars. Echles glanced nervously down at his phone, still hidden under the table. He looked to Samzen for help, but the infernal wasn't giving any; his eyebrows were raised and he was waiting for the same explanation Tom and Maxine wanted.

"She is an innocent bystander!" Echles blurted out, the attempt convincing himself more than anyone else. "And her act of charity should not put her at risk."

Maxine planted her hands on the table and half stood from her chair, pinning down the sweating celestial. "There better not be a fucking chat group talking about me right now. Look me in the eyes, Echles. Are all the celestials you know waiting to hear more about the least desirable human on the mortal plane?"

"I must go!" Echles sprang from his chair and fumbled the phone into his pocket. His eyes looked pleadingly at Samzen. "She must be kept safe. I cannot say more."

And then the celestial hurried away, ignoring Maxine's voice as she called out after him, "Get back here, you coward!"

With only a small, hunched pause that proved he'd heard her, Echles hustled away, the door swinging closed behind him. Other people milled around the coffee shop, some of whom also took note of the celestial's abrupt exit and glanced curiously at Maxine.

Samzen tilted his chair back again. "Huh," he said, calmly. "Never seen that before."

"What the... what *was* that?" Maxine fumed. She was still standing, unsure of what to do with her hands and tempted to run after him. She swayed uncertainly side to side, as if she might bolt for the door herself.

"So, what do you say, am I posting someone across the street to keep an eye out for more weirdos knocking down your door?" Samzen grinned, delighted to be without a partner.

"I don't... um." Maxine and Tom hadn't discussed details, but he said he'd follow her lead. "I thought you weren't allowed to talk to humans alone."

"If I only did what they said I was 'allowed' to do..." Samzen air-quoted with his fingers with derision, "...I'd wait all day for permission to take a shit." He grimaced. "Yeah, I'm not supposed to talk to humans without my walking lightbulb, but when I've *got* him, he sprays awkward everywhere. He means well, but the guy's still new to the mortal plane. He doesn't 'get' humans yet."

Maxine was distracted from the disaster of her personal life. She'd latch onto anything to avoid thinking about a bunch of celestials gossiping about her.

"How long have you been here? And... how did you get hired with the FBI?"

Her own fear of infernals aside, she hadn't been wrong, before. There were laws against hiring infernals, yet here one sat with a badge and a self-satisfied smirk.

"About fifteen years now." He looped an arm around the back of his chair. "And I knew a guy who was willing to give me a chance a few years back. We figured out some workarounds, got me a babysitter, made a deal. I thought maybe I could change some opinions about infernals if more people actually got to know one."

"How is that going for you?" Tom interjected.

The infernal's eyes lingered on Maxine for an uncomfortable second. Despite herself, she felt a twinge of fear at the situation. He'd been jovial and working to put her at ease earlier, and as much as Echles had been socially inept, the presence of a celestial *had* made the infernal seem less dangerous. Samzen's mouth turned down and his eyes went a little flinty.

"I think you already know the answer to that question, beefcake."

"Samzen—" She cut herself off, not sure if she was about to be unspeakably rude. "I'm sorry, but *why* would you—"

"Lady, you think I don't know what people say about infernals?" He interrupted, frustration in his voice. "But why *wouldn't* I wanna help humans? You're delicious. And c'mon, what better way to find easy victims, right?"

Perversely, his frustrated sarcasm was exactly what Maxine needed. Up until that moment he had been performing, but now she could see his *actual* body language. He might be a sarcastic asshole, but he sincerely wanted to help. His frustration came from people like—like Maxine, who put obstacles in his way. She took a deep breath, suddenly trusting him much more.

"What kind, I mean... is it okay to ask—"

"Normally I'd make a joke to keep you squirming, lady, but you might actually explode." He didn't sound upset, but he did seem nervous. He started fidgeting again. "Yeah, usually you're not supposed to ask, but I get it. I'm, uh... I'm an incubus. And I'll ask you to keep that to yourself please."

She failed to keep her response neutral. She stared at him, trying to see if there was a physical indication she could discern, but he just looked like any normal infernal. He wasn't a normal infernal, though.

It explained a few important things; if he was an incubus he didn't feed on fear. He got energy from human pleasure. But incubi were *rare*, and they were some of the most powerful infernals to visit the mortal plane. They didn't just have the ability to influence human minds, they could *control* humans outright by manipulating their desires. It wasn't technically mind control because the human was always in the driver seat of their own brain. But there wasn't a meaningful distinction between influence and control when they could change the thing you wanted more than anything else in the world into whatever *they* wanted.

"What? But—but how—"

"I care about the M.T., lady." He used the common abbreviation for Mortal Treaty. "And I know the stories, but half of those are sensationalist crap used by the goddamn porn industry. Y'got nothing to worry about."

This was important. She was supposed to be impartial to species. And as much as she'd always said "people are people" and that everyone could find common ground, she'd never realized there was a quiet "except infernals" in her own head. It was a prejudice that might have killed Amanda.

"Agent Samzen, you've been the first person with authority to actually try to help me ever since I got the egg." Eye contact was uncomfortable, probably for them both, but she held it. "And you're the first one to *tell* me anything other than to go away. So... thank you."

"Ugh, there's already sugar in my coffee, lady." He cleared his throat and stood up, but Maxine thought he was secretly pleased. It sounded like he was more used to fear than gratitude. "So am I gonna call an intern and tell them to watch your place, or do you wanna swing in the wind?"

She made a few quick decisions. "I'm staying at his place for right now. I'll need to stop by my apartment to get some stuff, but yes. Please station someone across the street from his house."

"Anyone except a celestial," Tom added.

She let herself be distracted as Samzen and Tom coordinated details. Letting the agents use her egg as bait might help them find members of the hate group, Exalt, but it would put the egg at higher risk. She'd let Samzen, and hopefully Exalt, think they know where she and the egg will be. But she wasn't about to sit around and wait for someone to come after it. Tom had said he'd follow her lead. Time to test that.

Hatching a plan

Their first stop was at her apartment to get clothes and basic toiletries.

There was still police tape over the broken door, but someone had wedged the door back into place so it looked closed. When she tried to open it, the door on its broken hinge fell outwards, just missing her head. She kicked random debris out of her way as she walked in, Tom following her closely.

"It's normally a little cleaner than this," Maxine joked, taking in the utter disaster of an apartment. Unlike the violation she had originally felt when Validus had broken in and torn it apart, she could barely muster a mild exhaustion. Compared to the other events of the week, having to pick her stuff off the floor didn't register as a problem.

Every drawer had been pulled out and their contents dumped on the floor. Every cabinet had been opened, with dishes and glassware broken wherever they had been haphazardly tossed. Several ceiling panels had been torn down, as Validus presumably climbed up to make sure the egg wasn't hidden in there. Ventilation panels were torn off the wall. A few of her nicer dresses had been shredded, probably out of spite.

Her suitcase had been in a closet, but now it was now lying open in the hallway. She started filling it with the clothes lying on the floor.

At least there was minimal structural damage. Maxine counted what thin silver linings she could find. She didn't smell any mold, which should mean all she needed to do once all this was over was fill a dumpster with anything that was broken and put everything else away. Maybe this would be her excuse to get a better dinnerware set. Maybe she could ditch this place entirely and find an apartment that wasn't haunted with memories of her brief happiness with Jehudin.

Wandering through her home, Tom kept his hands mostly to himself until the manly urge to start fixing things got too strong. He righted the bookcases and furniture that had been knocked over, putting books back on the shelves in unorganized stacks, but then got distracted by looking through her books.

Her bathroom was mostly just messy, but the shower curtain had been torn down for some reason. She tossed the curtain into the tub along with most of the other bottles and toothbrushes and sanitary napkins scattered across the drip rug. Her toothbrush and toothpaste were salvageable, and she grabbed those along with her shampoo, conditioner, and body wash.

What was she doing with Tom? He had been forced into this at first, but there wasn't anything to stop him from walking away now. He had proposed casual sex while they thought they had time to kill, but was that all he wanted? She wasn't a "casual sex" kind of person, even back when she was a "has sex at all" kind of person. What if she still had a chance Jehudin would change his mind before they signed the papers? And how long would she put her own life on hold for that delusion?

"I think I've got everything!" she called out, carrying her suitcase back into the living room and shaking herself out of the emotional spiral. Tom was lying out on the floor trying to re-attach a leg to her coffee table. It was a cheap table and was not worth the effort, but he seemed happy to be doing something. His shirt had ridden up, revealing a stretch of skin that drew her eyes down.

Nope, definitely not. She over-corrected her gaze by jerking her eyes up. Stains on the ceiling. Fascinating.

"Some wood glue and no one will know." Thankfully he was too absorbed in trying to save worthless furniture to notice her wandering eyes. "Ready to go?" He stood, dusting off his hands and giving her a friendly smile.

"Yeah..." Her voice trailed off, distracted by her own doubts. They could be adults about this. She put a torn cushion back on the couch and righted one of her chairs. "Can we talk?"

"If you're gonna break up with me," he said flatly, "you've gotta date me first."

But he did sit down on the chair, patiently waiting for her to get her thoughts in order. Even this showed an unusual amount of consideration for her, and made her wonder what he was getting out of this arrangement. She wasn't *offering* him anything. She'd said no to sex, then proceeded to stumble into dangerous situations that made him put his life on the line to protect her.

"I'm putting you in danger. You shouldn't have to fight for me, and you don't even care about the egg."

She wasn't making eye contact, too uncomfortable with the entire situation to look at him. Two people had been hurt or killed because of Maxine's mistakes. She didn't want Tom to become the third.

"No, I don't care about the egg, but I care about you. If dracks are involved, and vamps and weres are being sent after you, you need me."

"I have no idea how long this is going to take, Tom. I can't ask you to do this."

"It sounds more like you're asking me *not* to."

"How long are you prepared to follow me around on open-ended protection detail?"

He opened his mouth to answer, then closed it. She didn't know if he was actually giving it careful thought, or if he was pretending so she'd take him more seriously, but either way he was mulling something over. Maybe he was finally reconsidering the decision to work as the unpaid bodyguard of a broken woman.

"As long as it takes."

Nope. He wasn't thinking this one through.

"And if it takes months? Are you going to let me move in with you long-term?"

"Sure."

"Are you going to quit your job?"

"I hate my manager anyway."

"Will you raise a draconic baby with me?"

That one got a reaction. He recoiled with an expression of horror that would have been comical if it didn't make her so sad.

"That's what I thought. Tom, it's *okay*." She stressed the last word, trying to let him off the hook. "Everyone has limits, and this has gone too far. You don't need to turn your life upside down. You shouldn't."

He rubbed at his temples with a soft groan, shoulders tense. "Gimme a minute."

Leaning back in his chair, he looked around the chaotic mess of her apartment as if looking for the right words in the detritus. She was having a hard time reading him.

"I get headaches." He said it like a confession. As though pain or weakness was something to be ashamed of. "I've also got some mild tinnitus. Leftovers from concussions. Doctor said I might always have them in the morning."

"I... I'm sorry to hear that."

"Eh, it's not a big deal now." He hunched forward, turning his eyes back to her. "Getting hurt? That sucks, but healing is the worst. I don't know how many nights I spent sweating out a fever 'cause some drack opened me up and it got infected. It's not something I like to think about. And it was always for shitty reasons. Did Fez tell you how I got involved with the dracks in the first place?"

"No," she said softly. She could tell that this was important to him, although she didn't know why it was so important to tell her.

"I was—in some shit. Didn't have a lotta options, and there's people who pay good money to see fights. The *problem* was when I wanted to stop, the dracks didn't wanna let me. But before—before it got to that point, I was making money from it. A buncha other people who never got their hands dirty made *more* money. No one walked away better.

"But y'know what?" His gaze was intense. "This is the first time that living through all that absolute *shit* did some good. Because you needed someone who went through it to help you now."

He took her hand in his, squeezing with calloused fingers. "Lemme help you, Maxine. Lemme be *good* for something. I'll follow you around until the goddamn thing hatches, if I have to. But you're smart, and I think you'll find it a home before it gets to that."

She felt a shiver go through her as his words settled in her mind and sank deep, raising goosebumps. She hadn't expected him to stay with her and didn't know what to do with the idea of an actual partner. But... even with her own revulsion about violence, she'd be a fool to think she could have talked her way safely through the previous day. Swallowing through the emotion stuck in her throat, she nodded.

"Okay. Okay, yes. But... I can't let the egg be bait for Samzen." She reached over for the suitcase she had packed, squeezing the handle with sweaty palms. "If they think it's going to be at your place, then it needs to be anywhere else. I want to walk in the front door and climb out the back window as soon as we get there."

He nodded, unfazed. He was really taking this "following her lead" idea seriously. It was a heady thought—a man like him doing whatever she said. She'd have to think about that more, later. For right now, she hoped she could effectively trick Exalt *and* the FBI into thinking they knew where she and the egg were going to be.

"Let's see if your car still has its tires," Tom stood, looking up and pursing his lips slightly as he thought through a plan. Her car hadn't been abandoned long, but they had left it on the university campus. For all she knew it had been towed. "We can re-park it a few streets away from my place and ditch my car out front. From the second floor I've got a fire exit up to the roof so we can get to your car without being seen."

"Have you done this before, Tom?" She added a flirty tone to her voice, trying to lift the mood.

"Done what? Gave cops the runaround, or had to sneak out the back before someone jealous got home?" Pausing for dramatic effect he answered his own question with a smirking irreverence that further brightened the tense mood of the room. "Because yes."

Sunny side up

Performing the most Scooby-Doo type nonsense she'd ever done, Maxine and Tom sneaked through his house and made their way to a nearby hotel.

Standing in the large open lobby at the reception desk, the carefully bland expression on the receptionist's face made it obvious he thought she and Tom were having an affair. It didn't help that Tom was constantly checking the doors and windows, looking for potential threats. She suspected he was playing it up a bit, leaning close and overacting to embarrass her further.

She avoided eye contact with him for as long as she could. She unlocked their door with the keycard, handed him his own key so he could come and go as he pleased, put her suitcase next her one of the two beds—because she'd made *sure* they would have two beds—and finally set up her computer on the little desk.

Maxine had been putting off research, but now that she knew the infernal wasn't going to be her ticket into Exalt, that left the draconic woman as a lead to follow.

Tom was moving around behind her in the small hotel room. His large frame made it difficult not to be distracted anytime he moved.

They were adults. They were mature adults who could get through this abnormal situation with dignity. But she'd have to be very careful if she wanted to hide her thoughts from him. He would be able to tell she was getting flustered if she wasn't—

"So, how do you want to do this?" His voice was amused, coming from the other side of the room along with some minor squeaking of bedsprings.

"Do... do what?"

"You can't pretend not to look at me forever." That bastard wasn't even trying not to sound smug.

"I want to respect your privacy."

"That's nice. You aren't worried?"

Confused, she finally turned to look at him. There were so many things she was worried about, she didn't want to start guessing and give him more options. He was sitting comfortably on the edge of the bed, still bouncing a bit.

"Worried about what?"

"You're not worried about me? That I'm expecting something from you?" He said the words without any clear judgment or intonation that would say whether he was or wasn't expecting... something. He hadn't acted like the kind of person tallying a score of what she owed him, but it was a question that showed he wasn't ignorant of power dynamics. Where was he going with this?

"*Are* you expecting something from me?"

He could have smirked or said something jokingly salacious, but instead he ceased his bouncing and clasped a hand loosely around his own wrist in what she now recognized as one of his "nonthreatening" poses.

"No." His eyes were serious, voice gentle. "You don't owe me anything, Maxine. And I don't want you to... to pretend to be interested in me or anything just to keep yourself safe. It's not... that's not necessary."

Stop. Drop expectations and reevaluate.

She thought he'd been teasingly trying to embarrass her with the weird situation, simultaneously flirting and pulling on her pigtails. But no... he was nervous. Why? It wasn't because of a confrontational conversation; he loved those. They'd already talked about his concern for her life. This felt different.

Research and egg momentarily set aside and forgotten, this was what she *lived* for. This was what she'd painstakingly built her own business around because she loved it so much. She'd found a man who initiated a conversation about power dynamics and sex. Next, she'd find a flying unicorn.

"Okay." She needed to dig in and get more of this catnip. "But do you want something from me?"

His eyes flickered down before he could stop himself and he refocused on her face. Maxine felt a burst of unfamiliar raw power. With Jehudin she had been eager and willing to take whatever he'd give. Was this what it felt like on the other side of that coin?

"I appreciate honesty." She smiled encouragingly.

"Uhm." He cleared his throat. "Well, I wouldn't mind more, but you don't—"

"What do you mean by 'more'?" She could get used to this. She probably shouldn't get used to this. But as it turned out, there was a point at which he would stop retreating when pushed. Her own attitude must have clued him in that she wasn't upset or nervous.

"I mean sex," he said bluntly, enunciating the word a little challengingly. "I'm attracted to you and would like to have sex with you." Then he waited, having passed the ball firmly into her court.

She had spent years working with clients who weren't able to communicate their needs, and until this moment she hadn't realized what a turn-on it was to hear someone express those desires so plainly.

He had taken a major risk, and at her prodding he had put himself in a vulnerable position. She should reward that with her own honesty; it would only be fair to tell him she was also attracted to him. Tom deserved to know she was holding back because of her own hang ups. But... she felt a flare of heat and a spark of mischief as he waited for her to respond with either an invitation or a denial.

"I appreciate your honesty, thank you." Her voice was bright, and bubbles fizzed in her chest. She hadn't had fun teasing someone since long before Jehudin.

And then she sat back down at her computer, conversation closed. From the corner of her eye she saw his face shift into incredulity, and then finally humor.

He stepped out of view for a few seconds, making her jump with surprise when he spun her chair 180 degrees to face him. This close to her, he was huge. His wall of a body blocked everything around her, narrowing her awareness to his half-smile.

"I'm glad you know you're safe with me." His voice was light, evocative of someone enjoying a game. He tilted her chair back, making her heart jolt at the unbalanced sensation of falling. "But you should know you're not *that* safe." And before she knew what he was planning, he closed in for a kiss that started soft—but quickly deepened.

She stiffened, freezing at the unexpected kiss before closing her eyes and returning it. He felt good, tasted faintly of mint, and this was a kind of excitement she hadn't had in a long time. Eyes drifting closed, she pushed up into him to enjoy the newness and exploration of a first kiss.

But the thought of Jehudin lurked as a ghost behind her thoughts. This was nice, but—

That thought evaporated in surprise when Tom slotted himself between her legs, lifting her body weight with one hand scooped under her so he could more effectively tilt her head back with the other. Clutching his shoulders for balance, she attempted to hold her own against him as he delved into her with teeth and tongue. When he finally broke away, they were both short of breath. Her lips felt swollen and cheeks flushed. She stared into his blown-out pupils until he broke eye contact to tuck his cheek against hers and brush his lips against the shell of her ear.

"I think we're going to have fun together."

Setting her back down into her chair, he turned and started unpacking his own clothes.

She might be in trouble.

⚬

Maxine had gotten tired of sitting at the small hotel desk, and she was lying on her stomach on her bed to continue her research.

The sun trickled in through the edges of thick curtains, and Tom was pausing his work-out routine to lounge on his own bed and read a battered paperback book with spaceships on the cover. He hadn't seemed like a "sci-fi" kind of guy to her, but she was starting to give up on trying to predict Tom.

Maxine was researching draconics and Exalt on her laptop to figure out what the hell was going on. The egg, she figured, was part of some kind of research. The draconic woman had said "millions in development." Maxine used her membership in medical journals to research the recent advances in draconic studies.

There were some promising leads. Draconics attending human universities were rare, and several studies on draconic egg viability rates over time came up in a medical journal search. Here was a promising paper that—

Her heart spiked to three times its resting rate when Tom surprised her by straddling her lower back and digging his thumbs into the base of her neck.

An instinctive complaint didn't have time to pass from her brain to her mouth when she realized he was giving her a back massage.

Oh, this she could get used to.

His hands kneaded the stressed tension out of her muscles, turning her into a puddle from her neck to her toes. She found herself sinking into the mattress with a groan, savoring the gentle pressure from his calloused fingers.

"You said," he began, his voice considering, "that sex was just kind of nice, but so was a massage. So there isn't a difference for you?"

Where was he going with this? She bit back an embarrassing noise as he stroked the knuckles of both hands down either side of her spine.

"They're... they're different." She fought to keep her voice even. "But essentially, yes. Compared to a... a direct connection to the astral plane, physical friction isn't as satisfying." He thankfully didn't stop the massage. "Still feels really good, though," she added for encouragement.

He hummed and his voice was curious. "But you haven't been with another person since."

"No," she admitted again. "I've never been the type for casual sex, and... ah... oh wow... no one should have to feel like they need to compete."

He didn't say anything for several pleasurable minutes.

"You're good at this." Maxine didn't want him to think she was unappreciative, and she was enjoying the increased intimacy of the contact. But it was hard not to include the comparison in her head—as much as she tried to tamp down the thought—that this wasn't the full-body explosion of pleasure Jehudin had given her. An explosion that lasted for what seemed like forever, until she couldn't bear it and—

She might have accidentally bucked him off if Tom weren't balanced over her when the at-first inexplicable sensation of his mouth on the back of her neck shocked her. With a hint of teeth, he sucked at a small patch of skin beneath her ear.

Her eyes rolled back and fists clenched to endure the unexpected pulse of arousal. "What are you...?"

And as soon as he'd started, he pulled off and blew cool air against her neck, making her shudder.

"It sounds to me," he said with a poorly hidden smirk, "that using the astral plane was a lazy shortcut."

"Wha?"

He gently removed himself, leaving her back feeling cold. "You're not as hard to please as you think you are."

Egg him on

One cold shower later, Maxine didn't have any new leads on her investigation of the draconic woman. She lounged on the room's uncomfortable couch while Tom did push-ups in the small space between beds.

"We need information," Maxine mused.

"Yeah."

"Samzen said they're interrogating that vampire tonight."

"If they can arrest him, yeah."

"There's going to be information in Samzen's office."

"I can't break you into an FBI building."

"No, I think… I have an idea." She didn't like it, but she couldn't be picky about the few tools available to her. "How much do you know about infernals and celestials?"

"A lot less than you, I bet."

"Honestly?" She grumbled about this internally. "I don't know as much as I thought I did. Jehudin hated infernals. He said they were all trying to debase humanity and I—I believed him. But Echles is working with one. I need… I need to figure out what's real."

"Okay. What's this got to do with Samzen's office?"

"There's something about my divorce that freaked out Echles. I'm going to use it."

She didn't have Echles' number, so she called Samzen. He picked up after two rings.

"Hey lady, these things take time—"

"Is Echles there?"

Samzen's voice stuttered into a long pause. "Ahh... he's working the case like I am, lady. It's only been a few hours, we don't have any—"

"I'd like to talk with Echles, please."

She couldn't make out words from their hushed argument on the other side.

"My partner isn't—"

"Echles!" she called louder. "Get on the phone, please."

After a shorter argument, the celestial's voice tentatively came through. "Ms. Hallis, is there a way in which I may assist you?"

Using every shred of acting talent from that high school play where she was an understudy and never actually got to perform the role of Lady Macbeth, Maxine put a tremor of fear in her voice and pushed through it to give the impression she was terrified but trying to hide it.

"I'm scared, Echles. They're coming for me, and I don't know how to... I need to protect the egg." Her playacted fear was more honest than intended, but as long as she could sell it, that was what mattered. "I want to be there when you question the vampire. I need to know why they're coming after the egg."

"Ah, uh, I am sorry to say, as part of an ongoing investigation it would be inappropriate for us to—"

"Are you saying you won't help me, Echles?" Tom was holding a plank position, watching her berate the celestial over the phone with the most gleeful expression she'd ever seen. She spared him a wink. "I would feel so much safer if I had all the information available."

"Ah... one moment, Ms. Hallis."

Now the argument between the celestial and his infernal partner was audible, as the celestial had apparently forgotten to cover the mouthpiece.

"We must comply with her need for emotional safety."

"Don't you dare, Echles! She's playing you like a fiddle."

"If her safety is at risk, it is my duty to provide for her needs and preserve her paths toward enlightenment."

"Since fucking when? The lady's in beefcake's house, safe from everything except beefcake!"

Tom pressed his ear against the other side of the phone so he could listen in.

"Even you can sense the violence in his bearing. He is not an oasis of safety; he is a threat to her gifts. She is compromised."

"Goddammit, don't pull this celestial crap."

"No!" The celestial sounded near tears. "He is indecent! He has already brought venal selfishness into her orbit! It risks her nature!"

"You celestials are being real creeps, you know that right? And... uh... Echles, did you put that phone on mute?"

"No he did not." Maxine rejoined the conversation. "And I'll pretend I didn't hear whatever that conversation was if you bring me in for your interrogation of the suspect."

After Samzen demonstrated his prodigious skill with profanity he took the phone back.

"It ain't that easy, lady. What, you think this is a goddamn circus? I'm not selling tickets and popcorn."

"Are you sure?" Without the infernal in front of her, Maxine glared into middle space. It was true Samzen had been the most helpful authority so far, but she wasn't above a little bullying when a potential life was on the line. "When I was talking alone with you at the Starbucks, I thought I smelled popcorn."

Silence on the line. That was, until the faint sound of Echles' voice in the background came through, distressed and unaware he could be heard on the other end.

"Her heart held only compassion, and now you see she is—"

"Shut up, Echles!" Sazmen's voice had the manic edge of someone babysitting an unruly set of children. "Lady, I owe you an apology. I thought beefcake was the dangerous one.

"Here's the deal, take it or leave it. Our guys are bringing in the suspect, and I was gonna let him marinate in a holding cell for a few hours anyway. You can watch on a monitor from another room."

"I need to ask him about the egg."

"You need a lotta things, lady."

Maxine huffed a frustrated sigh. "You'll ask him about the egg for me?"

"My investigation," Samzen spoke through gritted teeth, "is ongoing."

"Fine."

"The intern watching your place is across the street in a blue car, she'll drive you to the office. Ask to see a badge, don't just take the first ride that offers you candy."

The phone line clicked off, and Maxine realized her jaw was clenched tight enough to ache. "One of these days..." she hissed, "I'm going to sit a celestial down and figure out what the *fuck* they see when they look at me."

"He wasn't wrong, though." Tom's teeth flashed. "I am indecent."

Was it possible to get muscle strain from rolling your eyes too hard? She'd figure it out if she spent much more time with Tom.

"Let's go talk to that intern." She paused. "Do you... have any other clothes available?"

They both looked down at his thin shirt and low-riding pants. With the air cooling his post-workout sweat, his nipples could be seen through the fabric. "Worried Echles won't approve?"

"It's not Echles I'm worried about. Samzen is an incubus."

"So?"

The only way to do this was with a clinical tone. Otherwise, she'd be in real trouble. "Celestials can be sensitive to negative emotions: anger, hate, and aggression feel like nails on a chalkboard for them. Infernals don't react poorly to those baser human emotions, but incubi are particularly sensitive to sexual attraction and... sexual frustration."

Tom burst into laughter.

"And that poor sonofabitch invited us to his office!"

———◆———

"Working within human institutions..." The vampire's voice was tinny coming out of the poor-quality security monitor, but disgust was laced through every word. "It poisons your mind."

The small, pixelated view of Samzen didn't look impressed. He was leaning back in a chair opposite the vampire, fiddling with papers to keep his hands busy. The vampire's hands were cuffed to the table.

"It poisons the coffee, maybe." Samzen yawned. "They make it weaker than herbal tea around here. So tell me, William... Bill? Do you prefer Bill? Will, maybe?" Samzen let the chair fall forward so he could put an elbow on the table. "Anyway, Billiam. We just want a few answers."

The vampire bared his fangs and said nothing.

"You've got a buncha charges to worry about, buddy. Trespassing, assault, vamping out like a cheap extra in *Buffy the Vampire Slayer*. But what I wanna talk about is the hospital footage showing you in Ms. Amanda Havelka's room prior to when she was found deceased next to a heart monitor that had been tampered with." He waved a paper that may or may not have been related to that report. "What's your relationship with the deceased?"

The handcuffs rattled, but he said nothing.

"Had a fling with her maybe? Sharing her with the draconics?"

"Ugh!"

That got the intended reaction.

"Humans are slime!" William snarled. "They crawl all over the city like cockroaches, spreading disease and filth."

"Hmmm." Samzen still looked bored. "You don't drink human blood, Liam?"

"You'll get nothing more from me! I demand a lawyer."

Samzen groaned, turning his head to crack his neck as he stood up to leave the room. "Call your lawyer, if you have one. You should know, if you qualify for a public defender you don't get to pick your favorite." He paused, smirking at the vampire. "And most of them are human."

He left the room.

Maxine and Tom, standing close together in front of the antique security screen, looked up as the infernal walked back in and shut off the security feed. Echles had been standing and watching with them along the back wall, scowling at Tom.

Leaning back into Tom's warm hand, which rubbed slow circles on her back to give her comfort for the difficult memories of Amanda, Maxine laid into Samzen as soon as he re-entered his office.

"That's it?" Maxine pointed at the dark screen. "That was nothing! Go back in there and ask about the egg! Who was the draconic woman in the room?"

Samzen shrugged. "He lawyered up, lady, I ain't that crooked. We're going to be playing paperwork tennis for weeks, if not months. I told you, the investigation is ongoing."

"How did Amanda die?" Tom said it softly. The hand on Maxine's back paused its movements but maintained its gentle pressure.

"Allegedly someone, either our boy here or that draconic you met, injected something into her IV after tampering with the monitoring equipment." Samzen was twitchy, fidgeting with the badge clipped to his belt. "Toxicology is still doing the bloodwork. It... it was quick, anyway."

Sazmen seemed to be struggling with something. His red skin was darker than usual and he couldn't focus directly on her, flitting his eyes around the office.

"The draconic woman is a suspect in the homicide investigation. Inquiries are being made but... but we don't have a name or address." The infernal was looking everywhere except at them. "I assure you, lady... ma'am... we're doing the best we can."

"And, she did have a cesarean section incision, right?" Maxine felt shaky thinking about it. "No records of a baby found or abandoned anywhere?" She gratefully leaned into Tom's side as he stroked gently up and down her back. He had not changed out of his thin exercise clothes, which smelled not-unpleasantly musky—

"I can't do this," Samzen choked out. He scrunched his eyes and covered them with one hand. Turning blindly for the door, his free hand groped for the handle. "You've got to be kidding me!" the incubus muttered mostly to himself as he got the door open and stumbled into the hallway.

Tom and Maxine exchanged confused glances, then looked towards Echles for an explanation. For his part, the celestial looked panicked at having been left behind but did his best to sound calm. "It would be easier to have this conversation outside. Without anyone in physical contact." At that, he glared pointedly at Tom's hand on her back. He then held the door open for them. "If you would please follow me, the main courtyard is out the door on the right."

"I... I don't know if I..." The thought of Amanda being murdered and the disappearance of her baby was awful. Maxine's voice shook. The office's fluorescent lights were blocked out by Tom enveloping her in a hug.

"It's okay." He pressed his cheek to her hair as he squeezed the outside world away. "We'll figure it out. It'll be okay."

"What do we do when they hate humans so much?"

"I don't know." His voice was careful. "But I'll keep you safe, I promise."

"If they hurt a baby, I don't know what I'll do." Her voice was muffled through her clenched teeth and his chest. She dug deep for the anger and fear, doing her best to visualize the murderer's destruction. "I want to kill them for what they did to her!"

"Shhh, don't say that. That's not like you." Tom squeezed her tighter.

"It's true though, she asked me for help... whoever hurt her deserves to—"

"I must go!" This came from Echles, wide eyed and horrified in the open doorway. "Courtyard! Join us in the courtyard!" He ducked out the door with more grace, but as much speed as Samzen. The door clicked shut behind him.

Tom and Maxine broke apart.

"I'll take the left side, I don't think Samzen re-locked that bottom drawer."

They moved quickly. The desk in Samzen's office wasn't large, but it was stacked high with folders and files. Working in tandem, they methodically opened every drawer they could and skimmed their way through the files.

"Found something on Exalt!" Tom dropped the file on the ground and kept searching while Maxine snapped photos of everything. She could read it later; they needed to gather as much information as possible before either of the agents came back to check on them.

When they joined Samzen and Echles in the courtyard, only a couple minutes had passed, and Maxine was sniffling into a tissue.

Samzen was dry heaving into the grass, crouched with a hand pressed against his nose and mouth. Echles, for his part, also looked queasy, glaring venomously at Tom as they approached.

"Lady..." Samzen pushed himself to his feet, turning his head away from them like he was trying not to stare at the sun. "I ain't even mad. But be careful with beefcake, there. You've got a bulldog on a leash made of string."

"That's rude." Maxine was offended on Tom's behalf. "He's a person, not a—"

"Did I hurt your feelings, beefcake?" Samzen interrupted, risking a look at them to squint a skeptical eyebrow at Tom.

Tom put an arm over Maxine's shoulders and winked at Samzen. "Woof."

The incubus' naturally red skin purpled. He spun fully around to face the opposite direction. Maxine could only wonder what emotional feedback he was getting from the two of them.

"You didn't answer my question, Samzen. About the baby. Were there any reports of missing or abandoned newborns?"

"Ugh, no. No, lady, nothing unusual reported." His voice sounded choked. "We're still sending out inquiries, but at this point? It's either in a landfill or a were-bear's stomach."

"Maliel!" Echles' voice boomed in the otherwise peaceful courtyard. "She should not hear such things!"

While hearing "such things" had caused a burst of grief and anger so visceral it felt like a literal gut punch, she still appreciated the candor. And did not appreciate the attempt to shelter her.

"Echles, why are you treating me like a stained-glass hand grenade? What do you celestials see when you're gazing into my soul?"

Before the celestial could respond, Samzen stepped between them protectively. He was still flushed but bravely managed to look at her directly.

"Lady, fair play today. I get it, you're a mama bear. But I can't let you walk outta here with whatever you got in my office."

Echles looked confused. No one bothered to explain; he'd figure it out when he grew up.

"I need information and no one is helping me, Samzen." Maxine glared. "Exalt and I are the only ones who care about the egg. Which, I can't believe I have to keep reminding people, is basically a baby!"

This small grassy courtyard tucked inside the FBI office building was perfect for smoke breaks. When a random agent chose this moment to join them, tapping a box of cigarettes against his palm, Samzen snapped at him.

"Not a good time, Alan!"

The man looked up wide eyed at their tableau, and then promptly exited stage right. That was better for his health anyway.

"That egg don't make any sense, and I got no idea what to do about it, lady," Samzen confessed, his accent stronger in his frustration. "But y'got a point. You're in danger and need help."

Uh-oh. Tom was already on the balls of his feet looking more anxious. Samzen's posture got more confrontational, and Maxine could tell his professional pride had been damaged. They had pushed their luck too far.

Echles, eternally on the back foot, started to catch up.

"They... they used their emotions to—"

"Echles, you had a good idea before," Samzen interrupted his partner. "The lady should be allocated a safe house."

"You can't lock us in a room and pretend we don't exist, Samzen." Maxine tried to use her "reasonable" voice when what she wanted was her "screaming banshee" voice.

"Lady, you think I don't have cameras? You've been recorded tampering with evidence in my office." Samzen's face was dark with anger. "This is me being nice. I've seen beefcake's rap sheet. You're lucky I'm not arresting you."

"Echles." Maxine knew this was a failing gambit. "Please don't let him do this."

The celestial's glow was subdued, and he was wringing his hands, swallowing and shaking his head apologetically.

"This will be... we will find the safest place for you." His voice was tight and he wasn't looking at her.

"Safest?" Cupping the egg with both hands and fighting for composure, she heard the crack in her own voice. "Are you going to lock us in a holding cell until the egg hatches?"

Crack under pressure

Technically, it wasn't a holding cell.

They were pushed into one of the spare interrogation rooms to wait until Samzen and Echles figured out whatever they were going to do with the nosy humans.

Before closing the door on her, Samzen grabbed the edge of her t-shirt sling to hold her still so he could get in the last word.

"Sam's a great name. Works for a boy or girl draconic."

The door clicked shut on his stupid red infernal face.

"Ugh!" She didn't have words for her disgust.

Their phones had been confiscated, but so far the agents had stopped short of arresting her and Tom. Legally, Samzen would have to arrest them and put them into the system in order to detain them, but Echles begged for a cool-down period, and no one argued with him.

She surveyed the small room. Two uncomfortable chairs, a table, one of those big mirrors someone could watch through from the other side, and an overhead light.

Tom had been quiet through the whole argument. He didn't put up a fight, just followed along with Maxine. She'd never seen him so passive.

"Rap sheet," Samzen had said. Tom had successfully overcome the prison system recidivism rate, and now he was waiting to figure out if he'd be put back into the system because of her.

"I... I'm sorry Tom, this is my fault."

He grunted in acknowledgment that he heard her, pulling up one of the two chairs and sitting down. His eyes were distant.

"I'm the one Samzen has a problem with, I'll make sure he—"

"Echles is afraid of something."

He was still staring into the distance, chewing on the inside of his cheek. Stumbling out of one train of thought and into another one, Maxine tried to catch up.

"He's a celestial, and I know my divorce was—"

"No, something else," he interrupted again. "Did you notice? He made sure we were detained together."

She had been so angry at Samzen that she hadn't focused much on Echles. If she had made the mistake of dismissing him as socially clumsy and harmless, Tom hadn't. Thinking back, she remembered Samzen had been about to follow a more standard protocol and have them detained separately until Echles intervened.

She pulled out the opposite chair and sat across from Tom.

"What... I don't know what you're implying."

"Neither do I. Yet," he grumbled. "Samzen made sense: we pissed him off. Echles though... I don't know what to think."

Maxine tried to remember what Echles had been doing. She was kicking herself for not paying closer attention to his body language, too upset to be thinking clearly. While Samzen had been willing to arrest her, Echles had been wringing his hands and desperate for any other solution. For someone in his position, it was even stranger to consider that he'd be bending the rules on anyone's behalf. From what little she'd seen of Echles so far, he'd been a stickler for rules.

There were a few reasons why a celestial would tolerate breaking the rules.

"I think—I think maybe I'm part of an active prophesy."

"What does that mean?" Tom's brow creased.

Not everyone knew, or cared, about how most celestials wanted to improve humanity. Tom was definitely the kind of person who would consider a celestial's definition of "enlightenment" meaningless. But helping people become better versions of themselves was her life's work.

"It might not mean anything," Maxine sighed, "but there's very little a celestial won't do to make a prophesy come true, if it will improve a human. Jehudin considered it his mission in coming to the mortal plane."

"You can't be 'improved' Maxine." His face was twisted in distaste, like he'd bitten a rotten lemon.

"Of course I can be—"

"Nah, I mean *they* can't improve you." Tom was sneering now, getting worked up on her behalf. "Who the fuck do they think they are?"

"Celestials just want to help." It was something she'd always believed, and marrying Jehudin only solidified that belief. It was all he'd wanted. To help humanity.

Tom stared at her. He was probably reading her expression and body language to determine how fragile she was feeling in that moment. He looked cautious, but based on how he was shifting his weight and pressing his lips together, he was holding something back.

"Just say it." Maxine rolled her eyes, "I've got a lot more than my divorce to worry about right now."

"Alright," Tom's voice was dark, "when did Jehudin *ever* help you?"

She had been braced for a question about Jehudin, but it still hurt. Stinging pain in her chest felt like the precursor to panic, but she did her best to stay calm. Despite her best efforts at remaining calm, her face felt hot with a flush of anger and defensiveness. She bit back her immediate response, which would have been "What do you know about it?" Maxine held herself stiffly in her seat, trying not to show him how much the words affected her.

"Our relationship failed," Maxine said the words just as stiffly as she was holding herself in the uncomfortable chair, "but he was a good man. *Is* a good man."

"So, what do you think your prophesy is?" Tom had softened his voice, maybe sorry about bringing up painful memories. Maybe he just didn't want to have that argument right now.

"I don't know," Maxine swallowed. "But if Echles is scared of me, there's two options: he's either trying to interfere because of a prophesy, which is dangerous. I could bring legal action if I think he's breaking the Mortal Treaty. Or he's trying to avoid the prophesy entirely, but forced to interact with me because I'm—" she chuckled without any real humor, "I'm somehow mixed up with the case he and Samzen are investigating."

"Or he's just a shitty agent," Tom suggested, smiling slightly.

"He doesn't like you either. Could you be projecting?"

Tom laughed suddenly, a lighthearted glint in his eye as he focused his attention back on her.

"You sound like a therapist."

"There might be a reason for that," she groaned, leaning back as far as the cheap plastic seat would allow. "You've been putting yourself in danger to protect me, Tom. I'm going to do everything I can to make sure you aren't arrested."

"Does it bother you?" He didn't sound upset. His tone was curious. "That I've got a record?"

"No." She smiled to put him at ease. "But I am sorry you went through it."

He turned away, avoiding eye contact. "It's just... it's another way we're different," he said, finally. "And I know they say 'opposites attract,' but from what I've seen, differences cause problems."

This wasn't about sex. He was worried about whether they could have a viable relationship. And he cared enough to bring it up and talk about it. This was better than chocolate and roses.

"Shared life experience can be important." She planted her elbows on the table, leaning in towards him. "But I've worked with couples who are still happily partnered despite being different species with completely different upbringings. What's more important, I think, is having shared values and the ability to communicate about sensitive or difficult topics with empathy."

He had taken enough of the risks in speaking his desires. Now it was her turn.

"For example, one of the reasons I haven't had sex with you yet is because I'm worried about making our situation awkward." His head whipped around to look at her, wide-eyed and eager. "Hah, *more* awkward, maybe. I don't want to—I mean, I think I'm going to be disappointing." She cleared her throat, barreling forward before she could lose her nerve. "I don't think normal sex is going to be satisfying for me anymore, and that's not fair to you—or any human. But I am attracted to you." She risked a small smile. "Obviously."

"I wouldn't mind if it were more obvious." His answering smile was slow, but she blushed as it spread over his face. "No wait, don't clam up yet." He rose from his chair, moving behind her so she couldn't see him. Her gut clenched in anticipation at the amorphous sense of danger—and excitement—right behind her. His lips tickled the shell of her ear, making her jump in her seat.

"I like a challenge," he murmured softly. Her hair shifted with his breath, making her shiver. "And I don't mind experimenting until we find out what makes you tick. You won't disappoint me, Maxine." She gasped as she felt his lips moving, featherlight against the back of her neck. "Just tell me when."

And then he pulled away and walked back to his chair, a satisfied smile on his face while she struggled to hold on to her stomach swooping in every direction.

"And if that perverted red asshole was watching us, he's probably blind right now."

⸻◆⸻

They ended up waiting only a couple hours. In the meantime, Tom and Maxine played a game of reflexes, trying to lightly slap the opponent's hands before they could pull away. Tom had the obvious advantage, but Maxine enjoyed trying to fake him out with twitches and facial expressions.

When the door opened they both stopped, turning to see two strangers standing in the doorway, two men, both wearing FBI jackets and badges, one of whom looked bored and the other looking nervous.

Maxine risked a quick exchanged glance with Tom to make sure he saw what she saw. He did. They were both vampires, which might be normal for the paranormal unit, but these men didn't have the right body language for FBI agents. One was too tense, and the other too relaxed. They were acting—about something—she didn't know what, yet.

"Ms. Hallis? Mr. Morgan?" the bored one drawled. "Please come with us."

"Where are we going?" Maxine stood, cradling the egg against her chest and stepping between them and Tom. "Where are Samzen and Echles?"

"Busy," the nervous one said quickly. "Hurry up, we're taking you to a safehouse."

The hallway was quiet behind them, but maybe that was normal. It had been late when she and Tom first arrived, and several hours had passed, so this must be close to the middle of the night.

The other agents they'd seen had been in plain clothes with badges. Maybe these two wore their jackets late at night in their own empty office for... normal reasons. Or maybe they just thought a couple props would sell their story before walking into a room with two people who specialized in body reading.

Standing behind her, Tom's hand was warm on her shoulder with an unspoken warning. She nodded. She didn't want to walk directly into a trap, but she also didn't love the idea of spending all night in an interrogation room waiting to be arrested.

"Lead the way."

The two false agents, or maybe they were real corrupted agents for all she knew, led her and Tom outside the FBI building using back hallways. After exiting a fire door into a parking lot, they saw a nondescript minivan which had been left idling. Its windows were blacked out.

"You'll be safe there," said the bored one, gesturing toward the van. "It's a short drive."

Never go to a second location.

Curling herself around the egg, Maxine darted to the side to give Tom room to move forward in a practiced lunge.

Tom engaged the nervous one first. His fists were up in his loose defensive stance while he measured his opponents.

The fake FBI agents didn't go fangs out, which was the only real indication they weren't trying to kill Tom. He got several punches through but didn't faze the vampires, who kept circling and baiting him.

Two on one, bare fists against vampires in the middle of the night in a wide-open parking lot, Tom was at a major disadvantage.

"Maxine, run."

Tom wasn't looking at her. He knew what he was demanding. But even so, she stood as if her feet had been frozen in blocks of ice. If she left to get help, she might never see him again. This time she didn't feel like she *couldn't* move—but she wouldn't. Which amounted to the same thing.

The vampires grinned around him, working together to keep him from focusing on either one. Maxine watched from the sidelines as Tom took a kick to the leg that crumpled him.

They were moving too quickly for Maxine to see what kind of hit landed, but Tom sprawled on the pavement and skidded several feet. With his forearms abraded from catching himself and his breath sharp and controlled, it probably wasn't a good sign he didn't get back to his feet. Crouched in a kneeling position he kept his eyes up and hands in front of his face.

It had been so easy to imagine that Tom was invincible.

Pushing off his knee, Tom grappled one of the vampires to the ground using some kind of arm bar that prevented the vampire from bending his knee.

The vampire went down with a crunch, but now Tom couldn't defend against the other one. A solid kick from the standing attacker had Tom rolling away and his target standing up.

Maxine watched in slow motion as Tom curled and tucked his head inside his arms to protect himself. The two vampires laughed as they kicked him carelessly. He couldn't uncurl, accepting the blows that rained around his back, legs, and arms because moving would be worse.

She could stop this.

"Stop!" Maxine couldn't hear her own voice over the sound of their laughter. It felt like a nightmare where she couldn't move or talk. She yelled louder, "Stop, I'll go with you!"

One of the two paused, looking over, and he nudged his friend to stop as well.

The one who seemed to be calling the shots smiled his fangs at her. Carelessly, he planted a foot down against Tom's neck to force the human's head up and expose his throat.

Tom's face was... he had a split lip, blood smeared across his whole face, and one of his eyes was swollen shut. Maybe he was trying for a defiant grimace, but he just looked pained.

"Get in the van if you don't want to hear me break his spine." His smile widened cruelly. "It makes a lovely pop."

When she spared a glance towards Tom, she regretted it.

He was gripping the vampire's foot with both hands, but he was struggling to keep it off his neck. With his face bloody and twisted with pain, his arms were strained, trying to prevent the vampire's foot from going through his throat.

"Move quickly! I want to see his blood spill, wasted on the ground." The vampire gloated, enjoying his position of power. "Worthless, unloved and unwanted."

What a fucking edgelord.

Second vampire wasn't as happy as the first. He had gotten to his feet and enjoyed the revenge of kicking a man while he was down, but Tom had clearly done some damage to him first. Staring with hungry eyes at their bloody victim, Maxine felt a panicked urgency to get them away from Tom. No matter what.

"That's not what your boss wants." She said it much more confidently than she felt it. When she turned her back, the image of the vampire standing over Tom still burned in her eyes. "Let's go."

Fox in a henhouse

Her goal had been to get them away from Tom, but that was also a failure. Soon after she'd climbed into the van, one of the vampires tossed Tom in after her. The dread of her own panicked idiocy started to sink in. She had jumped blindly into their van in desperation to help Tom, without any knowledge of what they wanted or where they were going. They had been *right behind* the FBI office. She hadn't even considered a little thing like screaming for help.

But maybe screaming would have killed Tom.

She sat in a brand-new minivan with the back seats torn out, leaving the driver in view. The other one, the hungrier one who had been more hurt in the fight, was climbing in the back door with greedy eyes fixed on Tom. This left her and Tom sitting in the back of the van as far from the vampires as possible.

Tom did have the wherewithal to adjust his protective fetal position and push himself back against the wall. His hands were up in front of his face and neck, but his eyes were unfocused and he was swaying.

Maxine planted herself firmly between Tom and their guard.

"Where are we going?" She didn't manage to sound defiant, but she wasn't aiming for dignity.

En route to a location where they'd have fewer allies and witnesses, Maxine was aiming for survival.

The hungry vampire was going to say something, but the driver barked at him not to fraternize. With a longing look at the blood coating Tom's face, he left them alone in the back of the van to sit more comfortably in the front.

There were bumps and exposed hardware from where seats had been removed, and they weren't replaced with any sort of comfortable cover. Trying to arrange herself with her back against the wall next to Tom, she guided his head onto her lap as he collapsed back down.

"It'll be okay," she murmured softly, knowing the vampires could still hear.

Gently brushing some hair out of his face, which had stuck into the blood crusting around his eye, she saw him squint up at her.

He was hurt, but still seemed alert and aware of his surroundings. Tom took a deep breath and sighed it out after holding it for several seconds.

His lungs sounded clear. That was good.

"Leave the lying to me," he muttered.

"You... you'll be okay, Tom." She'd do whatever she could to ensure that. "I'm the one they want. I'll get you to a hospital and—"

"Bruised," he interrupted softly. "Got a good hit on my head and I'll be spinning for a while. Nothing broken, nothing torn. I'll be fine."

"You might have internal bleeding."

"Nah, don't think so." He prodded his own midsection tenderly. His hands were scraped and the knuckles on his right hand were broken up and sluggishly bleeding, dripping on the thinly carpeted chassis of the minivan. "Didn't get m'spleen or kidneys. Liver's fine."

Pain was written clearly across his bloody face and he spoke with a split lip, but his voice was analytical.

"You need medical attention, Tom."

His automatic smile made the lip bleed more, and he winced.

"Yeah. I've been making some... self-destructive choices lately. Think I need a shrink?"

She couldn't help but laugh. Hunched over him and crying at the same time, she tried to throttle her wet sobs, but they kept bursting out of her. Her palms were bloody from where they'd been stroking back his hair, so she used the back of her hand to wipe the tears from her face.

"I'm so sorry Tom."

He let her cry for a little while. Not that he could have stopped her. But with his head resting in her lap, he lay a hand heavily against her knee for a comforting squeeze and he closed his eyes and rested.

He shouldn't be comforting *her*. She was the one who dragged him into this mess. He was a broken, bloody mess because of her and this egg.

None of it was the egg's fault, of course. Maybe when the kid hatched, and "Auntie Maxine" visited the loving foster family to bring whatever treats young draconics like, she could tell the child about how hard someone had fought to keep it alive.

It didn't matter that Tom wasn't technically fighting for the egg. His intentions didn't matter as much as the results.

The drive didn't take long. Wherever Exalt was taking them, it had to be in or near Crestfield. When the minivan rumbled to a stop, the back door next to them opened immediately. The light that poured in was artificial; they were parked in an indoor garage.

Waiting for them outside the opening van doors was the draconic woman from the hospital, flanked by a younger female draconic.

With her eyes immediately latched onto the egg, kept warm against Maxine's chest, the older draconic woman sagged with relief. It was only after she'd laid eyes on the egg that she quickly inspected Maxine, Tom, then the two vampires who were climbing into the back of the van to "welcome" their guests to the destination.

"They weren't to be harmed!" she barked at them. "You could have damaged the egg in your carelessness."

The hungry one snarled at her, unrepentant. "He attacked us first!"

"It was a simple task." A clawed hand with faded green scales gripped the metal door hard enough to dent. "And your life is worthless compared to that egg."

"I do not answer to you!"

Maxine and Tom, who hadn't even left the van yet, watched impassively at the dissent in their ranks. Despite the fear and anxiety of her helpless position, Maxine felt a mild embarrassment on their behalf. How gauche to argue with your minions in front of the prisoners.

The hungry vampire, still limping from whatever Tom had done to his leg, was posturing aggressively at the draconic woman. He pulled himself out of the van to snarl into her face.

"You came bleating to us for help, turned away from every other—"

Even older draconics had terrifying strength. Without hesitation or warning, the woman pulled a reinforced wood-tipped knife from her lab coat and drove it into the chest of the posturing vampire.

He crumpled in disbelief, staring down at the hilt protruding from left of center in his chest. It had been perfectly angled to drive through his sternum but avoided being fatal by missing his heart. The draconic woman turned away from him in disgust, leveling her glare and baring canines at the other vampire.

"Unreliable assistants are worse than none at all." The other vampire was gaping as his friend crumpled on the concrete floor of the garage. "Will you do as you are told?"

"Y—yes ma'am!"

"Good. Now get out."

He escaped quickly, dragging his injured companion behind.

Vampires could recover from almost any wound that missed their heart, but the placement of the dagger made it obvious this woman knew how close she was to it. Maxine didn't know if this was typical "discipline" for them.

The draconic woman stepped closer and extended her claws in a facsimile of welcome.

"None of this was my intention," she apologized, dipping her head. "If you are willing, Mr. Morgan, I have a medical team to assist you. I wish only to speak with your woman; no harm will come to her unless she seeks to harm me or the egg."

"I won't be separated from him," said Maxine. It was bad enough they were in this unknown location. "What do you want?"

"You are both safe here, Ms. Hallis. I believe we want the same thing." The woman clasped at the collar of her own lab coat, bowing slightly. "My name is Luculenta, and I deeply regret the terror we have put you through. I asked for you to be taken from incarceration because I want to work with you, Ms. Hallis."

Maxine cautiously stretched a leg out to step down onto the smooth concrete of the parking garage floor. Was this what a cat felt like, brought to the vet and cautious about the dubious safety of an opened carrier?

"What... why do you have a medical team?" She swallowed, looking between the two draconics. "What are you doing here?"

"We are conducting vital medical research." A light of excitement in Luculenta's eyes reminded Maxine oddly of Professor Jiminez. The same manic joy of discovery. A clawed hand gestured around them. "Please allow me to show you my work. This is my old facility, and sensitive operations have been moved. I do not... it is not my intention to separate the two of you..."

At this, Maxine felt Tom's hand, still bloody and scraped, grasp at her shoulder as he pulled himself out of the van to stand at her side.

"…but our time is limited." Luculenta continued. "If you will consent, my aides can assist with Mr. Morgan's medical needs while I answer all your questions. If I can, Ms. Hallis."

The draconic woman was consummately polite, exercising deference in her body language and tone. She didn't look nervous, but Maxine deferred to Tom, knowing he would be able to read her better. Leaning in close to Maxine, he didn't bother lowering his voice. "It's okay. She's telling the truth."

That was a better guarantee of safety than she'd had all year.

"Get to medical, then." Maxine risked a gentle hug, trying not to jostle his injuries. "I need my answers."

The younger draconic stepped forward to assist. "Please follow me, sir," she said softly, nodding at the elder for approval.

"Thanks." There was no gratitude in his voice, but given the circumstances no one was offended. He was limping slightly, but it was doubtful anyone here would make the mistake of thinking he was easy prey.

The older draconic turned her slitted eyes back onto Maxine.

"Please come with me."

⚊⚬⚊

The draconic woman led her out of the underground garage up industrial metal stairs. She strode swiftly through undecorated hallways past unmarked doors. They had started in an underground parking garage, and Maxine never saw windows to indicate they'd climbed aboveground. "This facility was our home for a long time, but with recent... changes... it has been retired. Ah, here we are."

They stopped at a door with a large window panel which allowed Maxine to see a laboratory too clean to be in current use. Tables with centrifuges and other equipment she couldn't recognize at a glance lined the pristine stainless steel counter tops. Luculenta opened the door, walked inside, and gestured broadly to welcome Maxine in after her.

The whole situation felt wrong. This facility was sterile and empty, but Luculenta walked through it like it was a beloved home. Stuck somewhere between being a guest and a hostage, Maxine wasn't sure how to behave.

"Where is Tom right now?" She might as well start with the important questions.

"Here, I can show you."

Turning to a computer monitor, the draconic brought up a security screen in a few clicks, navigating through black and white views of empty rooms and hallways. She stopped when the view provided a small but high-definition video of Tom sitting up on a hospital bed.

He was talking to two draconics wearing scrubs. They stood at the far side of the room and he was dabbing at his own head with a small cloth. A few bottles of what might have been disinfectant sat on a table next to him.

"He does not trust us." Luculenta sounded amused. "We are a skeleton crew at the moment. Our operation has been turned upside down and we may need years to fully recover. But you, Ms. Hallis..."

Turning away from the monitor, the woman's eyes were bright. Her expression looked open and... eager? Happy?

"Ms. Hallis, you have done us a great service. When I first learned of the egg's theft, I thought it had been destroyed. When I learned that...

somehow… the infamous Thomas Morgan had claimed ownership of it, I could not imagine it was for a good reason." She clasped her clawed hands together. "But I have looked into you, Ms. Hallis. I have seen how you care for and protect the egg. If not for you, I believe it would have been lost. And you have my gratitude."

"What is going on?" Maxine swallowed; her mouth was dry. "I don't understand. Are you with Exalt?"

"Not… technically, no. They are extremists. Closed-minded and irrational when it comes to humans." Luculenta opened a drawer under the desk and pulled out a folder thick with paper. "But they have money and have agreed to fund my research.

"Ms. Hallis, do you know the hatch rate of an average draconic egg?"

"Um… I understand they're low?"

They were discussing hatch rates? Luculenta had not turned off the monitor showing Tom. One of the nurses had apparently tossed him some more supplies and he was in the process of wrapping his open cuts and scrapes himself.

"They are exceedingly low, Ms. Hallis." Luculenta shook her head sadly. "We can fertilize and lay one egg in a year, and there is a one in five chance it will be viable. But because of the stigma against weakness in the Holding, very few families discuss this pain while trying for children. I have dedicated my life to finding ways to improve our hatch rate."

"Where does this egg fit in?"

Spreading out the pages from her folder, Luculenta laid out comparison charts and data analysis tables, but Maxine was too busy studying the draconic and distractedly checking on Tom to be able to focus on the papers.

"I will happily bore you with the details, Ms. Hallis, but suffice it to say, that egg you have been protecting contains a rare genetic mutation which makes its shell more permeable in utero."

"...Okay." At what point would her life start making sense? Maxine desperately hoped it would be soon.

"This allows for more nutrients to cross the membrane wall!" Luculenta's overjoyed smile was terrifyingly full of teeth. "When we are able to access the genetic material of the child after it hatches, we can start the real work of determining what therapies and genetic selection could be used to replicate its success."

The little black and white Tom on the monitor had taken off his shirt to access some abrasions along his side and had thrown a metal tray at a nurse who was trying to take pictures.

"And... why did Amanda have it?"

The excitement on Luculenta's face dimmed. She leaned back from her research, suddenly more solemn.

"She was a research assistant working with our subjects. But she was also... *fraternizing* with a colleague." The way she said "fraternizing" one might think it was a war crime. "When their relationship soured, she had to be let go. But..." Her tail lashed and she clenched a fist against the table, scoring ragged lines in the papers. "Instead of simply leaving, she decided to ruin us with her petty revenge."

The egg was in its sling as always, a comforting presence. Maxine looked down at it, then back up at Luculenta.

"If you are the guardian of this egg... I will give it to you." Uncertainty churned, but this was her goal. She didn't understand how they were using the egg for research, but it did seem as though this woman wanted it safe.

"My impression of you was correct. You are a good woman, Ms. Hallis." Luculenta was shaking her head. "But my operation... my study is in chaos." She looked down at the torn pages on the table, gently piecing them back together with precise claws. "Amanda's betrayal has given us unwanted attention. I am... embarrassed to say that we cannot perform our research legally due to red tape and requirements for working with live subjects. Bureaucracy is always opposed to progress! But I assure you all our participants have consented."

Maxine wished she had Tom with her. She still couldn't read draconic expressions, but Luculenta sounded sincere.

Maxine knew all about psychological research studies, but very little about clinical research. From her layman's knowledge, however, she did know that medical research required a lot of work to prove the safety of an experiment before being allowed to perform it on any sentient species. The rules and regulations were there for good reasons. It was easy to complain about bureaucracy holding back progress, but those rules and regulations had been built on pain and suffering.

Luculenta continued, "Because of you we have a chance. It might take years to find another egg with a similar genetic mutation. When Amanda stole this one she was attempting to kill a generation of potential eggs. But... it shames me to say that I do not trust my current staff during our transition. I am asking for your continued help to keep the egg safe, until we have finished settling in our new location."

Silence. A metaphorical tumbleweed meandered across the vacant desert of Maxine's mind. Seeing the complete shut down of higher-level processing, Luculenta nodded sympathetically.

"You, Ms. Hallis, have been the best advocate for the egg's safety. I am reviewing my team to ensure they are trustworthy. My research assistants are all being surveyed, and our methods audited. Many of my assistants were assigned by Exalt, and now... any one of them may decide to leverage this egg against us. They know how valuable it is. And how delicate.

"You and I want the same thing, Ms. Hallis." She stepped back, gesturing around. "We both want the egg where it belongs. Safe. Loved. And when I realized we had this in common... it became clear to me that everything I had done to get it back had been a mistake. Please accept not only my apologies, but my request: keep it safe until I know it will be safe with me again."

At this point Luculenta seemed to be expecting some kind of response.

"...And Tom?"

They both looked at the monitor again. Tom had his shirt back on and was in the process of tying a brace around his knee. The security camera was distant enough from him that small details of his face weren't visible, but he looked much better. His injuries were wrapped, and he was moving more smoothly. The remaining draconic nurse had her hands out as if she wanted to help him, but whenever she got too close, he yelled at her until she backed away again.

"I don't... know what you see in him." Luculenta sounded doubtful but was trying for a diplomatic tone. "But if he is protecting you, and you are protecting the egg, he has my gratitude as well."

There were too many questions. Maxine was powerless in someone else's territory, not knowing what to believe. This woman had stolen a baby as leverage and killed Amanda, maybe? Or told the vampire William to do it so her hands could stay clean?

How much was true?

Maxine was going to ask more questions, but they were both interrupted by a painfully loud siren. Lights flashed from the corners of the room, turning the whole laboratory into a heart-stopping rave.

Luculenta's scales actually fluffed up in shock; Maxine had never seen that before. With panicked speed, the draconic tapped through security screens again. She landed on a hallway monitor showing Agent Samzen, in his FBI jacket, breaching the facility. He was carrying a gun this time and based on his silhouette, seemed to be wearing a bulletproof vest under his jacket.

"How has that demon found us?" Her voice had changed completely, from a reasonable and compassionate tone into a harsh snarl. She turned back towards Maxine. "I have to go. But here..."

After pulling a pen from her coat pocket, Luculenta jotted down a phone number on the top page of what looked like clinical research results. She spoke quickly, trying to fit as much information as she could into only a few seconds.

"I thought I'd have more time! I will call you soon. Read the papers; they will show you the need for my research! I am trusting you with our future generations, Ms. Hallis." Her gaze was intense as she pressed the papers into Maxine's hands. "You could be the reason thousands of loving mothers get the chance to hold their own children."

The draconic turned and disappeared through a back door, tail swishing behind her.

Deviled eggs

The lights and siren of the alarm were drilling through Maxine's head like railroad spikes. She gritted her teeth, not knowing what to think about Luculenta's story.

The papers with charts and data analysis were in her hands, promising either answers or lies. She folded them over and tucked them under the egg in her sling. Folded, they were about as thick as a novella. She didn't think they were visible from the outside, but they poked her chest uncomfortably. Maxine decided her limited time would be best spent looking for more information.

She typed at the computer until it became obvious it was only a security monitor. Rifling through drawers and cabinets revealed only the occasional piece of scientific equipment, but no printouts or other data.

At some point the alarm turned off, soothing her nerves. The ear-piercing siren had clearly been designed to instill panic and urgency into everyone inside the facility. As far as Maxine knew, the only other members of Luculenta's team were the two vampires and draconic nurses she'd seen on the cameras. The security cameras showed nothing but empty hallways. Either the alarm had a time limit, or Samzen had turned it off.

After only a few more minutes the door opened and Samzen walked in, followed by Tom.

"Lady, I turn around for five goddamn minutes, and you get yourself kidnapped?"

He had holstered his gun, probably also realizing this was an empty facility. His tone was somewhere between utter exasperation and relief, like a frantic parent finally finding their lost child after imagining every possible worst-case scenario.

She barely heard what the infernal was saying; her eyes were fixed on Tom.

Something was wrong. He was moving wrong, his face was wrong. He was looking at Samzen as though the agent was the center of the universe, leaning towards the smaller man like a flower following the sun.

"What did you do to Tom?"

Samzen gave a scant glance backwards and shrugged. "Nothing. I think the guy took a hit to the head. C'mon, lady, let's go."

"No. What did you do to Tom?" His face was uncanny, holding an expression that didn't fit his personality. He hadn't looked at her once, his attention fixed devotedly on Samzen. "Tom? Are you okay?"

He didn't respond to her, but Samzen groaned.

"Lady, I came here to rescue you. Let's goooo." He drew out the last word with a sarcastically exaggerated gesture towards the door.

That was probably true but... there was no light in Tom's eyes. The man looked hollow.

"Undo it." Maxine had felt a lot of outrage in the last week, but this was a new peak. Tom would have preferred to be beaten back into the ground than to have anyone take over his mind. "Right now, Samzen. Whatever you're doing, turn it off."

The infernal clenched his fists, sullen and frustrated.

"Lady, we don't have time for this."

Before she could react, everything about Samzen shifted.

Even though nothing about him physically changed, Samzen suddenly became someone... different. Instead of looking like any average infernal, in a blink he became shockingly, unbelievably, and unnaturally attractive.

Maxine had only heard of what an incubus could do. Violations, Jehudin had called them, but this didn't feel like a violation. This felt like seeing a sunrise for the first time. In awe that she had met this incredible person, and he deigned to even talk to her, made her desperate to be worthy of that attention.

Her mouth was suddenly dry, and she felt nervous—like she was trying to build up the nerve to ask out a crush for the middle school dance. Intellectually she knew this was not a natural response, but her outrage had completely disappeared. Her stomach flipped. What if he didn't like her? It felt like a matter of life and death that this man should be impressed by her.

Standing behind Samzen, Tom's empty expression served as a reminder. *That* was what the infernal was trying to do to her. She had to move, close her eyes, turn away, but... she couldn't tear her eyes off Samzen.

Moving fluidly, the infernal's steps were graceful and deliberately placed until he was standing close enough to touch. The butterflies got stronger. She'd give anything for him to touch her. Maxine gritted her teeth and used all the self-control she could muster to slam her eyes shut. It didn't help; her knees wobbled, weak at his proximity.

"Incubus," she said, although the word sounded raspy coming from her dry mouth. "Stop."

"Oooh, but why would I want to do that?" he purred in a chocolate voice. The feeling of his hand on her cheek made her gasp and instinctively open her eyes. His thumb stroked her cheekbone, setting her blood on fire. "You two have become a real problem. You don't want to be a problem for me, do you darling?"

"N-no," she said breathlessly, helplessly caught.

"That's good. You're gonna be just fine, sweetheart."

He was so kind, sympathetic to her confusion and anger. He was also patient, more patient than they deserved after all the trouble they caused. His hand was perfect, soft and warm against her cheek. She leaned into him, beyond grateful for his kindness.

Everything went black.

———— ◆ ————

Consciousness came with what felt like the worst hangover of her life. Maxine groaned, an icepick of light stabbing through her eyelids and she squeezed her eyes tighter against the agony.

All other sensations trickled in slowly. A throbbing ache pulsed through her body as if she had the flu. Sticky sand and crud itched in the corner of her eyes. Her butt was numb and she was sitting against the wall of a small cargo van propped up next to a warm body which... yes, a painful peek through her eyelids confirmed it was Tom, who had apparently also been put to sleep and was still unconscious. The van was messy, with boxes stacked against the walls and men's clothes tossed carelessly on the floor.

The van wasn't moving and the back doors weren't fully closed. Sunlight stabbed through the crack. How much time had she lost?

Now she could hear Samzen's voice filter in from outside.

"...figure, anyway? Should have been— ... But fuck me, right? Now I've got— ... -complicated mess."

He sounded normal again, no longer her idea of perfection. He sounded irritated, but that was also normal for him. She didn't have time to do more than slowly acclimate to the pounding headache and brace herself to pry open her eyes more before the door to the van was abruptly pulled open.

"Augh!" she yelped involuntarily at the fresh light stabbing behind her eyes.

"Oh good." Samzen's voice was achingly sarcastic. "You're awake."

"What the *fuck*, Samzen?"

"I had to get you two outta there, lady. For all I knew they were gonna put nerve gas in the vents."

"And you couldn't have said something like, 'it's time to go'?"

Glaring through watery eyes had no effect on him. The incubus groaned in response, a teenager being told they had to clean their room.

"Look, all I actually know about beefcake there is that he's a scary motherfucker pretending to be your lapdog, and I didn't have any backup. If he'd wanted to get me outta the way, I'd be pasted on the floor of that shitty secret lab and no one would ever find enough of me to scrape into a jelly jar for my funeral. Which no one would attend, by the way."

"What did you do to us?"

"Power drain." Samzen inspected his nails for dirt in an exaggerated air of nonchalance. "I took the energy you needed to stay awake. He'll sleep until he builds it back."

She tried to remember what else she knew about incubi. They did have the ability to drain energy from humans, but if it went too far it could kill. There was a reason that humans were afraid of infernals.

"That's illegal."

"Wanna report me for violating the treaty? Up to you lady, that's your right."

He had... sort of broken the treaty, but there were enough exceptions for using powers in the defense of others that she wasn't sure if this counted. Exhausted and aching, Maxine tried to dredge up anger, but it wasn't there.

How much did he know about what Luculenta was doing? How much of what she had said was true, and would Maxine be risking life-changing research by talking about it with the FBI?

She needed to review the papers she'd taken from the lab. Samzen was doing his job in a haphazard and rules-optional kind of way, but he'd also been the only person in any sort of official capacity to try to help her. If he had been following the rules, he wouldn't have given her the time of day back when they talked at Starbucks.

"Were we kidnapped by real FBI agents or fake ones?"

Samzen flinched. "Yeah, no, they were fake. I fucked up when I left you alone. I mean, I didn't actually fuck up, but apparently our security is shit and those assholes waltzed in like headquarters was a goddamn public park. It's not my job to run security, y'know."

"Do you know how impressive it is," Maxine said, after having adjusted to the light so she could glare more effectively, "that that's the worst apology I've ever heard?"

"Boss is doing a security review," Samzen grumbled, bitter and resigned. "And everyone looks at the infernal first. I'll need laxatives to get the auditors outta my ass while golden boy gets a free pass. Speaking of which..."

He took another look outside.

"Echles was supposed to be here by now," he grumbled. "Fucking celestials. He's not usually this flaky but he's got a bug all the way up his nose about you."

The headache was starting to ease, and relief from pain was a visceral pleasure in and of itself. She was more inclined to be generous about the violation now that it hurt less. Stretching out her legs, Maxine readjusted so Tom could sleep more comfortably with his head in her lap, steadfastly trying not to think about how Samzen called him a lapdog. He had taped up several cuts, and the bruising was bad, but it seemed he had successfully avoided real damage.

"How much did you take from him?"

"More than a bit." Samzen still sounded casual, but there was a worried crease in his forehead as he looked back at her from the edge of the van. "He'll, ah, he'll be fine of course. But I didn't know he was, I mean—" The incubus was subtly *blushing*. Maxine hadn't known that was even possible. "I rolled him the way I would have if he were totally straight and it ended up being more... ah... effective than I expected."

"Sexuality makes a difference?"

"It's like when you think you're picking up something heavy, but it turns out not to weigh anything. I overshot. But, can you blame me? ...I mean, I shouldn't profile. That's my bad. But, c'mon lady, look at him!" He blushed harder. "He looks like he eats smaller alpha males for breakfast!"

"I don't know what you or Echles see when you look at him. Or me, for that matter." Maxine brushed her fingers through his hair. "But he's a good man."

"I ain't arguing it, lady. And between you and me, we can't see if someone's good or bad. That's not a thing. It's more like... like how many voices in a choir are in tune. I mean, it's nothing like that, but it's more like that. Celestials can get real weird about it. I dunno, I can't see the so-called 'virtues.'" Samzen said the word "virtues" like he was condescendingly indulging a child's absurd idea. "But if he's got a bunch of voices out of tune, you're the goddamn Tabernacle Choir."

"Huh. I appreciate you telling me that. Thanks, Samzen."

"Yeah, yeah. Don't mention it, lady. You know the drill. Really don't mention it."

Tom woke up several hours later, and Tom woke up angry.

Lay into it

Samzen had given up on his partner showing up, and Maxine had tried to make Tom's sleeping body as comfortable as possible with a jacket folded into a pillow. They had driven in the van to get breakfast, parked in an industrial lot in the middle of nowhere to avoid attention, and were sitting together on the back of the van drinking coffee. Not sure how long Tom would be out, Maxine set aside a couple breakfast sandwiches and a coffee for him, hoping to mitigate the excruciating hangover he was going to have when he woke up.

Samzen was sharing a story about getting his celestial partner drunk and Maxine was laughing so hard she didn't hear movement from the van behind them.

It happened so fast that she didn't realize there was a problem until after Samzen had disappeared from her side. When she turned, her brain froze before she comprehended that Tom was strangling the incubus in a choke hold. His arm squeezed around the smaller man's throat. Samzen's red skin was turning purple as he slapped ineffectually at the elbow under his chin.

"Tom, no!" Maxine spilled her coffee as she scrambled over to pull Tom off Samzen. She hauled down on Tom's arm to give Samzen some room, but she'd have more luck pulling down a building.

"Tom, it's okay, let him go!" He was in his own world, pinpointed on Samzen, unaware of her with his single-minded goal of erasing Samzen from the mortal plane. Tom's eyes were black, his face stuck in a mask of fear that chilled her blood even as she desperately tried to get through to him. "You're safe, Tom! We're safe, please stop!"

Samzen's struggling became weaker, but finally she saw a light come back into Tom's eyes. He loosened his grip, letting Maxine catch the incubus before he could collapse onto the floor of the van. Tom was breathing too quickly, fingers curled halfway into fists and balanced on the balls of his feet as he battled his instincts to either fight or fight harder.

On his knees and wheezing, at least Samzen didn't seem injured. His normal reddish color came back quickly, but as soon as it was obvious he would recover, Maxine's attention turned to making sure Tom wasn't lost out of his mind without a map.

"You're okay, Tom. And I'm okay." She repeated it softly, carefully holding her arms out in the universally known gesture to calm a spooked horse. "You were out for a while and Samzen and I had a chance to talk."

Tom's face contorted in anger and pain, and even though she knew he'd never hurt her, she stepped back instinctively. It was her fear that finally got through to him.

"What the fuck just happened?" His voice was cracked and gravelly, but he didn't try to clear his throat. He trained murderous eyes on the man struggling to breathe at their feet.

"Samzen wanted to get us out of there, but he was worried we'd fight him, so he did... that... to get us out quickly."

"He fucked with my head." Tom's teeth were bared in a feral promise of violence as he turned his glare from Samzen to Maxine. "He fucked with *your* head."

"Yes." She tried to maneuver Tom away from the incubus, but he wasn't budging. "It's not permanent. It was a misunderstanding."

"I can't imagine..." Samzen wheezed, thready and barely audible, "why I thought you'd fight me."

"Shut up, Samzen," Maxine snapped. Tom still looked a hair's breadth away from dismembering the incubus. "How are you feeling, Tom? I woke up with an awful headache."

His breathing slowed and he shifted his weight back onto his heels. Although his hands were still prepared to strangle the man recovering at their feet, his expression came closer to his normal sardonic wit.

"It feels like my skull is cracked open." He finally cleared his throat a little, trying to sound more human and missing by a few evolutionary leaps. Maxine's coffee was a puddle on the floor, but she had put Tom's breakfast off to the side and she grabbed his drink to help him out. He managed a small, grateful smile only slightly marred by his scabbed lip. "It's just pain. It won't slow me down."

"You're flirting... now?" Samzen didn't sound good. His larynx might be damaged. Now that it seemed less likely Tom would murder him if he so much as twitched, the incubus scuttled backwards to get further away. "Fuck, it hurts to talk." He cradled his throat with one hand, slowly standing and pressing his other hand against the van wall for balance.

"Good." Tom's voice was more human, but still rough. "You're a sick sonofabitch, and you're going to tell us everything you know."

The way he said "us" made something in Maxine's chest light up. He was still thinking about an "us" even while his body must be screaming in agony.

Samzen, she belatedly realized, was an incubus sensitive to romantic energy. He was still holding his throat defensively, but his face had turned incredulous.

"You two deserve each other. Fuck, I need a drink."

"It's okay, Tom." His sharp attention on her from the moment she'd started talking made her wonder what her face and body were communicating. "Samzen put a tracker in my sling when he pushed us into the waiting room. After we were taken, he followed as fast as he could."

"I *thought* you were gonna bust out through the mirror and I'd have to chase you down," Samzen wheezed, getting back to his feet. "Boy, was my face red."

"Really, Samzen?"

Even holding his throat and wincing in pain, he couldn't help looking proud of himself at the bad joke.

"Are we under arrest?" Tom glowered at the infernal, as if daring him to put them back in a holding room to be kidnapped again. "Where are we going now?"

"I still have the egg," Maxine said quickly, making eye contact with Tom. She hoped he could read her mind and know she didn't want to talk about it in front of Samzen. "But if the FBI is still willing to have someone watch your place, I think we can go back to being bait. Samzen?"

The infernal managed to sound sheepish with his damaged voice. "Yeah, uh... y'know what? I won't say any more about your evidence tampering or assault on my person if you don't say anything about the... mind control and energy drain. I don't think either of us want more shit on our records."

Of all things, this made Tom's glower break. He actually smiled at Samzen. The incubus startled slightly. Until this point he'd only ever seen Tom look like either "blank-faced bodyguard" or "imminent death." He seemed surprised the human *could* smile.

"Deal." Tom relaxed enough to look around the van. "Let's call it even."

"So... since we're all being cool about it, I've got a question for you, beefcake." Samzen still sounded rough but wasn't upset anymore. He was analyzing Tom like a puzzle piece. "How are you able to stand right now? I've taken less from people who couldn't move for hours after waking up." His eyes darted to Maxine and back to Tom. "Entirely consensually, I assure you."

Tom puffed himself up, by all appearances happy to show off for an appreciative audience. Tom would be much more comfortable with Samzen now that they had dirt on each other and legal action was off the table.

"This is nothing. I've beaten off a seven-foot draconic while my leg was broken and my right hand was crushed." Tom's teeth flashed in a smug display of machismo Maxine suspected was at least partly faked to push through pain.

"Bullshit." Samzen grinned up at him. "That's not humanly possible."

"You've looked me up, right?" Tom crossed his tree-trunk arms over his chest in a not-very-subtle showcase. "I'll bet my file doesn't tell the half of it. This other time I had two vamps in my ring, and I made them both go down at the same time."

Maxine was beginning to suspect Tom was fully aware of the double entendres and was doing it to provoke Samzen. From the way the incubus' eyes were lighting up in delight, it was working.

"Sorry to interrupt whatever this is," she cut in. They could flirt on their own time. "But I need to eat something and take a shower before my next scheduled kidnapping. Samzen, can you take us back to Tom's place?"

"You got it, lady."

Scrambled

"First, I will assume a basic understanding of aplacental viviparity in synapsids such as draconics."

Fez had come over as soon as Tom called him and explained the situation.

Tom's experience with entertaining guests involved yelling at the TV, and he didn't have a dining room table, so she and the professor were sitting on the couch with the slightly torn research papers she'd received from Luculenta splayed on the coffee table.

Immediately upon entering Tom's home, Fez had made a beeline for the fridge and started raiding its contents. Tom had apparently expected this, and was dicing vegetables for a stir-fry.

"Professor," Maxine interrupted, "you are operating under a false assumption."

"What?" His eyebrows furrowed. He was talking around a mouthful of hummus scooped into his mouth with sandwich bread. "But you've had the egg for days. Have you not reviewed the basic principles of ovoviviparity?"

"We've been a little busy." She cupped a hand over the egg on her chest to prevent it from hearing this conversation. "Can you explain in layman's terms?"

"Keep in mind, this is not my area of expertise." He was good-natured about her ignorance, at least. "But based on these curated documents, this research is a breakthrough in improving the draconic hatch-rate."

"Curated? What do you mean?"

He picked up one of the papers and pointed at a paragraph with a crust of bread.

"She has only provided a portion of her research methods and results. There are processes referenced in the abstract which have been omitted from the descriptions. If I had students, I'd fail this paper."

"...You... you don't have any students?"

"I'm a member of the research faculty staff, funded almost exclusively on grants." He avoided eye contact while scooping up more hummus. "The administrative body and I have agreed my studies are too dangerous for students."

"They tried, didn't they?" Tom called out over the sound of sizzling, proving he was actually listening to the conversation. "You wrote a curriculum on cults and made me sit through a goddamn slide-show."

Fez stammered for a second.

"It... it was a primer on social groups defined by their belief structures in—"

"You compared Amway sales to that Kool-Aid guy. I remember that part."

Fez was blushing, glancing quickly between Maxine and Tom. Maxine narrowed her eyes at him, suspecting that for Fez, a PowerPoint presentation was the most romantic gesture he could think of. Tom probably never caught on that Fez had been trying to flirt with him.

"Back to the topic at hand," Maxine smoothed over the interruption, noting the relief in Fez's eyes. "Do you have a guess at what Luculenta's hiding?"

"Hah! Everything!" Crumbs sprayed. He took a pen and started circling blank spaces between sections and the beginning sections of sentences. "The success of her results is credited to improved incubation, but she's cut all descriptions of the incubation methods. She describes the genetic mutation in the egg you're carrying, but the genetic tests had to have been conducted while it was in utero, and she doesn't describe how she performed those tests."

"She's already conducted the experiment; why does she still need the egg?"

"Because doing something once isn't science." He was scribbling in the margins of the papers. "Without her methods I don't know how she sampled the egg's genetic material in utero, but the process of replicating its permeability in other eggs was destructive and can't be repeated without more genetic material. She needs it to hatch so she can take living tissue samples from the, uh, the child to repeat the experiment."

Maxine's background was in the softer social sciences. She glared at numbers and charts that might as well have been written in ancient Sumerian for how much sense they made to her. Or Khmer, a small voice said in the back of her mind. The official language of Cambodia.

"Professor, I believe you are still operating under the assumption that I understand what you're saying. My last lab science class was... a long time ago." Never was a long time ago.

"He does this on purpose," Tom cut in, handing over a couple piping hot bowls of stir-fried vegetables and rice. The steam wafted a pleasant garlicky warmth on her face. "It's also why he wears a lab coat. He just needs people to know he's smart."

"Excuse me!" Fez's outrage was at least partly faked. "Specificity is important for a thorough understanding of—"

"Since when are you an expert on eggs, Fez?" Tom was smiling indulgently around his food, perching himself on a nearby stool with his own bowl. "You're all about cults."

From the sour expression on Fez's face, he didn't like Tom's use of the word "cult," but he had already exhausted himself trying to get Tom to change his terminology. In this one thing, Maxine could sympathize. Language shaped thought, and using the wrong words could create or exacerbate prejudice.

"This study represents a controversial schism within the draconics." Fez slowed down his speech, emphasizing this mostly for Maxine, but still talking both to her and Tom. "If it can be repeated, the experiment these papers describe would drastically improve their hatch rate, but their strength-based value system glorifies a low hatch rate as the initial proof of strength in a newborn."

They ate in relative silence, Maxine's thoughts spinning through the incomplete information she had.

"I believe Amanda stole the egg to extort them," she commented, interrupting the sound of industrious chewing from the two men. "She was looking for a way out."

"Hah, a nest egg!" Fez was comfortably leaning back into the couch holding his bowl the same way the egg was tucked against her own chest.

Maxine ignored him. "And when Luculenta figured out I'm not interested in money and I'm actually keeping the egg safe, she asked me to keep it until she's sure she doesn't have any greedy staff who realize the entire experiment hinges on this one, exploitable item."

"They really shouldn't keep all their eggs in one basket." Tom added, leaning forward to initiate a high-five with Fez for his own joke. He looked far too proud of himself. Maxine continued to ignore them.

"I need to know what Luculenta kept out of these reports." If humans like Sophia were being used to conduct the experiment, she needed to know how.

"How are you going to do that?" Fez was scraping the side of his bowl distractedly, presumably trying to figure out a third pun he could squeeze in.

She sighed, trying to push down the stress headache that was beginning to throb at her temples.

"I'm going to cross the road and see what's on the other side."

✦

The clandestine location Samzen had given her so they could talk without interference from pesky FBI regulations and/or celestials was the back of a smoky bar. It wasn't cigarette smoke, but it had a musky organic scent she couldn't place. She counted more vampires than humans, several other infernals, and at least one were-bear. At least, she hoped it was a were-bear. It was currently shifted into bear shape and taking up an entire booth.

Tom was on the other side of the room trying to get someone's attention at the bar. For once he wasn't the biggest person in the room thanks to a couple of half-giants standing hunched against the wall.

"Lady, as much as I love you..." Samzen looked more comfortable here than she'd ever seen him. His smile came easier and he was sitting in a slouch on his side of the booth. "... you're nuts if you think I'm gonna give you any information more sensitive than the weather. I'm in administrative hell already, I don't need any more reasons to get fired."

"You don't love me at all, Samzen."

"Not true!" He leaned forward, and as much as she tried hard not to fall back on old stereotypes, his red grinning face truly did look demonic. His horns gleamed, reflecting the yellowed lighting amidst shiny black hair. "I love all of humanity. I'm a loving kind of guy."

This was her own fault; what did she expect when she asked an incubus for a secret meeting?

"How about if I give you information, then?" Maxine pulled the research data from her egg sling. The papers were creased and soft from having been folded and unfolded so many times, but still readable. Fez had marked them all up to some degree, including several which had doodles of draconic uteruses on the sides. Uteri? She hoped Samzen didn't know what they were, but his frown as he unfolded and reviewed the pages implied that he at least suspected.

"If you have pertinent information to our case, why are we meeting without my glowy buddy?" For the first time since sitting down with her, Samzen started to tense up. "Whattayou want from me, lady?"

"Echles is only there to keep you in line, right?" She watched his eyes, looking for micro-expressions. "And he's trying not to get involved in an active prophesy, so he's been leaving you in the lurch as much as possible wherever I'm involved."

Samzen swallowed.

"Here's what I think, *Agent* Samzen." She grinned, mildly put out that she'd never look as devilish as he did. "You've found signs of human trafficking but not enough evidence for a warrant. And the only reason you've been bending the rules with me is because I'm the best potential lead you've found."

A gin and tonic with lime appeared next to her, and she scooted over on her side of the booth to give Tom room. Even while he took up the majority of the booth, he leaned back and tried to fade into the background. Maxine continued.

"I think Luculenta is buying humans to use for her experiment. I can get you into her new facility if you can help me figure out the egg's mother."

Samzen's face went from serious to grim. "Lady, I don't gotta tell you to *stay away* from the human-hating extremists, do I?"

"A reminder wouldn't hurt." Tom's voice was dry, his expression long-suffering.

"I need to find out where the egg belongs."

"You're looking for a home with the worst kinda people, lady."

"I don't need to find a home that loves humans." This was something Maxine had already agonized over, but she was confident in her decision. "I need to find a home that will love *it*. Whoever comes out of it."

That was only part of the truth. The egg needed to be her top priority; she had taken responsibility for it, and that *meant* something. But a larger picture was emerging in which she suspected she was an unwilling pawn. Sophia had shown up at Planar Parenthood during Maxine's shift, which *could* have been a coincidence. But the timing was suspiciously perfect. Maxine had been primed from the failure of her marriage to put her life on the line for *any* excuse to feel useful, and her connection to Amanda had put her on this path.

Sophia, who had done nothing except ask for help in a place where she couldn't speak the language, was likely to be as much of an innocent victim as the egg. The thought of that woman, injured and betrayed where she'd thought she could get help, twisted painfully in Maxine's chest. Grateful for the drink Tom had acquired, Maxine took a sip.

Her drink was strong. She wrinkled her nose and put it back down; she hadn't realized she now associated the taste of gin with being at the courthouse getting a divorce.

"Samzen," Maxine wasn't sure how much help she could expect from the incubus, but so far he'd been the most willing to talk. "I want to be a helpful lead. I want to get you wherever you need to go, so you can help the trafficking victims. I just—I also need help with the egg."

"Lady, d'you know about infernals and contracts?" Samzen pinched the bridge of his nose as if he had a headache.

"That the um… that infernals can be bound if they sign a contract?" Assuming you could get one to sign something, which wasn't easy.

"I signed a contract with the FBI, lady. I gotta follow certain rules and it ain't a choice or a preference, it's a goddamn compulsion. Even if I wanted to, which I don't, I would not be able to help you go somewhere dangerous."

Her hand choked her glass in excitement, and the condensation made her grip slip. She'd never heard of an infernal actually signing a contract.

"What—do you…" She needed to calm down. She could interrogate him on the fascinating implications of this kind of contractual control in her free time. "But they assigned a celestial to prevent you from using your powers, and you were still able to control me and Tom. What are your limitations?"

"None of your business, lady." There was a bitter note in his voice. "I signed by choice, and I could quit any time I want, which would end the contract and leave me free. But the thing about trafficking? A lotta times they sign contracts too."

Samzen was deliberating on something. When he seemed to come to a decision, he pulled out his phone, tapped a few times to open a file, and spun it around on the table to show her.

"This was what put us on to your girl, Amanda. We found a contract she signed as witness. All nice and official. These people are being told they owe money. They usually don't speak the language, and they're afraid'a getting arrested as illegals. It ain't the same, I know, but this is personal for me. No one should be bound to a contract they don't even understand."

"This is a lot more sensitive than the weather," she mused, zooming in on his phone. "Why are you showing me? *How* are you able to show me this?"

The incubus licked his lips and looked a little smug.

"I didn't promise to follow the law, lady. I promised to keep civilians outta harm's way to the best of my ability, and to help where I can within reason."

"Who defines what's reasonable?"

"*I* do."

"That seems like a pretty big loophole."

He gave a half shrug and wobbled his hand. "Eh, kinda? Thing is, I really gotta think it's reasonable, and unless I go legit crazy, my reasonable is probably about the same as anyone else's."

Maxine had met some people with wildly different ideas of reasonable.

"So you can't help me find the egg's mother?"

"I can't. Help you. Put yourself. In danger." He overenunciated the words. "And these people are dangerous, lady. Amanda was one of them, and they *still* killed her."

Operating off of muscle memory, she took another sip of her drink and winced.

"How much do you know about the prophesy I'm in?"

Samzen raised eyebrows at the topic shift. "Lady, if you're in a prophesy, it means jack shit about the future. They ain't reliable, and I think half the time they only happen because celestials love to meddle."

"Yes, I understand that." Not really; from what Jehudin had told her, prophesies were like directions guiding humans to the choices which would better themselves. "But Echles is freaked out, right? He was at the parking garage when you and I first met. I saw him out of the corner of my eye, and he ran away?"

In her mental state at the time it had seemed like a beacon from Jehudin, but in retrospect it was much more likely she'd seen Echles' glow just before he ran away in a fit of awkwardness.

"...I dunno about it." Samzen didn't look like he was lying. "And if I did, I wouldn't mess you up by telling you."

"I'm pretty sure I know what they're doing with the trafficked humans."

Samzen seemed suddenly off balance—mildly confused by the topic shifts and not sure what she was angling for.

"Yeah? You gonna share with the rest of the class?"

"No, I wouldn't mess you up by telling you." She took bitter, petty enjoyment in this. "But you can stop looking for Amanda's missing baby."

"Lady... what are you up to?"

She stood up, leaving her mostly full glass on the table.

"Mostly cloudy." She couldn't look at Tom, or she'd probably start laughing and ruin the moment. "Chance of rain."

Which came first?

Back at Tom's place, Maxine decided she could cancel the hotel. Luculenta wasn't going to send more kidnappers after her and the egg, and Tom couldn't cook for her at the hotel.

It was vitally important Tom be able to cook for her. She wasn't just being selfish here. Cooking was obviously part of his long-term seduction plan, and it would hurt his feelings to hold him back. She'd just have to be gracious and let him keep trying to seduce her.

Technically, Maxine was now working with Luculenta, complying with the draconic's request to keep the situation secret from the FBI and keep the egg safe.

Moral relativism formed a lump in her throat. She wasn't doing it *for* Luculenta, but it was still what the draconic wanted. It was still playing into her claws while she did whatever her awful "cleaning house" processes were to ensure loyalty.

"I don't like what you're planning." He was using his muscles for the best possible purpose; kneading fresh pasta dough. A dusting of flour had made its way onto his cheekbone somehow. "I don't know *what* you're planning, but I don't like it."

"That makes two of us, Tom." She stretched out on his couch, feeling her back pop. Her laptop was precariously balanced across her legs with one of Fez's papers about draconics on the screen. "I'm still figuring out what to do."

"Samzen wasn't helpful."

"I wouldn't say that."

"He specifically said he couldn't help you."

"Hmm." Samzen had said he couldn't help her go into a dangerous situation. She didn't know if the implication had been deliberate, but she thought that maybe he'd be helpful getting her *out* of a dangerous situation. With her back arched over the arm of Tom's couch, she looked upside down at him. "Have you heard of the trolley problem?"

"Sure." There was a shade of annoyance in his voice. He knew she was obfuscating. "Don't pull the lever, people die. Pull the lever, one person dies."

"Exactly, but it's all about responsibility. If it makes you *responsible* for the person who dies, what do you do?"

He rolled the dough into a smooth ball and laid a cloth over it. Then he put a kettle on for tea. He was going for gold with his seduction plan. She shouldn't tell him it had already worked. Let him keep going.

"This is one of those questions academic type people go crazy over, isn't it?" His voice was wry, and he leaned his elbows back on the counter while they talked.

"Just... just go with me. Do you pull the lever?"

"Um. Yeah, I guess? It's one person versus five people, right?"

"Yeah." She nodded. Chewing over dark futures would have to happen after she ate delicious fresh pasta. "Saving lives while causing a death."

"It's a ridiculous question."

"Why's that?"

She waited while he poured hot water into two mugs. "You never know what you'll actually do until you're in the life-or-death situation," he said finally. "And people don't make smart decisions under pressure."

"You're smarter than most academics I know." She accepted the hot mug with her fingertips, scooting over so he'd have room on the couch.

He sat next to her, looking comfortable with the casual domesticity they'd somehow developed in just a couple days. Maxine hadn't even realized at first how easily they'd clicked together. They both read each other's emotions and automatically adapted to the others' needs. Despite loving Jehudin, she'd never had this level of comfort with him. Throughout her marriage, she'd always felt like she had to *be better*. She wasn't worrying about being an imperfect human when she spent time with Tom.

She liked this feeling—this level of comfort. She wanted more. There was a thrill in knowing she was about to do something dangerous. In that moment, sitting next to him on his couch was close to the sensation of sitting at the top of a roller coaster.

"I'm curious about something. It's kind of personal though, you don't have to answer if you don't want to."

He shrugged, unconcerned. "Yeah?"

"Are you interested in another serious relationship so soon after your divorce?"

His expression implied he was deeply unimpressed with the question.

"I'm honestly not sure how I could be *more* obvious."

"I know you want sex." She rolled her eyes. "But that doesn't mean you want more."

He bought himself some time by sipping tea. She'd teased him enough by now he was probably trying to figure out if she was actually going somewhere with this.

"I'm interested in more than just sex," he said. "Maybe on the first day I wasn't. But I am now."

"What does 'more' mean to you?"

"Ugggh," he groaned, leaning his head back to look at the ceiling and resting his tea on his chest. "Are you a couples' therapist before there's even a couple to... therapy?"

She couldn't help but laugh. "You don't think it's fun?" She nudged him with her feet, then felt comfortable enough to tuck her toes under his legs. "Exploring what the other person wants?"

That made him perk up, smiling at her suggestively. "I'll talk about what I want. I love it when a woman—"

"You know that's not what I meant."

"I'm a simple man, Maxine." He shrugged, hugging his tea in a mirror of how she was holding her own. "I cook, I go drinking with friends, I work out, I enjoy sex because sex is awesome, and if shit gets serious I like monogamy because anything else is too damn complicated. What do you want to hear?"

"I like how you talk about what you want. You're always... straightforward."

"Simple man." He gestured down at himself. "What you see is what you get."

"Hmmm." She allowed her tone to ramp skeptical. She raked her eyes down from his head and allowed her gaze to linger. "I don't know if I've seen enough."

"Oooh, now it's getting good!" Energized, he set his tea carelessly on the small table and pushed himself to his knees, crouching on the couch to lean over her. "How much more would you like to see?"

Leaning back in an instinctive retreat, Maxine swallowed. Her throat suddenly felt tight as she shielded herself with her tea held tight to her chest. He waited patiently. He'd figured out her tendency to chase the car and then not know what to do when she caught it. His grin turned sly.

"No wait, don't tell me yet," he said, preempting her answer. "I've got a few ideas about what's going on and I'll tell you what I think. Nod or shake your head if I'm on the right track, yeah?"

She swallowed again, clutching her mug of tea a little tighter, and nodded.

"I think you let your ex make all the moves because you thought he was out of your league."

That stung. She felt a stab of—maybe anger, maybe defensiveness. But it was true, so she narrowed her eyes and nodded.

"He wasn't, you know."

She didn't nod or shake her head this time, but she gave a half shrug.

"I think you've enjoyed having someone pursue you. And you're worried if we start fucking I won't want you anymore."

Her teeth started to grind together. He didn't sound unkind, but it grated harshly. "Since when are you the therapist?"

"I've been watching you, Maxine."

He was still crouched on the couch, leaning over her. This conversation was not going where she had expected. But as soon as she started to feel trapped, he rocked back on his heels to give her breathing room.

"You're worried that celestial douchebag left you damaged?" He pulled his shirt over his head, voice muffled in its fabric. "I know a little about being damaged."

His skin was littered with fresh bruises and old scars. Many of them were obvious claw marks. One long silver line ran from his collarbone across his chest, ending above his stomach. A spattering of light brown hair decorated his chest and formed a treasure trail that led the eye down. But her eyes stuck along the way, stopping at a raised edge of a ridge of scar tissue that made it look like he'd been disemboweled.

Taking her mug and setting it aside, he guided her hand to press it against his chest. He was warm, muscles tensed, and she experienced the difference in texture as she ran her hand across his skin. Still unable to think of any words, she traced the hard ridges of his pecs over to his shoulders, then back down.

He still exuded confidence, but his heartrate sped up the longer she touched him.

He chuckled. "Okay, now it'd be great if you said something."

But she kept her mouth shut as she explored. She got a momentary thrill as she made him shiver, using the barest pressure on her fingertips to feel the edges of his old injuries. Her own heart was racing as she leaned forward. Pressing her mouth against his, she steadied herself with her other hand on his shoulder as she closed her eyes to enjoy the sensations of a gentle, chaste kiss.

Having expected him to push for more, she pulled back and blinked at him when he didn't. He looked pleased, flushed, and she could feel his heart racing, but he didn't move. He was waiting for—oh, of course.

"Yes. I want this."

"Finally," he gasped.

Maxine felt the ground fall away as she was scooped against his chest in a princess carry. She shrieked in surprise, but found herself laughing as he gracefully maneuvered her through the hallway, despite her instinctive flailing.

"Ahh, no, don't you dare—!" she laughed as he tossed her onto the bed. He was over her again in less time than she had to blink; he was also laughing as he held a finger against her lips.

"I've been desperate to try something." He was talking quickly but interrupted himself by nuzzling under her jaw to suck gently at the sensitive skin under her ear. "I think... I think *he* had the ability to turn pleasure on. Like a light switch."

She wasn't sure what to say, but she still opened her mouth to either defend or dismiss the reminder of Jehudin. The finger against her lips became a hand gently covering her mouth.

"But I don't think he ever made sex fun. Did he?"

Maxine didn't have a response, which was just as well because Tom didn't wait for one. Tom had lots of fun ideas to try.

She didn't think about Jehudin once.

"Don't do this."

She was at the kitchen counter eating an omelet, which Maxine was certain had been a passive aggressive breakfast choice on Tom's part. She thought mournfully of the fresh pasta left unfinished. What she *got* was better, but even so.

Maxine had told Tom what she thought was going on in Luculenta's research. Now came the difficult work of convincing him to let Maxine put herself in danger.

"She's evil to humans, but she might be the best person for the egg. More than that, she knows who donated it and who will want to raise it."

"You!" Tom leaned closer from across the counter, pointing his finger in her face. "You are human! If you think she's the best person for the egg, leave it in a goddamn basket at the door."

"I need to do more than that."

He gave a strangled scream of frustration. It sounded like he'd been wanting to do that for a while.

"Why did we have all those conversations about relationships if you were planning to get yourself killed?" Real hurt crossed his face. "Why make me think there was more here if you were gonna leave me the morning after?"

That one pierced with real guilt.

"I'm not leaving you, Tom. I need you to make this work. But if you won't be a part of this, I understand. I'm responsible for a life, and that—that's important."

"*You're* important. But you're so fucked up over your divorce you're going to kill yourself for that egg, and you're asking me to help you do it."

Her blood felt hot and sparks of adrenaline fired with nowhere to go, making her skin itch. Tom continued before she could argue.

"Don't leave me behind. Maxine. Don't walk right in because you don't value your own life."

They both sat with that hanging in the air between them.

"I am going to walk into that building," Maxine said firmly. "But I'm leaving you behind because I'll need you on the outside."

"Don't do it." His voice was barely a whisper. "If you leave me with that egg, I'm going to drop it out the goddamn window."

"No, you won't." Maxine smiled confidently. "It's weak, and you're strong." Her smile widened at his darkening expression. "And if you do, I won't fuck you when I get back."

Goose that lays the golden egg

Walking into the building was easy. She wore her egg sling, but instead of the egg she had a small balloon inflated inside to give the correct shape. It felt wrong. It was too light, cold against her skin instead of warm. She cradled it lovingly anyway.

This appeared to be an office like her own where multiple businesses rented space. Even with the address, there would have been a lot of paperwork hoops for Samzen to jump through if he'd wanted to investigate. He didn't have any evidence, just rumors and guesswork, and there were dozens of perfectly legitimate businesses here that would make a big stink if their operations were interrupted without the proper subpoenas or warrants.

A bronze placard next to the elevator listed different companies along with their suite numbers, but she didn't see *Exalt* or Luculenta's name on anything. And Luculenta hadn't given her a suite number, either because of her rush to escape or because she didn't want Maxine to give the information to the FBI.

Very inconsiderate of them not to label their secret lair clearly.

Maxine wandered the lobby and the first floor for several minutes, ignoring the odd looks from people walking by.

"Can I help you?"

A security guard, who seemed mildly annoyed at having to get up off his chair, looked her up and down. His job was probably mostly shooing away solicitors.

Her heart pounded against the false egg. "I'm looking for a draconic woman named Luculenta?" Maxine chuckled and shrugged at the elevator placard. "But I'm not sure where she works."

He nodded and walked to a small desk near the entrance where he consulted a directory. He was in the process of picking up his phone when someone interrupted them.

Striding quickly into the lobby, a man with thick brown hair and a tall, lanky frame called out.

"It's okay!" His voice was too deep for his thin frame. "She's looking for us."

The man was wearing a loose shirt tucked into slacks and slip-on black shoes. His movements were fluid, but his feet hit the ground too heavily. As if he wasn't used to wearing shoes. He wasn't wearing a jacket or belt.

Werewolf, probably. There were other kinds of weres, but wolf was the most common. And as much as she knew it didn't make a difference, the guy looked... wolfy. Was this the same one who had been waiting in her car? There probably wasn't a polite way to ask "Hey, did you try to kill me that one time?"

"Do you work with Luculenta?" she asked politely, trying to pretend this was a normal social visit.

"Yes." His eyes were focused a little *too* sharply on her. "She wants to talk to you."

Maxine forced a smile and gestured back towards where he came from. "Lead the way."

Luculenta's office was on the third floor. Maxine knew she couldn't hide her heartrate or flop sweat from the werewolf while standing in an elevator with him. But they didn't make small talk, and she kept her posture as confident as possible. She thought about how Tom walked through the Holding, her own posture a poor imitation of that confidence.

After leading her to a corner office, the man opened a door labeled *Principal Investigator* and loomed, waiting for her to walk through it.

Tom's phantom voice played in the back of her head. *"You fucking idiot."* Yes. Thank you, Phantom Tom.

Luculenta was waiting in front of her desk, still wearing her lab coat, her draconic smile wide and terrifying.

"I knew I was right about you. Thank you for coming."

Maxine looked around. There was a small loveseat facing a chair with the cutout in the backrest showing it was designed for draconics. Turning her back on Luculenta and the werewolf, Maxine took several steps inside to sit on the edge of the loveseat.

"I have questions before I'll feel comfortable giving you the egg."

The softer yellow lights made her green scales look warmer.

"You would not have protected it as fiercely as you have, if you did not care." Luculenta's voice was compassionate, but her tail was lashing with unspecified emotion. "As I said, I will answer all your questions."

"I need to know." Maxine said firmly. "I need to know how you are conducting your research. What it entails. I need to know there's a good home waiting before I give the egg back."

This was why she had to walk in helpless. This was what she was gambling her life to get. If they thought she was any kind of threat, they'd treat her like one.

If they thought she was utterly helpless, her only power the fragility of the egg on her chest, they'd lower their guard... and might give up their secrets. Why not? The egg would be safest if she handed it over willingly, and the deeper they brought her into their lair, the easier it would be to take it and make sure she never left.

Standing, Luculenta gestured for her to follow her to the back of her office.

"I will show you, and happily, Ms. Hallis. But..." There was a hint of challenge to her tone. "I will require discretion."

There was a panel at the back wall, which, when Luculenta entered a code, opened a private elevator.

Maxine was pretty sure she had sweated through her deodorant at this point. If the werewolf was a member of Exalt, he probably hated the smell of humans, so at least she could take some petty enjoyment in smelling *extra* bad. After pausing to wipe her palms on the fronts of her pants, she walked into the tiny elevator.

"Your phone please, Ms. Hallis. No recording is permitted in the lower levels."

She handed it over with a waxen smile. This wasn't the phone she was planning to use when she called for help later.

***

The goal had been to get confirmation about what Luculenta was doing with her research. Maxine had achieved that goal, and more.

Following the draconic through a guided tour of the two lower levels under the office building, she saw the research laboratories with clean, advanced machinery and chemistry equipment. Unlike the last location, this one was fully stocked and in use.

"After incubation and extraction, this is where we measure the viability of the eggs."

Her voice held the passion of any scientist excited about her research. It was exactly as she'd said; her life's work was to improve the hatch-rate of her fellow draconics, and she had found a solution. After seeing what Luculenta was doing, Maxine felt an odd mixture of sympathy and hatred.

Luculenta had tried for a child her whole life—until she became too old to lay and those dreams were lost. She worked for years to help other draconic women who wanted children of their own. And then she made an incredible discovery.

The egg that Maxine carried had a genetic anomaly. It could be fed extra nutrients during incubation, drastically increasing its chances of becoming viable. If this mutation could be studied and replicated, they might be able to increase the viability of other eggs as well. But Amanda interrupted that research and came close to sabotaging it entirely.

Maxine walked past an egg chamber where dozens of hard-shelled eggs lay swaddled in heated plastic cribs. She listened while Luculenta discussed science Maxine could barely follow.

"Just like you humans, our women carry many more eggs than we can reasonably lay. It is a safe, if not simple, procedure to extract eggs from their ovaries for the study. We incubate and increase nutritional input until we can confirm viability and measure the vitals of the newborn. All lineage is anonymized during the study to prevent any bias or favoritism, and I am personally in charge of unencrypting their information so we can match a child back to its mother. Many women of the Holding are desperate for children."

"Are you not in the Holding, Luculenta?"

"No." Her tail lashed. "I needed to attend a human university for the research I conduct. It required too much association with humans and I was pushed out."

Maxine's heels clicked and echoed in the pristine, undecorated hallways of the brand-new medical facility where eggs were extracted after incubation. She watched through one-way glass as a human woman, maybe in her mid-twenties, slept through the surgery to extract an egg that had been incubating inside her.

"We use state-of-the-art medical equipment and have several anesthesiologists on staff," Luculenta said proudly, not noticing Maxine choking back bile in an attempt not to vomit in their hallway. "Amanda damaged herself when she left. We do not recommend physical activity for several days after the procedure, but she was determined to ruin our progress."

Hatred and anger laced through Luculenta's voice, but it was muted. Presumably killing Amanda had laid some of those grievances to rest. It was not a comforting thought—especially since Maxine planned to betray her and create some new grievances.

"The humans," Maxine cleared her throat, "they consented to this?"

"Of course!" The draconic's voice was dismissive.

Of course they hadn't. Even in the elevator ride and walk down into the bowels of her research facility, Luculenta had paid only the barest lip service towards the idea of informed consent. The humans had been purchased by Exalt, whose ideology supports the idea of using humans as meat. Amanda's job, as Luculenta had explained it, was to communicate with the human incubators and keep them "happy."

Reading between the lines, Amanda's job had been to tell the humans whatever they needed to hear to stay docile. She'd written up contracts, discussed fictitious "end dates," and been a friendly, human face that was the victims' only connection to the outside world.

For a person untroubled by moral quandaries about the worth of a human life, it was a perfect solution. Luculenta had discovered that human women's physiology was similar enough that they could be used as stand-ins for draconic mothers. Since draconics didn't discuss their pregnancies until after their egg proved itself viable, a viable egg could be harvested from its human incubator and given back to its genetic mother, who would gleefully announce her good fortune without suspicion.

Maxine had seen enough.

Maxine knew enough. Too much.

Maxine cleared her throat again to make sure we wouldn't sound too croaky.

"And how many uses do you get out of the human incubators before they're too damaged?"

"Their contracts are single use, at the moment." Luculenta's draconic smile gleamed under their clinical lighting. "In follow-up trials we will seek to improve the efficiency. This has been an exceedingly expensive venture, but the results will convince Exalt to continue their support."

Luculenta's expression was challenging. Perhaps subconsciously, the draconic woman's stance was similar to the young draconic Maxine had seen on the university grounds before Tom had beaten him up. Luculenta knew that Maxine had seen too much. Now the draconic woman was waiting to see what Maxine would do next, and whether she'd allow the human to leave this facility alive.

Standing just behind Luculenta, the werewolf man was waiting. From what Maxine had seen so far, Luculenta preferred not to get her own claws dirty. She kept a clinical distance from everything she was doing, and she delegated the evil deeds to others who would enjoy them more.

Not so long ago Maxine had sat in her office after a disastrous therapy session with a werewolf and his human partner, wondering if she was too damaged to help anyone. The purpose she had given her life seemed to be slipping out of her grasp, the color bleaching out of her world.

Now, with her heart pounding and her blood roaring in her ears, the colors had never looked brighter. Maxine walked further down the hallway and stopped when she was standing under the neon "exit" light that marked the stairwell which led up to the ground floor. It also led further down, to the facility where the humans lived—before they were killed as part of Luculenta's "research."

"Thank you for showing me, Luculenta."

"Do you believe I will keep the egg safe? Give it a good home and a healthy start to life?" She held out her claws expectantly.

"Yes."

Maxine gently, lovingly removed the t-shirt sling. She held the false egg inside it, while the draconic and werewolf stood in front of her, and a staircase leading down to the lower level was behind her.

Dropping the sling, she turned and squinched her eyes shut, covering her nose and mouth, as it exploded into a cloud of chili powder. Fez had helped with the recipe. As an expert at running away from paranormal threats, he had cheerfully explained how it was easier to run away when your pursuer was busy with stinging eyes and could only smell burning. It did make it more important that they never catch you, of course.

Maxine ran the other way. Deeper into the facility.

Benediction

S he only had a few minutes, tops, before they recovered from the chili bomb. It would have burned Luculenta's eyes and made her uncomfortable, but the wolf was her real target. He'd need to recover before he could track her down. Hopefully.

The phone she'd handed the draconic was gone, but she'd never planned to get it back. Finally clattering to the bottom of the stairs and bursting into the lower level, she ignored the exclamations and stares of the trafficking victims who lived there as she pulled two small objects from her shirt and jean pockets. It was her work phone, and in case they had technology to detect signals, Maxine had removed the battery.

Several dozen humans stared at her as she pressed her back against the exit door. Maxine forced shaking fingers to pop the battery in place.

The phone lit up but... it had no reception. She was too far underground or they had something to block the signal. She'd have to either find her way back up—which was tantamount to suicide right now—or figure out another plan.

Her knees wobbled as she pressed her back more firmly against the door. She pocketed the phone, fingers now slippery with sweat. If the phone was useless, she'd have to buy time. Maxine looked at the humans who had been trapped down here. A few were talking quickly, but she couldn't understand them. From a quick glance they were mostly Asian, but a few looked Hispanic or South American.

"Does— does anyone here speak English? Um... ¿hablas inglés?"

If her life could be saved by using her broken Spanish to ask someone where to find the library, she might just have a chance here. If not—she might be in serious trouble.

With all eyes on her, Maxine pointed back at the stairwell she'd come from, and then pointed both of her index fingers down from her own mouth to simulate fangs.

"*Werewolf* coming after me," she said, trying to talk quickly but enunciate as clearly as possible. She held up her useless phone. "I want to *help*. I need *help*."

If that wasn't the understatement of the year.

"I need to *call* for *help*."

A few of the humans, nearly all of them women, were hesitantly shaking their heads. Maxine could tell none of them had understood more than a word or two, if that. One of them pointed at the phone, then gave a thumbs-down with a pitying frown and shake of her head.

Well. Time to improvise.

—◇—

Maxine was hiding in the back of an industrial kitchen several floors underground, hoping the smell of cooking food hid the scent of her fear from the werewolf hunting her. It had been hours. She was actually rather proud of herself for lasting this long.

The original plan, perfect in its stupidity, had worked—right up until the last part, the part where she was supposed to call for help and tell Samzen what was going on here. All wasn't lost though. She'd never removed the tracker he'd planted on her sling, and Tom was going to tell the infernal to look for it. It was probably still somewhere in the building. The werewolf would be using that damn sling to track her like a bloodhound.

Without any real evidence other than a hand-written address and Maxine's word that it came from Luculenta, a warrant would be a slow, legal process. But while Samzen had been precise about how he couldn't help her get *into* trouble, if a civilian needed help from *inside*, he could presumably rally the troops and actually do something useful. All Maxine had to do was spit in the face of potential torture and refuse to say where to find the egg until she was rescued.

It was the perfect time to do it; they were understaffed and overworked. After Amanda's betrayal, Luculenta had become paranoid and started auditing everyone for loyalty. But because their operations were time sensitive, they'd had all the human "subjects" transferred and in place already.

Hypothetically, Maxine could have walked out again. If she promised discretion and apologized for subterfuge with a false egg, she could have given the location of the real one. Her mission would have been successful, egg safe and back where it would be well cared for.

But after seeing what Luculenta was doing, there was no way Maxine could leave. Luculenta's claim that the human incubators had consented would have been laughable—if bile hadn't already risen to the back of her throat. As Samzen said, they had signed contracts. They had not *consented*.

These were the human trafficking victims Samzen was looking for. Maxine didn't know the details, but typically people in their situations were promised jobs and better lives; then they were transported and their passports and identification were taken. They were kept in the lower levels like cattle until needed, then were brought up to the clean, professional research lab to be used and discarded.

She couldn't leave them there. They would be transported to another location—or killed—if Luculenta thought her operation was at risk.

If Maxine was going to be rescued, she would be rescued down here with everyone else. If she wasn't going to be rescued... oh well. Tom was pretty. And smarter than he gave himself credit for. He'd be fine.

Hiding under stainless steel kitchen counters, Maxine hoped that the loud ventilation hood would cover the sound of her labored breathing. The werewolf had her scent, but everything probably still smelled like chili pepper to him, and this complex was large enough to house over a hundred humans. Maxine had spent her head start getting in as far as possible. Her problem now was trying to figure out how to get word out from a place specifically designed to keep people isolated.

If she had to give Luculenta any credit at all, Maxine had to admit that the humans were being kept in humane conditions. These areas had been designed to keep them healthy and reasonably comfortable. There were cramped sleeping quarters with bunk beds, an exercise room, clean bathroom facilities, and this lovely kitchen in which Maxine was hiding. But providing a humane prison before using and discarding people didn't deserve much credit. And it had probably been a choice of practicality, not compassion.

Under other circumstances, perhaps Maxine would have been as helpless as the other trapped humans. It was, after all, a facility specifically designed to keep humans inside. But Maxine had learned a little from Luculenta about how this place worked, and she knew a *lot* about werewolves.

Maxine had worked with quite a few werewolf couples and knew some very *unhelpful* things about werewolf physiology. But interspersed with stories about bedroom antics that had strained her ability to maintain a neutral, therapeutic presence, she knew about their enhanced sense of smell while shifted. And how they had to shift if they needed to use thumbs. Shifting didn't take long, but doing it too often was tiring and disorienting.

She'd been exploring the humans' holding facility as quickly as possible, but made sure to keep doors closed behind her. She looked for obstacles that would be difficult for a wolf, climbing and moving boxes to force him to shift frequently.

In the kitchen, several people were actively cooking, walking around her and preparing what smelled like chili. In an act of incredible bravery they were helping obfuscate her scent. An older woman with a lined face handed her a small bowl of chili and a spoon.

It was delicious.

The people here didn't speak English well, or at all. She was pretty sure that, like Sophia, they were mostly Cambodian. There were some Brazilians she had been able to speak to in broken Spanish. When they responded in their native Portuguese, a few words could be understood between the two. They weren't all female, either. Maxine wasn't sure whether maybe some families had been transported together and Luculenta had been forced to accommodate for "useless" humans along with the ones she wanted.

Having successfully caught her breath, she crouched close to the floor near a back door, waiting until one of the cooks walked past and gave a small nod to indicate that the coast was clear.

Finding the kitchen was a blessing. Maxine had been through it multiple times to hide in its mélange of scents and noise, but the constant pressure to keep moving or get caught by the wolf pushed her forward.

Tom had to know something was wrong at this point. She had always known she'd have to buy time. Without being able to call for help from inside she couldn't expect anything to move quickly on the outside. Tom saying "That dumbass woman I've been following around went into the office building and hasn't come out" didn't carry any real urgency.

This better not have been in Jehudin's prophesy. Maybe Echles had been avoiding her out of sheer embarrassment to be associated with her.

Maxine was playing a game of "terror Jenga," stacking a few boxes behind herself which the wolf would have to shift if he didn't want them to crash down on top of him.

She paused. A slip of paper taped to the outside of the box caught her eye. Luculenta had moved her "research" into this facility only recently. There were boxes waiting to be unpacked in most of the rooms. This was a packing slip, scribbled and slapped onto a box so that the moving company would put it in the correct room.

Tearing the page off the box, Maxine tried to read the scribbles as she continued on an escape route she'd already looped through twice. She needed to be less predictable if she wanted to avoid capture. Maxine thought she had seen every room available, but there was another one listed on this form. "Office."

Maxine backtracked half a hallway and ducked into a side room. She approached the first person she saw, a young Asian woman who was sitting on a small chair eating a bowl of chili that was still steaming, fresh from the kitchen. Holding the packing slip in front of her, Maxine gave the girl an anxious smile and pointed at the word "office."

"Office?" Maxine asked, helpfully, "Uh... d-donde está... the... office?"

The woman's look of polite pity was getting depressingly familiar. Maxine didn't have time for another game of charades. She grimaced apologetically at the Asian girl, attempting to communicate something along the lines of "I'm going to go die of shame, now." Leaving the room, Maxine looked back down at her slip of paper.

From what Maxine had seen, this floor had a kitchen, a communal living space, multiple rooms with bunk beds packed tightly enough you could smell the farts of the person three bunks over, and a gym. If there was an office on this level, it wasn't accessible from these hallways.

She looked up at the ceiling tiles at least three feet above her head.

Maxine had an idea. It wasn't a *good* idea. Good ideas were for people with options. And friends. And functioning prefrontal cortexes.

There was a bathroom she'd been avoiding for fear of getting trapped inside, but during her last terror-pee she noticed a ceiling tile that looked movable.

Listening for footsteps, Maxine pushed her way into the bathroom and climbed on the sink to test it.

Yes! There was space above the ceiling tiles. Now she just had to... pull up her body weight...

Balancing on a bathroom sink with sweaty hands pushing up on a ceiling tile was not the best place to try and remember the last time she'd ever done a pull-up. She hadn't *needed* to do pull-ups. She had Tom to do pull-ups *for* her. But if she was going to be fully honest with herself, even if they had been building a "brains and brawn" kind of partnership, she wasn't exactly holding up her side of the "brains" equation.

In a neighboring room a mass-produced wall clock emitted a loud tick-tick... tick-tick... there was one in every room. Maxine had started taking out their batteries to avoid the auditory reminder that her time was running out.

Jumping a little to give herself momentum only made her feet slip on the sink and lurched every internal organ several inches down in expectation of crashing before she caught her balance. The sink was too slippery, but there weren't any boxes for her to stack in the bathroom. She'd have to risk going out to find some.

She was about to climb down when the door opened and her heart leapt into her throat—but it was one of the Brazilians. Maxine got a glimpse of that Asian girl from before. She must have gone to find someone who actually spoke Spanish. He was harshly whispering something too fast for Maxine to follow. She pointed up at the ceiling to say *yes I'd love to hide, but I'm too weak to climb into the ceiling!*

He hurried close, helping boost her up. Then, because he was incredible and if she weren't currently involved with Tom she'd ask this complete stranger to marry her, he slid the ceiling tile back in place.

She was going to save every human in this godforsaken place if it was the last thing she did.

⸎

Crawling through the ceiling was slow going. She had to be quiet, and she had to distribute her weight carefully to make sure she didn't fall through.

By pressing her eyeball against the edges of every ceiling tile, she had mapped the layout of this floor. Every time she pushed her face against the tile to take a peek, she imagined the snapping teeth of the werewolf coming up at her.

The office wasn't connected to the quarters where Luculenta kept her human victims. But up here, she could see wiring and cables amongst the pipes leading somewhere. If Amanda had worked closely with the humans here, she'd have been put somewhere nearby, somewhere she could pretend to have a normal day job, translating and signing contracts. Amanda was dead, so they'd have to find some *other* morally apathetic human who spoke multiple languages and had a fetish for draconics.

Luculenta would probably try to find one without the fetish, this time.

Maxine struggled to crawl with unnatural slowness through dust and cobwebs, all of which came along for the ride thanks to her full-body layer of sweat. It would either make her much easier to sniff out, or the sludge of dust and grime sticking to her skin would become camouflage; she didn't know which.

There were wires, cables, dead spiders, pipes, and insulation panels to navigate around. One small comfort was that anyone much heavier than she was wouldn't be able to stay up here, so the werewolf couldn't follow her up here.

Okay. The office was directly under her. The lights were off, but Maxine was... pretty confident it was the office. Reasonably sure. Scraping her nails against the edge of a tile and pushing through muscle strain as she tried to shift it silently, she poked her head down for a breath of fresher air. No, it was another bunk room. Back into the ceiling.

Frustration and fear pricked tears at the corners of her eyes, but stopping wasn't an option. She had to be close.

When she finally found it, the strain in her arms made her clumsier. She had slipped and knocked down a few ceiling tiles in the previous bunk room and desperately hoped one of the humans would put them back before the werewolf noticed.

But this was the office. She struggled to get through pipes and cables, all of which were a lot thicker in this section and didn't leave room to crawl. Sliding a tile to the side revealed a desk six feet below. She dropped down.

Her leg twisted and she crumpled with the landing, but that was fine. Maxine hissed through her teeth and curled herself around her throbbing leg. It was *fine*. Her leg didn't matter. If this didn't work, she wouldn't be getting far anyway.

There was a phone. She picked up the receiver. No dial tone.

Maxine curled herself under the desk.

After a minute to cry it out, she pulled up the inside of her shirt to wipe her face clean. Cleaner. That werewolf could choke on it if he didn't want to wash her first.

There was a computer tower and a monitor, but all the cables had been removed. No power or ethernet. The same had been done for the phone. But... there were still cables in the ceiling. Her arms and shoulders burned as she looked up at the hole she'd fallen through. She didn't have a Brazilian man to push her up, and her leg wasn't going to hold her weight.

Think. She didn't do the punchy-punchy, she did the thinky-thinky. So do it. Survey the room, see what she had to work with.

It had been Amanda's job to "interview" new candidates and explain their contracts. Luculenta had apparently wanted a friendly human to tell their trapped "workforce" all the pretty lies about how they'd get their passports back when they'd paid their debts. Amanda added enough credibility and doubt about what was going on that most of the people trapped here could cling to hope. It kept people civil. Placid.

Groaning with the effort, Maxine tilted the desk over on its side so that it was braced against the office door. That would take... no time at all for a werewolf to break through. Excellent. If nothing else, the wolf would have to figure out that she'd left the humans' holding facility and made her way... wherever she was.

Going for speed more than silence at this point, Maxine dumped several boxes out onto the floor. She didn't see any ethernet or phone line cables as she rifled through random objects that had apparently been packed and delivered in a rushed facility change. A small black shape caught her eye. An old cell phone?

It didn't power on; the battery was completely dead.

After pulling out her work phone from her pocket, Maxine powered it on to check its signal. Still nothing. But she painstaking wiggled out the SIM card from the new phone. If they were compatible, maybe the new card would have better connectivity here.

She held her breath as she switched SIM cards and... yes! Euphoric joy at seeing the tiny single bar of reception. She dialed Tom's number by memory.

"Maxine?" Tom answered immediately.

"Tom!" She kept her voice hushed, but every cell in her body lit up upon hearing his voice. "There's a werewolf tracking me, I have to be fast."

She heard scrambling as he moved on the other end. "Are you okay? Where are you?"

"Shut up and listen." She spoke as quickly as she could. "Tell Samzen and Echles: there's almost two hundred people trapped down here. The egg Amanda stole has a genetic mutation that makes humans suitable incubators and they need it to continue their experiment."

"I'm getting you out of there."

"No! Give the egg to Samzen. Get it somewhere safe! We can't give it back, no matter what!"

She was talking too loudly. She hushed to hear the scraping noise of claws filtering through the door. The big bad wolf was right outside.

"Thank you Tom, you've been an incredible... thank you."

"Maxine!"

The wolf broke in.

Nest Egg

Having expected to be eaten, it was a unique indignity to be dragged upstairs like a recalcitrant child.

"Ms. Hallis, this is demeaning for us both." Luculenta's claws tapped against her desk as Maxine was deposited back on the couch, right where she'd started. The werewolf was still in primal form; its eyes were bloodshot and it was snarling at her. There were traces of chili in his fur. "I am forced to relocate my study—*again*—after just arriving here. This only delays and distracts me from my work."

It was easy to be covered in grime while fleeing for ones' life, but while sitting on an otherwise clean couch in a nicely decorated office it just felt wrong. Itches and cramps she'd previously ignored flared into awareness. Sitting up, trying to ignore the streaks of pain shooting up from her left leg, there was a dreamlike surreality to having a polite conversation while picking dead spiders out of her hair.

"I won't help you find the egg." It was her only leverage. They didn't know where to find Tom, and as long as she kept her mouth shut there was a chance of rescue.

Luculenta peered down her long, scaled nose at Maxine. She'd been getting better at reading draconic expressions, so Maxine wasn't sure why this looked like... pity?

"Ms. Hallis, I believe your heart is in the right place. You are an honest woman with strongly held convictions."

Unsure of how to respond, Maxine looked around for the punchline. Other than Luculenta and the primal werewolf, she was alone in an office. The faint background sound of the ventilation system and the buzzing of fluorescent lights gave the impression of hell's waiting room.

"You have partnered with someone who does not share those convictions," Luculenta explained with disdain. "Mr. Morgan has already negotiated your safe return in exchange for the egg. We will go to your workplace to avoid further disruption here."

No. He wouldn't, he—of course he would. Had he even waited ten minutes before betraying her plan? The best chance to get the trafficking victims out was to *be* with them and close to the tracker Samzen had planted in the egg's sling. Unless Samzen was in hot pursuit, he was stuck in the bureaucracy quagmire. And Luculenta's researchers were barely unpacked from their *last* move, so they'd be able to transfer their victims out more quickly this time.

The young draconic she had seen in the other facility walked into the room with a small medical kit. She was wearing scrubs that were too clean. Brand new.

"Tom's lying," Maxine spat out, but she could already tell she was losing this gambit.

"No, Ms. Hallis." The younger draconic approached with clinical sureness, ignoring Maxine's attempts to get away as she pulled a small syringe from the med kit. "You have lost."

The needle jabbed into her vein with precision. It didn't take more than a couple seconds for the room to start spinning around her. The grip on her arm loosened, but the edges of the room disappeared and it became impossible to keep her eyes open. They kept experienced anesthetists on staff after all.

Maxine didn't ask "where am I?" She knew exactly where she was.

She was lying on the couch in her own office. Someone had turned the place over at some point. Her files describing clients' petty interpersonal problems scattered across the floor, and random decorative objects broken for no apparent reason other than amusement. The plant had been fake, but someone had still bothered to knock it over.

Maxine had her hands tied behind her back, but clearly no one expected her to do much more than flop around. Even that would be ambitious, actually. Sagging into the couch, Maxine bit the inside of her cheek to resist the drug cocktail. She couldn't do any *good* from here. All she did in this office was talk to people with small, manageable problems. She had finally been in the place she could *really* help people who needed it. And her efforts had amounted to a mild inconvenience.

Luculenta had been staring out the window, agitation making her twitch and shift her weight. When she realized Maxine had woken up, she nodded a perversely polite greeting and turned away from the window.

"Ms. Hallis. Your hero is approaching."

She'd made herself comfortable where Maxine usually sat. The chair wasn't designed for draconic tails, but she perched on the edge, watching as Maxine returned to coherence. The werewolf which had been terrorizing her in the compound lay recumbant like a large dog by the door, yellow eyes gleaming from behind its thick brown fur.

Luculenta might have been worried about facing Tom alone, but with a werewolf at her side not many people could oppose her.

"I never thought I would hear the mighty Thomas Morgan beg," Luculenta gloated. "Did you know that he's used as a cautionary tale in the Holding?"

As the drugs wore off, her aches and pains were coming back with a vengeance. A move made more difficult with her hands tied, Maxine struggled into a seated position. Stabs of pain in her leg and dull aches everywhere else, Maxine swayed slightly. If she focused carefully, she could bring the two wavering Luculentas together into one.

"What, like... if you don't eat all your veggies, Thomas Morgan will come and take you away?" She coughed, still trying to clear the coat of dust from her throat.

"The lesson of Thomas Morgan is: pick your battles carefully. What appears to be an easy victory will bring greater shame if you fail."

Maxine would have nodded if she didn't think it would make her head fall off.

"Very wise," she croaked. "I'm glad you've decided to surrender."

The draconic woman had a loud, hissing laugh.

"My work will improve draconic lives, and give us a new generation of children." Luculenta's many sharp teeth gleamed. "I would have gladly traded my life for the egg. Your life for the egg is a bargain on my part."

"I've got to know." Maxine wished she had the use of her hands to keep her skull from exploding. The throbbing pain of her headache was rivaled only by her leg, which was either sprained or fractured. "Why did Amanda participate? Why was she incubating an egg when she didn't have to?"

"That fool was obsessed with Validus." The draconic stood again to look through the window facing the parking lot. "She thought she could carry his egg, have some kind of... grotesque relationship. When she learned how meaningless she was, her petty vengeance and blackmail almost destroyed us."

"What—what happened to *her* egg? Hers and Validus'?"

"Destroyed, and good riddance!" Luculenta snapped, "Validus should never have fraternized. You humans provide a method for transferring nutrients, nothing more. He forgot that, and thought he could *extract* lineage from one of the research subjects, pathetic fool."

Maxine swallowed, thinking back on the months of therapy sessions she'd had with Amanda. Amanda had insisted that Validus loved her. That he cared for her, and that his draconic background made his violent behavior understandable. Maxine wasn't sure exactly what Validus had thought about Amanda, but this did make it seem likely the man had truly cared for Amanda. In his own, shitty way. Not that it mattered now.

Tom was going to give up the egg. How could she stop the trade from happening? Turning her head made the office swim in circles around her. She tried to think of something through her half-drugged thoughts, but she ran out of time.

The door crashed open, pushing the werewolf aside with a yelp. Tom, in his combat gear, took up the entirety of the doorway. A small backpack was on his chest to carry the egg, similar to her t-shirt sling. Eyes wild and face flushed from the run up here, Tom focused on her immediately, but his lunge forward was halted as soon as Luculenta wrapped a clawed hand around Maxine's throat. An almost human sounding chuckle came from the werewolf, prowling behind Tom.

"Ah, ah, ah!" Luculenta scolded. "Egg first, Mr. Morgan. And gently, now."

Extending her other hand out towards Tom, she waited for him to give her the innocent life she was using to kill hundreds.

"Don't!" The draconic didn't even bother tightening her grip to prevent Maxine from talking. She didn't care what Maxine said. "Don't do it, Tom!"

He didn't care what Maxine said either.

"Take your claws off her." His whole face was twisted in that ugly hatred which had scared Maxine the first time she saw it. All of his attention was on Luculenta—he never gave the werewolf a second glance. "I'm not giving you shit until I know she's okay."

"By all means." Luculenta stepped back graciously. "She has been harmed only by her own stupidity, not by us."

That was probably—mostly—true. The funny thing was, Luculenta had been completely honest. It was Maxine who had broken her word. If she'd told them where the egg was, she could have walked out free as a bird, only weighed down only by the knowledge of the people enslaved and suffering, used and discarded by a mixture of non-human races enjoying their vision of a utopian world built on human pain.

Turning his back to both the draconic and the werewolf, Tom knelt in front of Maxine and gently cupped the side of her face with his hand. He patted her down clinically with the other hand, checking for injuries.

"Tom, you can't—"

"I'm not following your lead anymore, Maxine." His voice was sharp. "You might have a concussion. Can you walk?"

"No," she said stubbornly, sullen as a child. "Don't make the trade."

Ignoring her, he leaned a shoulder against her stomach before standing, smoothly lifting her into a fireman's carry over his shoulders. Turning towards the draconic gracefully, his voice was harsh when he spoke.

"Parking lot."

Not waiting for the draconic to argue, the world swirled around uncomfortably as he carried Maxine outside. The motion jostled her leg prompting an involuntary groan of pain. He hesitated only for a moment at the sound, but continued. She felt precarious on the moving shelf of his shoulders, but she wouldn't be able to fall off if she tried.

"You can't... please Tom." She couldn't get much air into her lungs, so she wasn't whispering so much as wheezing the words. "If they can replicate its permeability in utero, they'll keep killing humans as incubators."

"I dropped out of high school."

"What?"

"Never bothered getting a GED. I don't know what you just said, and I don't care."

The werewolf stayed close to Tom's heels in case of any escape attempts, but Tom ignored him. Maxine struggled, just to be a brat, as he tried to deposit her gently in the back seat. Not bothering to untie her hands, he closed the door with a hard slam, leaving so she could watch him walk back to Luculenta.

Maxine watched in slow motion as the egg she'd spent so much care and devotion towards keeping safe went to a draconic who would do anything to protect it.

There was love in Luculenta's scaled face. She cradled the egg with infinite care, inspecting its shell while the werewolf stalked around Tom. Satisfied, she turned her back on Tom and Maxine, leaving to take the egg somewhere safe.

The wolf snarled threateningly, as if worried Tom was going to strike when the draconic turned her back.

Maxine didn't know the wolf's deal. Was it Luculenta's bodyguard? Enforcer? Furry boyfriend? With a snap of Luculenta's clawed hand it bounded to her side, its snarl turning into a toothy grin.

Trade accomplished, Tom came back to the car and used his combat knife to free Maxine's hands before sliding into the driver's seat and starting the ignition.

"Tom, there are hundreds of—"

"Get some rest, Maxine."

Maxine was sprawled in the back seat, leaning against the door with her injured leg elevated next to her. When he started driving, she grabbed at the seatbelt to strap herself in.

"This wasn't the plan! She's going to go into hiding to protect the egg." Desperation tinged Maxine's voice. "They might liquidate the humans if it's cheaper than moving them again. We have to get back there and—"

"You have to be kidding me!" he yelled from the driver's seat, tilting the rearview mirror down to scowl at her. "Maxine, have you seen yourself? You look like a fucking zombie. I'm taking you home."

"I don't matter Tom, there are hundreds—"

"You matter." He said it softly, and the contrast to the earlier yelling was jarring. "Hate me if you like, but whatever the fuck you said about what they're doing, you're still more important than that egg. I'm not pulling the trolley lever to kill you."

All the energy drained from her bones and Maxine lay back as the world rumbled outside the window. She'd lost the egg. Her presence in the lab would have been the best way to get those people rescued. Were they being killed right now? Transferred to a third location?

"The people down there, they helped me. They've been enslaved for her research, shuffled around and used like cattle."

"What do you think you can do about it?" His tone had turned challenging. "If I drove you right back to that office, what would you do?"

She could... pull the fire alarm? Yell in the lobby like a crazy person? Luculenta wasn't the only one using that office building. They relied on dozens of other legitimate businesses aboveground to cover their operations.

"I can't leave them there, we have to—"

"Get some rest Maxine."

At this point her body wasn't giving her a choice. Still fighting the drugs they'd pumped into her, and now fighting the adrenaline drop, darkness closed in around the edges of her vision until the last pinprick of light vanished.

All in one basket

"**A**nd you didn't think to tell us this?"

The voice that woke her up was coming from Tom's living room. She recognized it as Samzen's, although the screechy quality was new.

Maxine felt like a used crash test dummy, but the world was in focus, and when she tenderly put both feet on the ground the left one held her weight long enough to limp on. Looking down at herself, she saw Tom had put her in one of his large t-shirts, and probably given her some kind of sponge bath. Her hair was still disgusting, grit and cobwebs coming away on her fingers, but her face and arms had been wiped clean.

Based on the sunlight coming through the window, only a couple hours had passed. Luculenta and company wouldn't have had time to evacuate all the humans. ...they probably could have killed them all though.

Zombie shuffling herself out of the room, she heard more of the argument.

"Well, I was going to..." That was Tom's "asshole" voice. They weren't getting anything accomplished. "But then I thought, 'would a whiny bitch and a broken light bulb really help right now?'"

"I've been trying to track down this human trafficking ring for—"

"Maxine was in danger," Tom interrupted. "And I don't give a shit."

"You had the opportunity for true heroism." Echles' voice was a mixture of outrage and disappointment. "With her as an example and inspiration, you could have risen above your base nature and flipped your balance towards enlightenment."

Turning the corner during that speech, Maxine got to witness the twin expressions of *are you kidding me?* on Tom and Samzen's faces. Echles' glow was dim and he was glaring flinty eyes at Tom as if the human had just slapped the Pope.

"Luculenta's office is on the third floor." Maxine limped with determination towards her shoes, which had been thoughtfully placed by the door. "She has a private elevator that goes to the lower levels. There's a larger service elevator, but I'm not sure where that lets out."

Tom reached out to halt her progress at the same time Samzen's dry voice drawled,

"Thank goodness! The cavalry is finally here!"

"Maxine, you are in no condition—"

"They have four different sleeping rooms on the second level below ground. Each with twenty sets of bunkbeds."

"Lady, slow down, you're not gonna—"

"I saw approximately one man for every twenty women down there. They might be planning to kill the men or leave them behind; they weren't necessary for the experiment to—"

"Jehudin sent you a message."

Echles' voice was a foghorn cutting through the room.

The celestial wrung his hands together, his glow so dim it was almost gone. His eyes were sad but otherwise he looked determined to get this message through.

Maxine became a statue. Her shoes in hand and halfway to the couch so she could sit down to put them on, she waited for the words to make sense. Jehudin? A message? The last message Jehudin had sent was that he couldn't be bothered to show up and sign their divorce paperwork. It had been a year since he left; did he want his stuff back? She'd donated his library of Latin dictionaries and burned his collection of modern dance videos in a ritualistic fire.

None of that mattered. The center of her universe after a whirlwind romance and elopement had dumped her like hot garbage, and she didn't owe him the time to explain now.

"I don't want to hear it."

"He says—"

"He can say it to my face!" Somehow she moved quickly enough to crowd the celestial, forcing him several steps back as she advanced into him. "Or better yet, his lawyer can send it to my lawyer. There are almost two hundred people whose lives are in danger, and the code to use Luculenta's private elevator is eight six fourteen."

That last part she said directly to Samzen, whose eyebrows were up to his hairline. He nodded, taking this in stride.

"Alright, lady. We've got a SWAT team outside the building now. They've been preventing anyone from leaving while they sweep the premises."

She hadn't loved the infernal this much when he had forced it with his powers. Relief threatened to take her knees out from under her.

"Why did—how did you get a response there so quickly?"

"I ain't just a pretty face, lady. You've been reported missing for almost twenty-four hours. Beefcake started panicking the moment you were outta sight. Considerin' how we've got security footage of you being abducted outta our offices, the uppity ups were pretty eager not to get egg on their face again."

Samzen paused with a sickeningly proud expression everyone else ignored. Tom was visibly upset with everyone, Echles was opening and closing his mouth like a fish, and Maxine was sitting on the arm of the couch to wriggle her shoes on. Her left foot was swollen, and she had to painfully corkscrew it in.

"I can give the layout of the lower levels. I only know a few names of the humans down there, but it might help the rescue team talk to them."

"Lady, we can call that in. You lie down and—"

"I'm getting the egg back."

Its loss felt like a phantom limb. She had become so used to carrying it with her that *not* having it felt wrong. But even more wrong would be letting Luculenta use it for the subjugation of humans.

"How?" This was from Tom, exasperated and throwing his arms in the air. "You're a stiff breeze away from falling down, Maxine. Your ankle is sprained, you're fatigued, probably still drugged, and you're not wearing pants."

Tom crouched to make eye contact with Maxine.

"The egg is gone."

"The egg is at the Holding." Maxine didn't know for sure until she said it out loud, putting the pieces together in her head. Ignoring their stares she started limping towards the door again. She had shoes, she had shirt—she'd get service. Maybe she'd start a trend. "Samzen, you're driving. She's not the leader of the trafficking ring, but Luculenta has been their top customer. She's at the draconic Holding to escape through their planar gate and you're in hot pursuit."

Clinging to the safety rail to get down three steps outside Tom's house, she limped towards the infernal's car. Maxine kept talking so the men would follow her.

"Validus had to stay in the Holding to keep an easy escape route. I'll eat my shirt if Luculenta doesn't think that's the safest place to take the egg. She's either going to hide there until she's got a new base of operations, or she's going to jump planes and regroup."

Samzen dutifully unlocked his car in time for her to slip into the passenger seat. Echles and Tom, both glowering but accepting their positions in life, got in the back. Tom still had his combat gear equipped and was grimly tying back his hair.

"Lady, all you've *got* is your shirt. If you eat it, beefcake is gonna lose his shit."

Maxine thought back to when Samzen had likened Tom to a bulldog being held back by a string. At the time she'd thought it was insulting, but for some reason she liked it more, now. Maybe because now he was *her* bulldog.

"How's that string holding up?" Maxine quipped.

"What string?" Samzen reached through his open window to slap a magnetic flashing light on top of the car and turned on a siren before pulling out of the parking lot. "The last thread snapped, lady. If I tried to kiss you right now, he'd rip my throat out with his teeth."

"Don't be so sure." Maxine smirked at the murderous glare Tom was giving both of them from the back seat. "As long as we've got a healthy dynamic, I think we can throw him a bone."

"Noted." Samzen had an odd light in his eyes as he wove around the cars that were too slow to get out of his way. "Pinned for later."

"This is a foul debasement of—"

"You're not invited, Echles." This time Tom spoke up to interrupt. Despite having death in his eyes, his voice was light. Knowing him, he'd decided that this kind of teasing would be the most painful for the celestial to hear. "And you haven't *seen* debasement yet."

En route to the Holding, Samzen called the lead of the SWAT team stationed outside Exalt headquarters and handed Maxine the phone so she could give a detailed layout of the lower two levels. It gave her something productive to do other than crawl into the back seat and join the angry staring contest that Echles was losing.

As soon as she got off the phone with the SWAT leader, Echles tried again.

"Jehudin is—"

"Will you shut up about Jehudin?" There were few things *less* important than her divorce right now. "Unless he shows up to—"

A glowing celestial hand thrust his phone in between the front seats of the car, with an active call ongoing.

"He is on the line right now," Echles said quickly to avoid being interrupted again. "He has asked to speak with you."

The call had been active for only a few seconds. Maxine watched the seconds tick upwards a few beats before she took the phone from Echles' hand. It was an incoming call from a number she didn't recognize. She didn't even need to lift the phone to her ear to hear *his* voice when he started speaking.

"Maxine." Yes, that was the voice she would have given anything to hear again. He sounded concerned. Serious. What the fuck was *he* concerned about? "You are on the wrong path. You must *not* continue as you are."

She didn't say anything. Seconds of phone call ticked upwards in an otherwise silent, speeding car. The siren on the roof of the vehicle was a minor background noise to the roaring of the ocean in her ears.

"You are a woman of unparalleled virtue," Jehudin continued. "Do not risk harming others with—"

"Did you get a new phone number?" Maxine interrupted. Now it was Jehudin's turn to be silent. "How long have you been back on the mortal plane?"

"You must not—"

Maxine rolled the window down far enough to toss the phone into traffic.

She couldn't hear Echles exclamation of shock over the rushing of air in through the window. By the time she rolled the window back up, she was back in focus. She'd see him at the courthouse. Maybe. Whatever.

"Why did you—?" Echles seemed to be too surprised to be upset yet.

"Because I am in the *middle* of something, Echles!" she snapped back, turning to see the contrast of joy and horror in the backseat. "And here's a hint for you: maybe ask how the fuck I'm doing first, and worry about my enlightenment later."

The celestial didn't have time to respond before Samzen skidded to a nauseating sudden stop at the foot of the Holding's marble steps. Without waiting, Maxine was out of the car and limping towards the front gate.

Samzen hadn't turned off the siren, and by the time they got to the top of the stairs a small group of draconics were pushing open the doors to see what was going on. Maxine limped right past them.

"Alright, lady," Samzen muttered sotto voce as she made her way to the desk. "What's your plan?"

Not responding to him, Maxine raised her voice and addressed the young draconic woman at the welcome desk.

"Excuse me, I need to register a complaint."

"Uh…" The woman didn't focus on Maxine; instead, she kept glancing up at Tom. "A complaint?"

"Yes." The desk made a nice place to lean her weight off her left leg. It was starting to give out. "There has been a challenge to Rex Invictus' authority."

A lot of draconics moved quickly at the sound of that.

The Premier didn't change his schedule for just anyone, so while lower hierarchy draconics panicked on the ground level, Maxine, Tom, Samzen, and Echles were left to wait in the lobby. Maxine ended up leaning her weight onto Tom while they all shuffled over towards the wall to stay out of the way. Samzen was faking authoritative confidence reasonably well as he sidled closer.

"Lady, my jurisdiction in a draconic holding is like a vampire without fangs."

"Ugly?"

"Well, yeah, but I was going for 'useless.'" He crossed his arms. "I can't arrest a draconic and walk outta here with all the parts I walked in with."

"Luculenta isn't part of the Holding." Maxine wasn't trying to keep her voice down. This was a public complaint, and she wanted as many draconics to hear it as possible. "If she's here, she's using the protection of the Holding without earning her place in it."

"Do you not feel compassion for her?" Echles' voice was low, and his expression told her he knew he'd already lost.

"Of course I do." Maxine rubbed at her aching leg. "She's doing everything in her power to help draconics."

"Then how can you—"

"Echles, do you know how many couples I've worked with who loved each other? Truly, deeply loved each other at some point in their relationships?"

She didn't wait for him to respond.

"All of them. Love isn't enough. Compassion isn't enough. Luculenta doesn't consider humans worthy of the basic respect and dignity of being people, and it doesn't matter how much compassion I have; she needs to be stopped."

"But what you are planning is—"

"I know."

Echles recoiled, eyes bulging.

"It is a monstrous—"

"I *know*, Echles!" She couldn't let him finish his sentence. "This isn't about me. It's about protecting the most people possible."

"Maxine," Tom murmured in her ear. "What are you planning?"

Maxine was operating on gut instinct, not *plans*. She'd spent so much of her life idolizing the virtues of higher reasoning over base emotions, but now those base emotions were in charge. But she was pretty sure she knew what Jehudin and Echles had seen in their astral prophesy.

She was going to make choices that would result in the deaths of others. Could Maxine look Luculenta in the eye and say the things that would almost guarantee the draconic woman's death?

Rex Invictus emerged from the elevator, saving her from needing to respond to Tom's question.

Maxine suspected there was no way to acclimate oneself to the sight of him. She found herself once again struck speechless. He was a dragon amongst lizards, and he knew it. His snarl was enough to curdle her blood, and he was directing it at her.

"You are not welcome here, human."

The tiles under her feet vibrated as he spoke.

"Your ruling has been violated, Premier." Her voice shook, not as confident as she'd wanted it to be. But the important thing was that she got the words out. "By rights I own the egg I challenged Validus for. But he is harboring the thief who took it from me."

It all came down to this. If he agreed with her, there would be nothing left to protect Validus or Luculenta. If he told her to fuck all the way off, she'd have no choice but to leave.

But as much as she didn't think Rex Invictus gave a single solitary fuck about her, humans in general, or this particular egg, what he did care about was was his authority. A challenge to a ruling he'd already made could not be ignored.

The Premier stepped closer, curling his head to the side so he could stare down at her. He ignored Tom completely, as if the man were a wall she was leaning against. Tom was doing a beautiful imitation of that wall.

"Why do you want a draconic egg so badly?"

It would be difficult for anyone to talk after they'd swallowed their own tongue. Maxine made the heroic effort to get her mouth working.

"It's got nothing to do with the egg," she lied. "The egg might not even be viable. But it's the center of an argument I already won. I won't let anyone steal my win."

That was something he would understand, and hopefully respect. It had taken Maxine some major mental adjustments, but she thought she understood their strength-based culture more. Strength was valued, but while being stronger was better, the strong understood the need for a society built of weaker individuals. To Rex Invictus, *every* other individual was weaker than he was.

The landscaping around this building was proof that they weren't completely single-minded on brute strength. It was a meticulous work of art requiring constant maintenance. The weaker draconics who kept the grounds must be considered valuable in their own way, but they also knew not to challenge a stronger opponent.

Maxine wouldn't choose a caste system like this one, but she could understand it. Someone who had left the Holding, stealing an object in direct contravention of the Premier's ruling, and then trying to hide that object within the Holding... it was a blatant disrespect to the Premier.

Rex turned to an assistant standing nearby.

"Has Validus returned to the property?"

She tapped and slid the leathery pad of her finger on a tablet. "Ah... yes, Premier. After the initial complaint he has already been apprehended with an outsider and is being held for questioning."

"We will meet at the arena." Rex was already walking away. "And I will learn more before a final ruling."

Cracked the case

Maxine entered the arena chamber alone. The agents had not been invited to participate or witness draconic policy, and were only somewhat politely pushed into a corner to wait. She could have invited Tom as "her man," but she wanted no confusion about how this wasn't *his* business with the draconics.

The slick, modern arena was slightly less clean this time. There was a background odor of bile she tried not to think too deeply about. Standing—cowering, really—between several draconic guards were a pathetically hunched Validus and a defiantly angry Luculenta, cradling the egg with her body curved protectively around it. It was a familiar posture Maxine had been holding for days. Her own back ached in sympathy.

"I will leave the Holding!" The words burst out of Validus, pushed by a cringing fear. "I am not challenging you, Premier; I will lose my place in the hierarchy and leave."

The Premier didn't acknowledge he'd heard. His eyes were fixed on Luculenta.

"You left to live within human society." She glared up at him, apparently uncowed. "Why have you returned?"

"I had an invitation." The draconic woman's slitted glare briefly turned towards Validus. She must not have realized until now how much cowardice he was disguising under the bullying and posturing. "But I will also leave, now that he has renounced his own membership. You will never see me again, Rex."

Her voice was familiar. Whatever history they had, it did not make the Premier generous.

"No, I will not." Rex stepped closer to the woman. "But first I will have answers. What have you done, that even from outside the Holding you have brought humans to our doors?"

Luculenta worked her jaw as she debated what to say.

"I made the mistake of forgetting the reasons we avoid working with humans," she spat. "They are stupid. Short-sighted. I trusted them and they rewarded me with betrayal. I will not make this mistake again." Tirade over, she maintained her protective curl over the egg, but levied a few more words towards Maxine. "You seek to destroy work that will help thousands! I will not forget your—"

"Even now you hide behind humans." Rex didn't sound angry, but the grave calm in his voice was still terrifying. "Will I get a better answer from her?"

Luculenta's eyes widened. "No!" she snapped, taking a confrontational tone that Rex Invictus probably hadn't heard in years, if ever. "She will say any lies to destroy me!"

"Sniveling weakness." The Premier eyed the arena, as if thinking how easily he could cut out this cancerous growth of weakness within his Holding. "You have learned too much from human society. Your destruction has come from within."

And then he stepped closer, ripping the egg from her claws the way a parent might pull a toy away from a screaming child. Luculenta gasped and cried out in protest, but she released the egg to him in obvious fear it would break in the confrontation.

Maxine was ready, gently cradling it when he dropped it back into her hands. But getting the egg back wasn't enough. Maxine needed to make sure this experiment could never continue, but the Premier was already done with this interaction and halfway towards the door. She'd have to talk fast.

"Luculenta, you have failed." She didn't need to raise her voice to taunt the other woman; this arena was built for acoustics. "Your research is flawed and based on pseudoscience."

Maxine couldn't think of anything more inflammatory to a scientist. And she needed Luculenta to damn herself while the Premier was here to witness it.

"Ignorant vermin," she snarled from between the Holding's guards. "My research will usher in a new generation of draconics. I am saving our people!"

"How many eggs have you infiltrated into this Holding, Luculenta?" The Premier stopped walking.

"What are you—" Luculenta cut herself off, suddenly realizing what Maxine was trying to do.

"Your hatch rates are low because only the strongest survive." Her words echoed in the chamber; the only other sound was hollow static from electric spotlights. "You had hundreds of "incubators," and that wasn't even your first attempt. How many eggs have you given women of the Holding, knowing they wouldn't have hatched without your interference?"

"None!" the draconic snapped, but her eyes were wild. She glanced around to the others present, seeing no assistance coming from Validus. "Once again your pathetic bleating is only to ruin me!"

"Not *only* to ruin you, Luculenta." Maxine calmly tucked the egg in her arm. "Also to ruin your research. And your partnership with Exalt.

And Validus." She gave a bland, therapist smile to them both. "If only there were some kind of cautionary tale you could have learned from."

The Premier was bearing down, and real fear touched Luculenta's face.

"She is lying!"

But instead of approaching Luculenta and Validus, the Premier towered over Maxine.

Shoulders back, head up, don't retreat. He stopped dismayingly close, but she glued her feet to the floor and didn't give him anything the draconic might interpret as intimidation. She tried to look up at him, craning her neck so much she got the uncomfortable vision of it breaking before she could make eye contact.

"Human, do you understand the accusation you are making?"

She needed to respond in a way he'd... if not respect... understand. It would be a sign of weakness to explain. It would show her own uncertainty if she tried to bargain.

"I don't need to." She spat the words up at him, once again trying to channel Tom's attitude. "I have my egg and I'm done here."

She did, though. By the Premier's ideology, Luculenta and Validus had weakened the Holding. An entire generation of eggs might be suspected of tampering.

Maxine holding the egg that Validus wanted had been an implicit statement that she was stronger than Validus, and the draconics interpreted that as a challenge. Luculenta and Validus had been conducting underground research that defied the Premier's authority, implying they knew better than him.

A challenge against the Premier was a death sentence.

But this wasn't about getting revenge. While Luculenta was alive, Maxine knew she would come after the egg to continue her research.

While Validus was alive... well, maybe that was a little bit about revenge. Maxine searched for the compassion Echles had asked her to find. She found a cold hollow in her chest, and a sense memory of the tea Tom had handed her when he said, "You never know what you'll actually do until you're in the life-or-death situation."

Pinned under the Premier's disapproval and general disgust with humanity, she swallowed any apologetic instincts that would make her look weak.

"Premier, am I free to go?

"Do you have proof of your claims?"

"Proof?" Maxine scoffed, "I'm not a cop. The two agents downstairs have proof, if you want to work with the authorities. I have my egg, and I'm done."

"An infernal and a celestial." And then he actually *rolled his eyes* in a sarcastic move Maxine hadn't known was physiologically possible for draconics. "A circus has come to my door." And the next part he said to his guards, still standing alert beside Validus and Luculenta. "Lock them in challenger rooms. I will face them in the arena for their insults to the Holding."

Maxine tuned out their protestations and yelling. Maybe the Premier would investigate to learn more about the accusations, but this was unlikely to be anything other than a death sentence for them. With a shuddering breath to harden herself, Maxine turned her face away from the two draconics she'd effectively killed with her own interference.

She had the egg back. A quick inspection confirmed it was *her* egg. It was unharmed, beautiful, and still reflected her warmth back to her with a comforting weight without which she felt naked.

She was... she was still mostly naked, actually. In all the excitement she forgot she'd strolled into the Holding wearing nothing but an extra-large men's t-shirt, her shoes, some bruises, and the kind of baldfaced overconfidence only people who said "hold my beer" were supposed to have.

The Premier wasn't quite done with her, though. After Luculenta and Validus had been taken to holding rooms to await their turns in the arena, he turned back to Maxine.

"Our eggs are rare." This sounded more personal to him. He didn't seem as disconnected as he had in his other, more disdainful comments in her direction. "Whose was this?"

Its shell gleamed in the spotlights illuminating the arena. She ran a hand gently over its unblemished shell.

"It was among hundreds of eggs harvested from volunteers in medical research," she said carefully, not looking up at the Premier. "It doesn't have a mother—or rather, its mother is a series of numbers on a database, and I don't know how to find her. Or if she would want it."

Now she looked back up, seeing herself in the Premier's shiny black scales. "Would a draconic in the Holding claim it?"

He gave her question actual thought, which was more consideration than she'd expected.

"No," he said, finally. "It has been tainted by human politics, and the ability to track our parentage is vital for a young draconic coming of age. It is yours to do with as you please."

That was what would count as dismissal. He turned and strode gracefully away, his tail sweeping the ground behind his clawed feet.

Eggilogue

Standing on the pavement in front of the courthouse, Maxine felt the jittery nerve tango constricting her chest. She accepted it, acknowledged it, and told it to go to hell so she could actually get shit done.

Tom stood slightly behind her and to her left, with his eyes alert in case any remnants of the Exalt research team were hoping to take an opportunity, but the risk was low, especially in such a public space.

She had only nervously texted the lawyer twice to make sure they were on track and they had added her new stipulations to the paperwork. The egg felt different in the little backpack Tom had given her. This was inarguably a safer and more secure way to carry it, but she couldn't feel the warmth of the egg anymore.

The lawyer, at least, was able to get them into a room so they weren't dangling in the waiting area.

In a room with a table so heavy anything signed on top of it would have to acquire some of its weight by proximity, Maxine gently placed the egg in its pack on the table. She sat facing the door. Tom walked behind her to give her a shoulder rub, which... oh yes, that was almost as good as a bottle of gin.

She was melting into her chair when the door opened and Jehudin walked in.

He was as gorgeous as he'd ever been. Somehow, not having seen him in a year, he had gotten more beautiful because her mind's eye couldn't retain his glory. His brilliant gold aura reflected off the wooden table and warmed the walls. He wore formal robes of the astral plane. They flowed in defiance of physics around his body, giving the impression of a waterfall constantly falling but never reaching the ground.

His human lawyer followed closely behind, but Maxine couldn't spare them a glance as she felt herself drawn to the vision of the man she had thought would be her partner for life. His face was somber, eyes down.

But that changed when he looked up, transforming into an expression comically similar to the way Echles had looked when he got his first good look at Maxine. Jehudin's robes flowed motionlessly around a statue of shock. His mouth even dropped open as he stared wide-eyed at her and Tom.

"Hi Jehudin," Maxine ventured, wondering whether having Tom's hands on her shoulders was particularly thoughtless. But she wasn't ready to give up the reassurance she felt by having his hands there. "It's good to see you again. You... you look well?"

Her voice raised as if the last part was a question. He did look well, but at the moment he also looked like he was in crisis.

"You went through with it." His voice was ice cold as he walked around the table towards her. She'd never heard him sound angry before.

"I don't know what you saw, Jehudin." Maxine stood, giving Tom's hand a gentle pat in thanks and pushing the chair back with a loud scrape. "But I was in an awful situation, and I did the best I could."

"You, no.... this is all wrong!" He stopped outside her reach, his cold anger sliding into despair. "You were never meant to have taken on that burden—*he* was to have been your guardian!"

Maxine's blood chilled. She'd had suspicions about why Jehudin had left her. If her plan was going to work, she needed him to spell it out more clearly.

"So it's true?" Her voice wobbled as she spoke, swallowing past a lump of outrage in her throat. "You arranged for me to meet Tom, so that he'd protect me?"

"No, darling, I swear to you it was so much more than that!" Jehudin's expression of despair only deepened. "He was a man of selfish desires with such potential to become a protector. He needed *you* to show him a better path." Jehudin's eyes turned towards Tom, going from soft despair into hard accusation. "*You,*" Jehudin's voice dripped with disgust, "you *tainted* her with your—"

Maxine felt the first two knuckles of her fist crack against Jehudin's perfect cheekbone before she knew what she was doing.

Jehudin's head snapped to the side and he staggered, a hand lifted to cup his cheek. His big eyes looked at her as though he'd never seen her before. Her whole body was numb with shock, floating in a sea of outrage so treacherous she needed a life raft to avoid sinking.

"You wanted to *use* me to push him towards enlightenment. I would never have been in danger if you hadn't gotten involved!" Her voice rasped in a harsh whisper, fighting rage tears.

"The man had such potential to be a guardian." Jehudin might never have been punched before. His eyes also shone with tears. "He would have—"

"You had *no right!*" Maxine felt Tom's hand wrap around her bicep, holding her back. She hadn't realized she'd been lining up another punch. Tom was right, though; one was enough. "You think my *virtues* are more important than my life? You were so worried about *improving humanity* that you ignored the draconics who were *killing* us!" Angry nausea filled her stomach.

"I would nev—"

"Shut your beautiful face, I don't want to hear it!" Casting her head around to see if either of the lawyers was still there witnessing her assault of a celestial, she pointed at her lawyer. "Is that enough proof?"

Despite his shock at the tableau, her lawyer nodded and held up the revised paperwork.

"Mr.... uh, Jehudin... due to your actions using astral prophesies in violation of the Mortal Treaty, we have revised the contract to state you will take sole physical custody of the egg rendered to be an orphan as a direct result of your actions."

Jehudin frowned at the updated documents, confused. Life was presumably perfect on the astral plane and they didn't have lawyers there.

"What do you—"

"You meddled and expected me to take responsibility for a child? Did your 'prophesy' say I should put my life on hold to find it a good home, or to raise the kid after it hatches? No," Maxine sneered, "*you* encouraged Amanda to come to me for therapy *knowing* it would result in my having the egg. It was a *year* ago that you knew what was going on? You ignored so much suffering just because it didn't relate to your precious *mission* to improve humanity."

He flinched, not looking guilty so much as sorry he got caught.

"This is your responsibility now, Jehudin. Find a home for the egg. Talk to fosters. Make sure it gets a safe, loving start to life." She slid the paperwork and the egg pack down the length of the heavy wooden table. "My lawyer will be asking for updates. And if you don't do a *good* job and find the best goddamn home available, I'm calling you out for your violation of the M.T."

Jehudin took the hand away from his cheek, revealing a gray bruise against his golden skin. He watched her with an expression of horror.

She paused to rest a hand on the backpack, giving a quiet goodbye before turning away and leaving Jehudin to clean up his mess.

— ◆ —

Maxine sank into her side of Tom's couch, which was already showing a permanent divot where she habitually rested. She looked up to where Tom was comfortably lounging on his side of the couch reading a magazine. He had one leg tucked up under himself, and the other lying off the edge to give her room.

"Tom..." Her voice trailed off. She'd hate herself if she didn't ask and know for sure. "What do you want to happen now?"

Tom put down his magazine on the table and did that thing where he looked at Maxine so closely she felt like he was reading her mind. He had a serious expression, but a lighthearted tone when he responded.

"You mean like, what toys I want to try, or..."

"No!" She needed to stop letting him get to her like this. Her cheeks felt warm. "I mean, I can actually go home now. I need to clean up my apartment, but I don't think I'm in danger anymore. Do you want... jeeze, do you want this—" she gestured between the two of them—"to continue? I won't hold it against you if you're ready to move on now that I'm not in danger."

He sighed and readjusted his position so he was sitting up and facing her. He had the suffering expression of long-tested patience.

"Do you think I was only interested in you because of the danger?" He raised a skeptical eyebrow. "Because I thought I made it clear I wanted more."

"I wouldn't hold it against you if you changed your mind. The situation has changed."

"Good!" He leaned forward to take her hand in his, rubbing his thumb over the back of her knuckles to savor the scrape she'd earned against Jehudin's face. "Maxine, I don't like dealing with cops and dracks. But you seem like the kind of woman who does stuff because you think you're supposed to, so... do *you* actually want to date *me*?"

He didn't react to her surprise other than to add, "Now that you don't need me anymore, do you still want to be with me, or would you rather find a nice uptight douchebag with a 401K? No judgment."

His voice definitely held some judgment.

"I didn't have sex with you to keep you close for protection, Tom." Cupping her spare hand around his, she squeezed his hand sharply and her voice came out a little harsher than she intended. "I'm not a sex worker."

"I wouldn't mind if you were. That's an honest living." He smiled. "I'd mind if you left me for some douchebag with a 401K though."

"What exactly do you think a 401K is? Do you have something against retirement?"

"Eh, it seems like something a douchebag would have."

"It's just an investment account, Tom."

"Yeah. Like a douchebag would have."

She knew they were wildly off-topic, and she knew he did it on purpose, but she would fall into this trap every time.

"Lots of people keep investments for retirement, it doesn't mean they're—"

"Maxine," Tom interrupted. "I'm not an idiot. But I am someone who keeps my cash in a lockbox in the closet because if I can't touch it, I'm not sure it's real. I dunno, maybe that makes me an idiot. We're very different, is what I'm saying."

"My career is helping very different people figure it out." Feeling more certain about this than she had at the start of the conversation, Maxine leaned in and initiated a chaste kiss. She tipped her forehead against Tom's and said softly, "I'm interested in seeing where this goes, but you should probably know..."

She paused for dramatic effect, leaning back and affecting an expression of anxiety. "I wasn't going to tell you this so soon, but in case it's a deal breaker for you... I've got a 401K."

He gasped, jerking away from her. "No!"

"Yes!" She laughed. "I also contribute to an IRA and.... I write it off on my taxes."

He clutched a hand against his heart and dramatically groaned in pain.

"Do you think you can bear to be with me, despite our differences, Tom?"

He stopped faking dismay and smiled again, leaning in to give her a much deeper, filthier kiss than she'd given him. He dug one hand into her hair and pulled her head back as he straddled her legs. When he finally gave her a moment to breathe, it was to nip at the sensitive spot under her ear.

"I forgive you."

"Thank goodness for that."

Kissing her neck, he faked a stereotypical hillbilly voice, because he wrongly thought he was hilarious.

"I ain't got none of them book smarts, but if'n you'd give me a chance, I can—"

He cut off as she grabbed a cushion to whack him on the head, laughing and ducking away from her assault. She knocked him off the couch and pillow-bashed him into the floor. Her face hurt with how widely she was smiling.

"Help!" He threw his hands up ineffectually, letting her hit him. "I can't handle this violence!"

"Do you forfeit?" She adjusted her grip to hold the pillow two-handed, but then shrieked as he flipped them over and pinned her to the floor.

His grin was more devilish than anything Samzen could have managed. "Never."

⋯◦⋯

Agent Samzen's Office, FBI

Samzen sat in his squeaky swivel chair and sulked. The fun stuff was over, he *still* didn't have the leader of the trafficking ring he was looking for, and now there was nothing left but grueling grunt work. His throat still ached from the fucking textbook chokehold that could have killed him if it had gone much further. His desk had so many forms to fill out he'd be lucky to get out by tomorrow night.

His partner had left Samzen all the work so he could console that other astral motherfucker who had his panties in a twist so tight that Samzen wouldn't be surprised if his balls popped off.

"I owe you a debt of gratitude, my friend." Gold light bounced off the walls as Echles nudged the door open with a shoulder and set a coffee on the desk, sitting across from him. "Had you not risked yourself for the woman's safety, she may have fared much worse."

"You done being real fuckin' creepy about her?" The coffee was perfect. Of course it was; the astral fucker never got it wrong.

"It was never my intention to cause her discomfort."

"Yeah... my man... intentions don't mean shit on the mortal plane. They can't see those here."

His shoulders slumped, glow dimming. "Of this, I am aware. I would like to make some recompense for my actions."

"She don't want to hear from you, pal."

"But if I could—"

"Just trust me. Don't show up and make your guilty feelings her problem."

"You are wise, as always, Maliel."

"Also, you shouldn't show up because there's a good chance she'll be in the middle of banging beefcake through the mattress."

"Maliel!" This guy was a riot. Partners for almost a year and he still couldn't deal with what he saw as humans' base instincts. "She is the most pure—"

"Yeah, no, shut up Echles. You and that other motherfucker thought she looked 'pure,' but I say she was repressed. Beefcake is good for her—she actually has, like, a full range of human emotion now."

Echles was silent, face drawn in grim contemplation.

"It is difficult. To exist on the mortal plane."

"Yeah, buddy." Standing to reach across the desk, Samzen clapped a hand on Echles' shoulder. "But you got me. That's gotta make it a little worse, right?"

He chuckled at his own joke, but Echles wasn't laughing.

"It pains my heart to say that our partnership will not continue further."

"What are you saying, Echles?"

The celestial pulled a letter out of his jacket, dressed up in an official looking envelope.

"You are being reassigned. It is believed your skills will assist on a different assignment."

After snatching the letter out of Echles' hand, he tore it open to skim his new assignment.

He stopped and went back to the beginning to read it more carefully.

"I can't—Echles, I know I complain, but I need you for this one, buddy."

"You have earned the trust of the—"

"Yeah, no, that's great, but this ain't about the uppity ups trusting me. Did you read this thing?" He waved the assignment and didn't wait for Echles to answer. "An isolated cult stuck in some black-and-white TV conservative wet-dream society? They're gonna burn me at the stake, pal."

"You will have assistance. A human turned our attention to this group, with a specific request for your talents. He is an expert in extremist organizations and cults. He will be an informative asset."

"Echles, unless beefcake suddenly became a lot more friendly and signed up to join the force, there ain't no humans can help me if I need extraction."

"It is not the—" Echles cut himself off. Samzen didn't know exactly what it was about beefcake, who had actually seemed pretty fun after he stopped trying to kill him, but celestials reacted to Tom like nails on a chalkboard. "Your work can be dangerous, my friend, but safety will come from knowledge, not violence. Dr. Frederick Jiminez will be at your disposal to assist during your investigation of demonic activity."

A quick internet search showed a picture of a weedy guy wearing glasses with one of those safety cords so they wouldn't fall off.

"Well, at least this guy can't get me in as much trouble as the lady and beefcake."

Thank you for reading!

If you've made it this far, I'd appreciate a review online. It really helps!

If you're hungry for more, you can join the newsletter at www.ssteere.com for exclusive content, updates, and upcoming book reveals.

——◆——

Keep reading for an early sneak-peek of the spin-off starring Samzen!

Samzen

Samzen watched pulses of sickly, electric fear flow through the crowd held back by police tape. They appeared to be made up of either people who worked at this shipping facility or at the nearby packing plant.

The human girl's body had already been transported to autopsy. Agents Echles and Samzen managed to arrive after most, if not all, of the evidence had washed away, but the lookie-loos weren't bored yet.

"Do you believe this victim will be like the others?"

Agent Echles was a celestial, and even while he wrung his hands fretfully, he glowed a supposedly divine light, illuminating chipped-rust stains on the shipping containers of this inter-planar holding facility. The logo on the corrugated metal container behind him belonged to the Humansanto corporation, exporters of food grade, shelf-stable blood packs to the vampire planes.

Exporting blood from the mortal plane was a major industry, dominated by corporations with deep pockets to pay for regular human "donations." Samzen didn't care about the blood export business. The one thing Agent Samzen Maliel could be reasonably sure about, was that this crime was too small for that corporation.

"We're here ain't we pal?" Samzen grumbled, squinting and moving the report closer to the celestial to see if it was easier to read by the golden glow coming off of him. "If I were taking you on a date, I'd be wearing tighter pants."

He was still wearing tight pants. If people were going to stare at his red skin and horns, they might as well also get to see how great his ass looked.

"What does the report tell you?"

"Not a damn thing." He huffed in disgust, giving up on trying to read the first responder's handwriting. "This is chicken scratch. Hey, you!"

Samzen waved down the closest police officer. "I need to talk to the lead detective."

The police officer in question, a human boy with pocked acne scars who looked as if his mom had just driven him here from his police academy graduation, jumped at being addressed. He stared at Samzen in shock, as though amazed Samzen could talk.

Less than patiently, Samzen waited.

Samzen was an incubus, which came with a bunch of weird, sometimes-fun but mostly-unfortunate stereotypes of being a sex demon. As far as anyone could tell from looking at him, however, he was a typical infernal. When he had come to the mortal plane he'd naively believed that humans would automatically accept him because they looked so similar. Two arms, two legs, etc., etc. In fact, the only differences were that his skin was a lovely dark red and he had short black horns above his temples, unobtrusively poking through black hair. Apparently, being identical in nearly every way wasn't enough.

Was this fresh faced police baby-man going to get over it?

No.

"Look, kid, I don't have all day. Am I the first infernal you've ever seen?"

"Uh..." He snapped out of his fugue state. "Uh, yes... yes sir?"

"Great. Congratulations, this is the first day of the rest of your life," Samzen reached into a pocket to throw a couple wadded up receipts and a gum wrapper in the air as confetti. "Now go ahead and just pretend like I'm a person and take me to your goddamn lead detective."

"Agent Samzen, that is littering." Echles' disapproving voice floated in from behind him.

Baby-man looked beyond Samzen, head tilting up in awe at the celestial. Celestials also looked human, but they were typically very tall and glowed. Humans were like moths; they loved the glowy stuff.

"Yeah, Echles, we're here because there was a murder," Samzen tilted his head up at his partner with substantially less awe. "I hope you're more worried about that."

"That is not an appropriate excuse for—"

"Ugh! Fine!" Samzen knelt on the filthy concrete and picked up his trash to shove back in his pocket. "Kid, am I gonna have to drag you down to the hell dimensions or are you gonna get the lead detective?"

Baby-man squeaked and dashed off.

"Agent Samzen," Echles scolded. "You should not threaten—"

"We don't have all day, Echles!" Standing, Samzen gestured at their surroundings. Towering shipping containers, heavy machinery for transporting and loading into the planar gate, and the echoes of his own voice reverberating back around them. "And I'm sick of finding nothing but cold blood and idiots."

Footsteps approached, turning the corner of a container to reveal baby-man hiding behind the metaphorical skirts of someone Samzen desperately hoped was the lead detective.

"Yeah, great, hi." Samzen pulled his badge as he approached and flashed it at the newcomer. "Agent Samzen Maliel, special investigator with the paranormal unit. I have reason to believe this murder is linked to a case I'm investigating. I'd like to take a look at—"

"You are in violation of the Mortal Treaty." The newcomer sounded very sure of himself while he spouted utter nonsense. He stood stiffly, staring just over Samzen's head instead of making eye contact. "It is against the agreement to endanger a human with your supernatural abilities."

The human was trying, but he couldn't prevent Samzen from seeing the fear oozing out of his pores. A miasma of dread writhed around him while he pretended he wasn't one "boo!" away from shitting his pants.

Samzen gazed up at the murky overcast clouds and imagined, just for a brief, magical moment, that he was back on the infernal plane looking at the iridescent ozone layer separating their atmosphere from the starless expanse. Even that dump would be better than dealing with these assholes.

"Echles, could you help me out here?" Samzen pleaded his partner.

For once, the celestial was useful. He could smooth over anxious human superstitions and provide a calming, reassuring presence that assured the humans "yes, this infernal is one of the good ones."

Finally granted access to the reports they needed, the infernal and celestial partners made their escape. Well, Samzen made his escape. Echles sauntered with unhurried contentment.

"They were very cooperative." Echles smiled faintly, jotting down the lead detective's name and number in a small notepad. Maybe he was going to send the human a thank you card for doing his goddamn job.

No point in complaining. Yeah, humans were very cooperative for Echles. Lovely. Great.

"How many times have I been accused of breaking the M.T., Echles?" Samzen complained anyway. "These ignorant human sons of bitches think I'm a goddamn demon, and suddenly just existing is using my evil supernatural abilities against them."

"They are inexperienced with your kind." The celestial's voice was diplomatic.

"If they were on fire, they wouldn't let me piss on them," Samzen kicked pebbles out of the way ahead of him, skittering them forward and kicking them again as he walked. "And I would, Echles! I would piss on them. That's just the kind of helpful guy I am."

"Vulgar."

"Nah, buddy. 'Vulgar' is draining humans dry before dumping them in convenient locations around town to become someone else's problem." He kicked at another pebble, but instead of going forward so he could kick it again, it veered to the side. "Fucking obscene is what they're doing to the humans before they kill em'."

"We shall find the perpetrators, Agent Samzen."

"Yeah, see, I don't wanna find them eventually, Echles," Samzen glowered up at his glowing companion. "I don't wanna find them when they're done. I want them last week. I want to find a fucking inter-planar time travel machine and catch them when they first came to the mortal plane so I can kick their goddamn teeth in before trapping them in the interstitial void between planes, never to return."

"To my knowledge there is no such time travel machine, Agent Samzen."

"...." Samzen pinched the bridge of his nose. "Thanks, buddy. Let me know if that ever changes, yeah?"

"I shall remain alert."

They were getting closer to Samzen's car. He had met Echles here, and wasn't sure where the guy parked, but it didn't matter because Echles always waited to leave until after Samzen.

"Thanks for yer help, Echles." Reaching up to clap his partner on the shoulder, Samzen unlocked his car.

"Will you require me tomorrow?"

Hm. Tomorrow was a "flail desperately for leads" kind of a day.

"Yeah. There's gonna be humans."

"Then I shall be present. Have a pleasant evening, Agent Samzen."

Samzen nodded, giving Echles a wan smile before the celestial walked away.

Taking one last look back at the crime scene, carefully outlined in bright yellow barrier tape, Samzen watched the crowd of humans dwindle. They were at least mostly human; he couldn't see emotions in non-human auras so a few blank spots could either be non-humans or humans experiencing emotions outside of Samzen's visible spectrum.

When they all stood together like that, the fear almost looked like a separate creature wrapped around them. People spoke to each other, and fear either spiked or diminished depending on whatever they were saying.

Samzen hated the look of fear. But, given the circumstances, it made sense. More concerning, in its own way, was a bright spot of excitement he could see somewhere inside the group. He blinked, shook himself, and got in his car. There was always at least one in every crowd.

He was going to have a pleasant evening, but couldn't tell his friend about it. He needed some stress relief, and Echles wouldn't understand.

⸻ ◆ ⸻

Fred

Fred's mother didn't love him, but he could fix that.

His plans, preparations, and quasi-formed contingencies lay scattered on the large dining table. Fred worked as a research professor, but his field of research frequently put in him into dangerous situations, and he had become proficient at planning ahead to stay alive.

He was a specialist in extremist organizations and societies, many of which had species-centric ideologies which rejected policies of the

Mortal Treaty. This resulted in tribal affiliations and belief structures which didn't respect pacifist ideals.

Or maybe as his friend Tom would say, "We taste delicious, and they aren't all vegans."

Better to have tools I don't need, he tried to convince himself, as he packed his hunting bow, than need tools I don't have.

Packing his arrows, he hesitated, but included the anti-vampire precautions he'd been obsessively developing ever since he realized that vampires made up over 80% of the paranormal population. He'd never had a chance to test this one, but at least it was non-lethal.

He'd run his sisters ragged with warnings and instructions on how to defend against various non-humans, but the only ones he could arm them against were vampires. At least they were armed against vampires.

Fred hated vampires. He knew he wasn't supposed to. Everyone living peacefully under the Mortal Treaty deserved a chance to—no. Why bother pretending? They were literal bloodsuckers! But it was social and career suicide to reveal himself as a "bigot," so he kept his mouth shut. And he quietly carried his precautions everywhere he went.

His nervous energy had ramped up, as he stood in front of a drafty farmhouse window feeling the brisk early morning breeze, staring out over untended wheat fields. His fingers rapped a fast beat against his thigh. He'd be pacing, but he didn't want to wake his sisters.

They were quickly running out of time.

The executives of the paranormal investigative unit had sent another polite meeting request, asking for an updated agenda and slides that Fred would present to a room full of bored FBI agents. He had covered this information already, with precise and detailed reports of demonic ritualistic sacrifices happening just hours away.

Did they want him to tap dance before they actually did something?

"Brother Frederick, are you feeling well?" Elizabeth's voice carried softly. She wrapped him in a hug before he could turn around.

He twitched in an effort to hold still. Fred was trapped between opposite urges to return the hug and flinch away from it. He had been away from the Family for years. The physical closeness was a phantom limb he ached to have back, but he had been alone for so long he had to re-learn how to accept casual touch.

"Yes, sister, thank you." Turning, he tucked her under his chin. "I am just... thinking."

"You are not—I mean... are you going to leave again today?" Her voice quavered slightly; she was trying not to show anxiety, but this was hardest on her.

Elizabeth had accepted the responsibility of taking charge when Fred was elsewhere, which meant she was the first line of defense if any of the brothers showed up, but she could not harm them any more than Fred could. Her tranquilizer gun was laid out on the table alongside all of Fred's other contingency plans. The gun had been the sisters' best hope to prevent themselves from being dragged back to be sacrificed, but even that had proved impossible to use against a brother.

"My—my efforts with the authorities are not... going as I had hoped." He admitted into Elizabeth's hair. "They move with caution that I fear we can not afford."

Sister Patrice had left a bowl of sourdough on the counter to rise, giving the room a lovely yeasty aroma. Despite the morning chill, the living area smelled warm. And comfortable.

But they were running out of time.

He needed the incubus.

With or without the rest of the FBI.

www.ingramcontent.com/pod-product-compliance
Lightning Source LLC
Chambersburg PA
CBHW051504150726
47997CB00001B/112